Tools
of the
Devil

ALSO BY BARBARA L. CLANTON

THE CLARKSONVILLE SERIES

Out of Left Field: Marlee's Story (Book One)
Tools of Ignorance: Lisa's Story (Book Two)
Going, Going, Gone: Susie's Story (Book Three)
Stealing Second: Sam's Story (Book Four)
Out at Home (Book Five)
Tools of the Devil (Book Six)
Going Under (Book Seven)
Stealing Hope (Book Eight)

THE WHICKETT SERIES

Art for Art's Sake: Meredith's Story (Book One)
Dani's Story (Book Two) … <Coming Soon>

THE GRASSE RIVER SERIES

Quite an Undertaking: Devon's Story (Book One)
Rebecca's Story (Book Two) … <Coming Soon>

THE GIRLS' SPORTS SERIES (Children's Books Ages 9-12)

Bases Loaded
Side Out
Live, Love, Lacrosse

Tools of the Devil

BOOK SIX IN THE CLARKSONVILLE SERIES

BARBARA L. CLANTON

eBook ISBN   978-1-953734-25-9

Revised First Edition 2022

9 8 7 6 5 4 3 2 1

Cover design by Sarah (Forcoverservice)

Published by:

Bibi Books Publishing Company, LLC

Dedication

To the memory of Jeanne Taylor

Teacher, Mentor, Colleague

Acknowledgments

Thanks to my ever-supportive family and friends for encouraging me in my writing. Thanks to the team members at Regal Crest for their expertise in putting the first version of this book together. And thanks especially to my team of Beta readers: Angela Mula, Andrea Danak, Sheri Milburn, Erin Saluta, Elaine Burnes, Dejay Garden, Christie Register, and Erin Register. I needed a big sounding board on this one, and you collectively came through beautifully. And, as always, thanks to my best girl, Jackie Weathers, who is the life of my party.

Table of Contents

Author's Note to the Revised Edition

I truly enjoyed this opportunity to look back and edit my earlier works. "Tools of the Devil" is Book Six in the young adult Clarksonville Series, initially published in 2015. It was written from Lisa Brown's point of view. Not much shakes Lisa, but she is rattled when her religious faith comes into question. This is the story about her exploration in terms of faith and religious beliefs. Naturally, the rest of the Clarksonville gang is on hand to help her in her quest.

And just a note that this is a *revised* edition, not a second edition. Nothing major has changed in the story plot. Only the grammar, punctuation, and awkward stuff (to my current ears and eyes) have been changed, updated, or eliminated.

I'm confident that the emotions and situations will stand the test of time and that you will enjoy more of Lisa's life story.

Cheers,
Barb
Central Florida (September 2022)

Chapter One

*"Submit yourselves therefore to God.
Resist the devil, and he will flee from
you." — James 4:7*

Lisa Brown didn't sing along with the choir like she usually did. Singing in church was a way to be free and let her spirit soar, not that she ever sang in tune. Off-key seemed to be her key. But usually, she could step back from anything troubling her and focus on being grateful for all the good things in her life. That was the point of church, wasn't it? But today was different because she had to give Sam an answer soon. It wasn't fair to keep her hanging like that. Unfortunately, she still didn't know what that answer would be.

Lisa had been going to the centuries-old Presbyterian Church of Clarksonville her entire life. All sixteen years of it. The ancient granite walls, the stained glass windows, and the musty tapestries made her feel part of something bigger than her and her stupid problems. Generations dating back to the 1800s had attended this church. Her family had history here. Lisa, her two sisters, brother, and mother had all been baptized in this church. Her parents and grandparents had been married here. The gigunda church organ, the dark wood pews, and the seemingly timeless traditions made the church her sanctuary. It was her weekly place to regroup, reground, and catch her breath. Usually.

1

At the moment, her sisters and brother were in Sunday school down the hall from the sanctuary. It was the same Sunday school she'd attended from age three to eleven. With her younger siblings gone, she sat alone with her parents in the unofficial Brown Family pew. She ran her fingers over her initials, LAB, that she'd scratched into the wooden seat with a blue pen when she was nine. That had made her parents furious, especially her mother who'd made her apologize to Reverend Owens. She even lost TV privileges for an entire month. Lisa never defaced anything ever again.

Lisa pulled her long, black braid over her shoulder and twisted the frayed ends. At almost six feet tall, she had to lean down to whisper to her mother. "Mom, where's Reverend Owens?" Over the years, she and her mother had mastered the art of whispering in church, although sometimes Lisa's father gave them the hairy eyeball when they did.

"Rochester. Granddaughter's graduation."

"In December?"

Her mother shrugged. "College graduation."

"Granddaughter in college? Geez, just how old is Reverend Owens?"

Lisa's mother smirked and nudged Lisa in the shoulder without answering. Her mother went back to singing.

The hymn ended, and Lisa sat down on the hard pew and pulled her coat tighter around her, not because she was cold, mainly because she knew Sam wanted her to say, "Yes," and Lisa wasn't sure if she could.

Mean old Mr. Muller was the reader for the service, and he stood and headed for the reader's podium. Lisa called him mean because he lived in their neighborhood and constantly yelled at the kids if they played near his house. Lisa's father fixed old man Muller's furnace on a regular basis, and he had never paid him. Not once. Not even for the parts. When Lisa asked her father why he kept helping Mr. Muller, he said helping your neighbors was the right thing to do. Lisa still didn't understand it.

"A reading from Psalm 42," Mr. Muller said, then paused for a moment. A few parishioners opened their pew Bibles to follow along. "When shall I come and behold the face of God? My tears have been my food day and night, while people say to me continually, where is your God?"

Yeah, Lisa thought, where was God when she needed help making this decision? Mr. Muller read on, but Lisa couldn't stay focused on his words. Either answer she gave Sam would somehow be the wrong one. Sure, the dance was miles away at Sam's high school, and not many people knew her there, but she couldn't decide. Only a very few select friends at Clarksonville High knew she was gay. Three, to be exact. Everyone at Sam's school, East Valley High, knew that Samantha Rose Payton, as she was known there, was into girls, but Lisa didn't want the entire world to know that she was, too. She was only halfway through her junior year, and she didn't exactly want to be out of the closet for another year and a half. That's why saying "No," had been her first instinct. When Sam was outed by a reporter in October, a lot of kids at her school had been mean, really mean, to her. Sam's picture had been taken at a gay pride event and printed in the local paper for everyone to see. Luckily Lisa hadn't been in the picture, too. In hindsight, it was probably pretty stupid to go to the pride festival in the first place. She thought it would be a place where she could finally be herself and hold hands with Sam out in the open. Neither of them had thought that one all the way through.

What made the decision to attend the dance at Sam's school tougher was the fact that Marlee and Susie had gone to Clarksonville's Winter Formal. Together. As a couple. Marlee outed herself to everyone at Clarksonville High School by going. Lisa's own mother had cut and styled Marlee's hair for the occasion. Since the dance had taken place the night before, Lisa hadn't had a chance to talk to them about it yet. They were probably still sleeping, anyway, but they had texted many pictures and said no one was harassing them or anything. Marlee even said they were having an awesome time. It sure looked like it in the photos.

Blocking out Mr. Muller, Lisa stilled her thoughts and put God first in her mind. She took a slow breath and let His empowering strength soak into her. She silently thanked Him for her loving and supportive family. She thanked Him for Sam, whom she hoped to marry and have babies with one day. Lisa almost laughed out loud. She wanted all those things but couldn't bring herself to go to a stupid school dance with her.

Mr. Muller adjusted his glasses and continued to read, but Lisa simply could not stay focused on mean old Mr. Muller's gravelly voice.

She looked around at the congregation. Many of her mother's customers were there. Mrs. Maynard was due for a touch-up with her gray roots looming large. Mrs. Winfred and her family, along with the Petrovs who lived next door to Marlee. Lisa had known these people her entire life. A few kids from school were also in the congregation, but she didn't have any classes with them and didn't know them well.

Mr. Muller finally finished and waited as the guest reverend made his way up the stairs. If she thought Reverend Owens was old, then Reverend Rinaldi was ancient. He shuffled to the pulpit clearing his throat loudly as he went. Lisa was amazed at the number of wrinkles in his face, and his hair was so white it looked like the dusting of snow that had fallen the night before.

"It is always a joy to visit the quaint hamlet of Clarksonville," Reverend Rinaldi said with a shaky voice that seemed like it had once held great power and strength. "The road sign on the edge of town told me that your high school softball team won the state title this year. Congratulations. You must be a proud hamlet indeed."

Lisa beamed. She had been the catcher for that championship team. And with most of their players returning, they had a really good chance of going all the way again next spring if that stupid East Valley team didn't get in the way, of course.

"God's glory shines down upon us, and the people I've met here have truly been God's people." The reverend smiled at the congregation. "Welcoming and kind and generous to my wife and me." He smiled down at his equally wrinkled wife sitting ramrod straight in the front pew; her bland dress was buttoned completely to the top. A reverend's wife, that's for sure. Lisa wanted to whisper that to her mother but didn't dare. Reverend Rinaldi seemed like a nice old man, and he was a guest of their church. She had been taught to treat everyone with respect, including guests and strangers.

The reverend cleared his throat and spoke about God's children acting with charity and grace. It was a nice message, but after fifteen minutes or so, Lisa was ready for the service to move on. Wasn't the choir supposed to sing or something? Anything? Lisa feared the worst. She'd seen it before. Guest preachers didn't have their own churches, so they got it all out of their system at the expense of congregations like hers.

Lisa tried not to let her eyes glaze over as he cheerily went on and on and on. She also tried not to let the real world creep back in either, so she worked out a study schedule for her semester exams which were a week from Monday. Algebra 2 would be fine; it was so much easier than Geometry. Spanish 3, hmm, she needed to make vocab flashcards. Thank God there was no exam in Art History, but she'd have to review her notes for U.S. History and English 11. And, of course, she'd start on Anatomy right away. She'd quiz herself every day because Anatomy was the one class she wanted to ace.

When Reverend Rinaldi's tone changed, Lisa's attention returned to the sermon. He was scowling, clearly unhappy about something. Geez, Lisa thought, everything was sunshine and rainbows a minute ago.

"We are gathered here in Christ's name," the Reverend said. "Yet despite the holy teachings of Jesus, a cancer is growing among us." His eyes flashed in anger. He pounded a fist on the podium, gripped both sides, and leaned toward them. "The devil has a firm grip and is spreading this cancer throughout our country, our churches, and," he paused for emphasis, "even here in this lovely church." He pushed back off the podium.

Lisa had to admit that Reverend Rinaldi was good. He had them all hooked like fish on a line and was about to yank them in. Mr. Muller looked around at the other parishioners as if trying to root out the source of this unnamed cancer. Who or what had dared infiltrate his happy little church? Funny thing, he wasn't the only one looking around.

But when Reverend Rinaldi spoke again, he uttered four words that crushed Lisa's spirit. "Homosexuality is a sin," the Reverend said simply. They were four words that the congregation seemed to support. These were friends and family she'd known her entire life. Lisa's heart broke when she saw Mr. and Mrs. Winfred and even sweet but gossipy Mrs. Maynard nodding in agreement. These were people she'd known her entire life, people who came to her house on a regular basis.

Had she heard him right? When her mother put a hand on her forearm, she knew she had. Every muscle in her body tensed.

What was happening?

The church she'd been baptized in, grown up in, and wanted to get married in had, in one instant, turned against her.

The congregation, like a surging mob, murmured its collective agreement. Shouting and carrying on was never the way of her low-key conservative church, but if let loose, Lisa was sure there would be communal cheers of agreement.

It was one thing for a stranger like Reverend Rinaldi to come into her place of refuge and say these things, but it was an entirely different thing to see people she'd known her entire life agree.

He went on to say that big changes were coming to the Presbyterian Church, and as soldiers of God, they had to be ready.

Ready for what? Lisa was too much in shock to truly register his words. Still not quite believing what she'd heard, she mumbled, "Ignorance is the sin, Reverend."

Her mother squeezed her forearm as if to say she agreed.

She scanned the congregation again and finally noticed a few parishioners who didn't seem to be on the same page as the reverend. Marlee's neighbors, the Petrovs, looked as shocked as Lisa felt. And some of the kids from school had expressions on their faces that said they thought the reverend had lost his mind.

Lisa was so uncomfortable that she was inches away from climbing over her parents and bolting out of the church.

Reverend Rinaldi finished his sermon, and the choir leaped to their feet faster than lightning and burst into song. "God of the Sparrow" echoed off the granite walls.

Lisa found it hard to breathe. How could they all go back to singing as if nothing earth-shattering had just happened? Through the tears burning her eyes, she looked around at her betrayers, her own personal Judases, and muttered, "Game on, people. Game on."

Chapter Two

"God saw everything that he had made,
and indeed, it was very good." —
Genesis 1:31

Although it was icy cold in the world outside, Lisa was warm and cozy in the passenger seat of Sam's convertible Sebring. She gazed at her girlfriend as she drove. Blonde hair loose over her white ski parka, cute button nose, full pouting lips waiting to be kissed. Sam looked so cute. No, Sam wasn't just cute—she was gorgeous. And Lisa was lucky to have her. It was late afternoon on Wednesday, and Sam had picked her up at home right after school. She was whisking her off to some still unknown secret destination to celebrate their seven-month anniversary. Lisa had no idea where Sam was taking her, but it looked like they were staying in Clarksonville.

The gray skies were turning darker as the sun set for another long December night. It had been three short days since Reverend Rinaldi threw the first punch, and it had taken great strength for Lisa to hide her anger and confusion from her sisters and brother when they came back from Sunday school. Lisa pretended that everything was fine, but inside she was seething. For the past three days, Lisa's mother would look at her in that certain way that her mom had, sending the message that she was ready to listen if Lisa wanted to talk, but Lisa didn't. Not yet. She was still in shock. Maybe if she ignored it or pretended it had never happened, the whole stupid thing would disappear. But then she would remember Mrs. Maynard nodding along with Reverend Rinaldi. Who was he anyway? He was just a guest reverend, probably returning to whatever lost-in-time town he'd come from. She shouldn't have been surprised, anyway. Most of the world seemed to feel the same way he did. But why think of him when she was finally alone with Sam. She kissed the hand she was holding and let her lips linger for a while.

"Mmm," Sam murmured. "We may not make it if you keep that up." She glanced at Lisa appreciatively from the driver's seat.

"Would that be such a bad thing?" Lisa sent Sam a smoldering look.

"Yes, because it's the middle of December, and they'd probably find us frozen in a compromising position."

"You're right. That would look bad." Lisa kissed Sam's hand one more time and pulled it into her lap. She sighed as she looked out the passenger window at the piles of snow on the side of the road. The now dark, gray sky matched her mood. Well almost. She was with Sam, so one corner of her world was bright. But then again, she still had to give Sam an answer about the Snowball Formal. Dark clouds drifted over the only bright corner she had left.

"What's up, baby? I can sense your funk from here." Sam flashed a concerned smile.

Lisa wished it wasn't so cold and they could park in one of their usual private spots to forget about the rest of the world for a while.

"I'm okay," Lisa said, even though she wasn't. She squeezed

Sam's hand. With Sam, she felt safe. "I love you, baby."

It was Sam's turn to pull Lisa's hand to her lips and kiss it, but she didn't stop there. She pushed the sleeve of Lisa's winter coat up with her chin and kissed her way up the wrist, lingering on certain deliciously sensitive spots known only to the two of them.

A spiral of desire flushed through Lisa. "Mmm. That's nice, but don't start something you can't finish, Samantha Rose." Lisa tapped Sam on the arm with her free hand. "We should probably call Susie. Don't cha think?"

"You're right." Sam pulled out her cell phone. She slowed down for a couple of deer crossing the county road. "I can't believe Susie's eighteenth birthday fell on our anniversary."

"It's so surreal."

"What is?"

"You and me," Lisa said. "We've been together seven whole months."

"And I've loved every minute of it."

"Me, too." It was Lisa's turn to flash Sam a smile.

Sam smiled back, looking happy. "Call Asswipe," Sam commanded her phone and then handed it to Lisa.

Lisa suppressed a giggle. Sam and Susie were best friends, but you'd never know it by the way they teased each other.

"Happy Birthday, Susie," Lisa and Sam shouted into Sam's phone after Susie answered.

After their quick rendition of the birthday song, Susie said, "Thanks, *muchachas*." Her voice sounded tinny from the speaker on Sam's phone. "Happy Anniversary to you guys, too."

"Two major holidays on one day," Sam said.

Susie chuckled and then was silent for a moment. Lisa thought maybe they'd lost the connection. It wouldn't be the first time a cell phone call was lost in the rural North Country of upstate New York.

Susie finally said, "Wednesday birthdays suck. I'm celebrating by myself today. Well, I'm sure *Mami* made me a cake, but *Papi's* not home again, and Marlee's doing homework." Susie's sigh was the most pitiful sigh Lisa had ever heard. Yeah, it would suck to be alone on your birthday.

"Hey, Susie," Lisa said and then covered her mouth to stifle a laugh, "maybe we can do something this weekend. You and Marlee, me and Sam? Hang out and watch movies at Marlee's on Friday?"

It was Sam's turn to hold her laughter in. "Movies?" Sam mouthed to Lisa.

Lisa shrugged. It was the first thing that came to mind.

"Can't." Susie still sounded dejected. "Marlee and I are doing a private dinner at *Le Grand Bistro* on Friday."

"Oh, God, let us not get in the way of your private time with Marlee," Sam teased, sing-songing the word private. "Lord knows it's hard enough for Lisa and me to see each other."

"*Madre de Dios*, you got that right." Susie sighed loudly into the phone again. "Okay, well, happy seven months, and have a great night out." She couldn't have sounded more dejected.

"We will," Lisa and Sam chimed together.

They said their goodbyes, and Lisa tucked Sam's phone into the center console. She leaned her head on Sam's shoulder as Sam drove. "So where are you taking me?"

"It's a surprise."

"I like surprises," Lisa gushed. Good surprises, not Reverend Rinaldi surprises. "I hope Susie likes surprises, too, because we have a boatload of people coming to her party on Friday."

"Marlee thinks Susie suspects something," Sam said.

"Oh, geez. Really?"

"Yeah, but I don't think Susie knows."

"You don't?" Lisa picked her head up.

"No. I mean Susie, Marlee, Alivia, Karl, Ronnie, Jordan, and me, we're all kinds of preoccupied with the Snowball Formal on Saturday and—"

"About the dance—"

"Baby, it's okay," Sam interrupted and squeezed Lisa's hand. "I get it. You can't go. It's okay. Really." Sam flashed a genuine smile. "You have a whole 'nother year and a half of high school. I know how stupid kids can be when they find out you like girls. Even people you thought were your friends…" Sam trailed off.

The hurt expression on Sam's face tugged at Lisa's heart. The thoughts in Lisa's head raced at lightning speed. Maybe she should go to the dance with Sam after all. Could she risk everyone knowing she was gay? Was it worth more Reverend Rinaldi attitudes?

Sam pulled her Sebring off the county road in a cutout near the railroad crossing. She turned to look at Lisa. "What's wrong, baby?"

The winter sky was pretty dark at that point, the only light coming from the instruments on the dashboard. Lisa took a deep breath for courage, still not sure what was going to come out of her mouth. Sam's concerned look tugged at her heart.

"About the dance—"

"It's okay—"

"Stop interrupting," Lisa said with a laugh. She grabbed both of Sam's hands in hers. "I like you."

"I like you, too."

Lisa grunted. Why did Sam have to keep interrupting? What she wanted to say was really hard.

"Lisa?"

"Yeah?"

"I don't have to go to the dance. I can stay home if you want me to. We can do something else together."

"Oh, no, no, no, no, no." Lisa put both hands up as if to push back Sam's words. "I would never ever ask you to do something you didn't want to do. I want you to go to the dance with all your friends."

"*Our* friends," Sam amended.

"Yep. Our friends. C'mere." Lisa pulled Sam closer until their noses met. She leaned in another inch, and their lips met, gently at first, but that never lasted long. Lisa let go of Sam's hands to cradle her face and deepen the kiss. Sam reached underneath Lisa's long braid and caressed her neck. Lisa's moan escaped before she could catch it. Who cared? They were alone. She wished they could keep kissing forever, but she had to say what needed saying.

Lisa reluctantly pulled out of the kiss but kept nose contact. She whispered, "I love you, Samantha Rose Payton. And don't ever forget that."

"Never."

Lisa took a deep breath for strength. She pulled back and looked down at her hands. "I'm scared, Sam. Too scared to be so out and open at that dance. And, I will completely understand if you want to ask someone else to go with you. I don't want to hold you back or make you have a crappy time during your senior year."

When Sam didn't answer immediately, Lisa's already pounding heart went into overdrive.

"Baby, look at me," Sam said softly.

14

Lisa looked up. Sam's face was calm and focused.

"You are the only one for me," Sam said. "From the moment I laid eyes on you, I knew you were the one I wanted. My soul knew."

Lisa swallowed hard at the emotion building in her chest. She couldn't speak.

"Baby, there is no one else I would consider going to the dance with. Who in the world would I ask, anyway?"

Lisa felt the heat rise in her cheeks again. She reached up and stroked Sam's face. "I'm insecure. I mean, I know I'm a good person—"

"Who said you weren't a good person?" Sam's eyes narrowed. She looked ready to take on anybody that hurt Lisa.

Shoot, Lisa hadn't meant to say anything about Reverend Rinaldi. Still, with some gentle prodding, Sam got her to spill everything about the reverend's ill-informed narrow-minded bigotry and the congregation's general acceptance of his words.

"Baby," Sam said, "I'm so sorry that happened. Why didn't you tell me sooner?"

"You're busy." Lisa wiped at the tears forming in her eyes. "Helene's leaving soon, and I know you want to spend every minute with her and not listen to my stupid problems."

Instead of answering, Sam pulled her close and held her tight. "Having my nanny of eighteen years leaving my life does have a lot of my attention, but so do you, baby, so do you. Always. And that reverend? He's an idiot. A throwback from some bygone era of ignorance and fear. Fear of the unknown and the unfamiliar."

Lisa nodded against Sam's chest and tried to get her tears under control.

"When he said the word 'sin,'" Sam asked, "what exactly did he mean? What's the definition of sin as you understand it?"

"A transgression against God." Lisa wiped away the last of her tears.

"Phht. You have not transgressed against God. God made you this way. How dare this idiot reverend criticize God's work." Sam waved a dismissive hand. If only Lisa could dismiss it as fast. "You are easily the most giving person I know, Lisa. If anyone transgressed, it's the not-so-good Reverend Rinaldi. And you know what else?" Sam rubbed Lisa's shoulder.

"What?"

"You *are* a good person. I'm pretty sure God is happy with who you are and how you conduct your life. You take care of your sisters and brother and don't complain. Hell, you take care of me, too." Sam chuckled, causing Lisa to smile. "And you honor your parents, all three of them."

"That's true."

"I'm sure whatever those other nine commandments are, you exemplify those, as well."

"I doubt I exemplify anything, but I get what you're saying."

"You know what else?" Sam said.

"What?"

"Word's gotten around East Valley about Susie and Marlee going to Clarksonville's dance as a couple."

Lisa sat up taller. "I know. I heard kids talking at school, but I haven't heard any mean comments. Not yet, anyway, but maybe they won't say anything in front of me because they know she's my friend."

"The tide is turning for us, you know? In a good way. Susie and Marlee broke the ice majorly on Saturday. They were themselves and weren't worried about ignorant people like Rear-end Rinaldi."

Lisa stifled a laugh. "I want to break the ice, too, but…" Her tears started up again. Geez, why was she so emotional? It was exhausting.

"Baby, you're okay." Sam stroked Lisa's back. "Remember that you've got me, and I'm always in your corner."

"But you're going to Switzerland," Lisa choked out. She hadn't realized how much that had bothered her until the words fell out of her mouth. She instantly felt bad; it felt like a jab at Sam.

"Believe me. I wish I were staying here over Christmas break, but Mother wants us to bond as a family because she finally has Helene out of the way." Sam's bitterness toward her mother spoke volumes.

"Listen to us. We're supposed to be celebrating, right?" Lisa tried to sound upbeat when she said, "Isn't there some surprise anniversary dinner awaiting us somewhere?"

"Yes, my fine lady. Onward we go."

After one last kiss, Sam pulled the car back onto County Road 62.

"The bowling alley?" Lisa laughed as they pulled into the parking lot of Valley Lanes, Clarksonville's finest and only bowling alley.

"The scene of our first date."

Lisa's grin widened as she remembered how nervous they both had been on that impromptu first date, especially because they hadn't really known each other at the time.

"I hear the snack bar has a wonderful selection of, er," Sam tapped the steering wheel, "seven-month anniversary food."

Lisa bit her bottom lip. One of the things she loved about Sam was how she tried to make Lisa happy. A flush of regret washed over her that she couldn't do the same for Sam by going to the dance. She bit down her regret and said, "C'mon." She threw off her seatbelt and bolted out the passenger door. "Last one in has to keep score." She slammed the door shut.

"You're such a cheater," Sam called after her. "I knew Clarksonville girls cheated."

Lisa easily beat Sam to the outer door of the bowling alley and held it open. She felt relieved at finally getting up the nerve to tell Sam about the ignorant stupidity at church. But if it was only ignorance and stupidity, why had she taken it so personally? And why did it still hurt so much?

Chapter Three

*"Wrath is cruel, anger is overwhelming,
but who can stand before jealousy?"* —
Proverbs 27:4

L isa shivered in Marlee's cold basement. Even though she and Sam had strategically placed space heaters all around, it was still chilly. Maybe it would warm up once the party got going. Meanwhile, everyone invited to Susie's surprise party was there and waiting for Susie and Marlee to return from their private dinner at *Le Grand Bistro* in Southbridge. Lisa stood at her self-assigned station at the window, looking onto the McAllister's long gravel driveway.

Earlier that evening, Marlee's mother let Lisa and Sam in the house, and Marlee's grandfather helped them get everything out of Sam's car that they had been stock-piling for several weeks. He said it was up to them to get everything all the way down to the basement. He whispered to Lisa that Marlee's grandmother would kill him if she knew he was helping them at all. He had suffered a mild heart attack recently, and he looked kind of tired. His hospital bed still sat in the living room, although Marlee said he'd been sleeping upstairs for the last few nights.

Marlee's basement was full of kids from East Valley High

19

School. Lisa had played on the same summer softball team with Abby and Rachel, so she knew them but didn't know their respective boyfriends. She'd met others like Ronnie and his boyfriend Jordan through the play Sam had been in at school. Ronnie was really good in the male lead role, and Alivia and Karl were good in theirs, too. Alivia was beautiful, with her soft chestnut hair draped across her shoulders. Thank goodness she was straight. Her boyfriend Karl was proof enough of that, otherwise, Lisa might have to keep closer tabs on Sam. She rolled her eyes at the thought. That's all she needed— one more thing to worry about.

With a start, she realized that every person in Marlee's basement knew she was gay. They knew that she was Sam's girlfriend. Could they be discreet? Would they blab to the whole world? Lisa's face flushed at the thought. How could they do that after watching Sam get harassed by the kids at school? According to Sam, the kids at her school dished out a lot of hatred toward her just because a reporter outed her in the paper.

With so many people knowing the score, Lisa wondered how long her stay in her self-imposed closet would last. And her friendship with Marlee. Now that Marlee had busted out of her own closet by going to the dance with Susie, being friends with her was also a risk, wasn't it? It kind of sucked that you had to gauge your friends by whether or not they could keep your secrets.

Lisa looked over at Sam sitting on the staircase with Alivia and Karl. Sam said something that made Alivia laugh, and at first, Lisa smiled at the sight but then frowned when Alivia reached out to playfully smack Sam on the knee and let her hand linger there. Lisa shook off her annoyance. She was just on edge. There was no way Alivia was flirting with Sam. They were simply two friends having a good time. Lisa stroked the mood ring Sam had given her. It was a comforting habit and one she often did without thinking.

Julie White sidled up beside her. Lisa and Julie had a lot of classes together, and Julie was as close to a best friend as Lisa had. Julie was also an excellent first baseman, always ready for a pickoff throw. Besides Marlee, Julie and her boyfriend Marcus were the only people currently at Clarksonville High School who knew about her. And, so far, they had all been amazing about keeping her secret.

"Any sign, Brown girl?" Julie asked.

"Not yet, White girl." Lisa liked it when they teased each other using their last names. The joke was that Lisa Brown had white skin, while Julie White had brown.

Lisa rechecked her phone. "No text, either."

They chatted for a while about the upcoming softball season. Their favorite sport might be months away by calendar, but it was ever-present in their minds and hearts.

"Hey, I don't want to pry, but are you and Sam doing okay?" Julie's tone suggested she thought something might be rocky between them. She looked over at the stairs where Alivia now rested her chin on Sam's knee.

"We're fine." Lisa waved a dismissive hand toward the staircase. "They're good friends." She hoped that was all it was.

Sam looked up as if sensing Lisa watching her and then smiled. It was that easy smile that said, 'I love you.' Lisa smiled back, hoping her expression conveyed the same. Sam turned her attention back to her friends, but not before Lisa caught the daggers that Alivia sent with her eyes. What the hell was that all about?

Lisa turned away and busied herself straightening the already straight stack of birthday plates and checking the already checked settings on her new digital camera. It was almost eight o'clock, and still no text from Marlee.

Lisa glanced out onto the snowy driveway. "Geez, how long does it take to eat?"

"It's a special occasion," Julie said. "Marlee might be stalling just to make sure everybody's here." She looked around at the people in the basement. "You know, I was nervous tonight."

"About what?" Lisa followed Julie's gaze to where her boyfriend Marcus stood, having an animated conversation with Ronnie and Jordan. "Being in a room full of gay people?"

Julie laughed. "No, actually, it wasn't about that at all. It's the first time Marcus and I have gone to a party, as a couple, without having to pretend we just go to school together."

"It's time for you two to come out of the closet, eh, Julie?" Lisa said with a wink.

"Maybe one day." Julie rolled her eyes.

"Me, too. One day."

It was obvious that Julie was as nervous as Lisa about bringing her relationship public. Julie was afraid of racial prejudice. Being one of the few Black kids at Clarksonville made Julie a minority, and she was worried that dating Marcus, a white guy, might be too much for people to handle. Lisa felt the same way about dating a girl. People just wouldn't get it and might be mean about it. *Right, Reverend Rinaldi?* Lisa wondered how Mrs. Maynard felt about interracial couples. Would she nod in agreement about that, too?

"But we're all safe here tonight, right?" Lisa added.

Julie nodded.

Lisa was about to add something philosophical, but then her phone dinged. It was Marlee. Sam had gotten one, too, because she stood and shushed everyone. "Find your hiding spots, everybody. Marlee wants us to wait until Susie's partway down the stairs before we leap out and yell, 'Surprise.' Meanwhile, we have to be pin-drop quiet." She narrowed her eyes at Ronnie. "That's going to be really hard for some of you, I imagine."

"*Moi*?" Ronnie held a hand to his chest, pretending to be hurt by the accusation, or maybe he wasn't pretending. You never could tell with Ronnie.

"Honey," Jordan said, leading Ronnie to a hiding spot, "she speaks the truth. C'mon, let's hide behind here."

"Fine," Ronnie said curtly. He turned dramatically and strode off-stage behind the furnace screen. Well, there wasn't exactly a stage, but everywhere Ronnie went, he was on stage. At least, that's what Sam said. The few times Lisa had hung out with him, that seemed to be the case.

"They should be here in a few minutes," Sam whispered so everyone could hear. "C'mon, everybody, find your hiding spots."

"Sam," Alivia stage whispered, "come hide with Karl and me over here." She and Karl were hiding behind some storage shelves.

"I'm good here," Sam said and dove under the table with Lisa.

"Shhh!" Ronnie hissed at Sam, causing everyone to giggle nervously.

Sam sighed, but it was a happy sigh. It was obvious she liked her friends. As the noise level in the basement finally fell to an eerie quiet, Lisa had time to think. But Lisa's thoughts didn't take her to the happy party ahead. No, she couldn't help wondering what Alivia was up to. Alivia clearly knew that Sam had a girlfriend, but she kept touching Sam's hand or leg while they sat on the stairs. And why the hell did Alivia want Sam to hide with her knowing full well that Lisa

23

was right there? Lisa's eyes grew wide as her blood boiled over. How dare that bee-otch try to upset her happy little apple cart! Was it aggravate-the-hell-out-of-Lisa week?

Sam wrapped an arm around Lisa's broad shoulders just in time. Lisa was about to implode. Sam leaned over and kissed Lisa on the cheek. "This is so exciting," she whispered so quietly that even Ronnie wouldn't hear.

Lisa let herself relax. What was wrong with her? Why was she getting jealous? Sam loved her and would never stray. Still, Alivia bugged her.

Lisa's heart jumped when she heard the crunch of gravel on the driveway. It had to be Marlee and Susie. Sam squeezed Lisa's arm as headlights flashed through the basement windows.

"Get ready, everybody," Sam whispered to the hidden crowd causing an excited twitter.

"This is so cool," Alivia whispered from across the basement.

"Shhh!" Ronnie hissed again. Everyone grew quiet as they listened to the van doors slam, followed by two sets of footsteps on the gravel. Lisa reached for Sam's hand when she heard footsteps overhead in the house.

"Mom," Marlee said from above, "we're gonna hang out in the basement, okay?"

Lisa couldn't hear Marlee's mother's response, but two sets of footsteps headed for the back stairs.

The basement door opened, and Marlee said to Susie, "After you."

Lisa raised the lens of her camera toward the stairs.

Susie took one step down and stopped. "*Mi vida,* look at these romantic lamps you lit for us. It's so sexy. I can't wait to get you alone and –"

"Surprise," Sam shouted in the nick of time. Everyone else erupted from their hiding spots shouting, "Surprise!" a second after Sam.

Lisa snapped shot after shot with her camera.

Susie clutched her chest and leaned against the concrete wall along the basement stairs. Her face had turned bright red. She slowly turned toward Marlee. "You! You did this, didn't you?"

Pink raced up Marlee's cheeks as she nodded. She smiled that sweet smile that made her so endearing.

"*Aay, Santo. Casi me orinaba mis pantalones.*" Marlee, Sam, and Alivia laughed. Of course, Alivia knew what Susie said. Alivia was probably fluent in Spanish. And French. And Greek, Latin, and a thousand other dead languages that no one cared about. Whatever.

Susie headed down the rest of the stairs. It took her at least twenty minutes to greet her well-wishers before heading over to Sam and Lisa. "*Dios mio, gringa,*" Susie said to Sam. "I think you saved me. I was about to say something really inappropriate in mixed company." She nodded her head toward the rest of the guests.

"Oh, please. I didn't do it to save you," Sam said. "I did it to save me. I didn't want to hear what was coming out of your mouth next."

"Shut up," Susie said.

"My ears would have been bleeding," Sam continued. "I'd be sick to my stomach—"

Susie bumped hips with Sam sending her stumbling a few feet away.

"And you!" Susie said with a scowl and pointed an accusing finger at Lisa. "I don't know how you put up with that one." She flicked her chin in Sam's direction. Her expression softened, and she pulled Lisa into a quick hug. "I know you were a big part of this deception, weren't you?"

"Guilty. Did you know we were planning this?"

"Everyone keeps asking me that, and, no, I had no clue." Susie leaned in closer. "I thought Marlee and I were going to, you know, have some time alone."

Lisa felt her cheeks flush with heat. "Uh, sorry?"

Susie laughed. "That's okay, *mi amiga buena*." She pointed to Lisa's camera. "Send me some of those, okay?"

"Okay."

Susie patted Lisa on the arm and turned to go but then turned back. "We're going to miss you at the dance tomorrow night."

Lisa looked straight down at the basement floor, ashamed at her cowardice. She looked back up. "Thanks. I'm going to miss you guys, too, but you'll text me pictures and stuff, eh?"

"*Sí claro.*" Susie smiled at her, but it was one of those sympathetic smiles you'd give a weaker opponent. It was like when they said, "Good game," to the players on the Northwood team. No game with Northwood was ever good because Clarksonville handily trounced them every single time. It almost didn't seem fair that they were forced to do that every year. Susie had given her a Northwood smile—a pity smile.

Angry tears formed in her eyes. She turned away from the crowd so she could get herself together. She headed for Sam's iPod. She was just about to turn on the music when she heard Alivia say, "And we rented a stretch Hummer for tomorrow night. Oh my God, Sam, you have to ride in the Hummer with us. It's settled, right, Karl? It'll be so much fun."

Lisa jammed on the music. It was a little loud, but she didn't care. She spun on her heels and marched directly across the basement floor to where Alivia had Sam captured against the storage shelves.

Doing it for all the wrong reasons, Lisa grabbed Sam's hand, looked her right in the eye, and blurted, "What time are you picking me up for the dance tomorrow?"

Oh, God, what have I just done?

Chapter Four

"This is the day that the Lord has made;
let us rejoice and be glad in it." —
Psalm 118:24

L isa glanced at her mother in their shared reflection. "Thanks for doing my hair, Mom." Lisa turned her head first one way and then the other to check herself out in the mirror. "I love it." Her mother had separated Lisa's long hair into braids of varying sizes and artfully piled it on top of Lisa's head. Most of the hairpins were sturdy and functional, keeping the mass of hair in place, but the ones with white flowers and crystal centers were strictly decorative.

"You look beautiful, Lisa," her mother said.

"Thanks. And, Mom?"

"Mmm?"

"Thanks for not getting too mad."

"For what? Springing this on us at the last minute? Expecting your father and me to give you permission to attend a dance at a different high school? What could we possibly be mad at? You only have exams in two days, and I haven't seen much studying going on."

Lisa cringed, but despite the hard expression on her mother's face, the twinkle in her mother's eye said it was okay.

"Yeah, all of that. I wasn't going to go. That's why I never said anything about it. But then everybody was talking about it at Susie's party last night and…"

"And you didn't want to miss out on the fun. We understand, and that's why we gave you permission." Lisa's mother stepped back from the salon chair. "You'd better finish getting dressed, so we have time for pictures."

"Thanks, Mom." Lisa stood and hugged her mother. "I love you."

Before her mother could respond, Lisa was out of the back room her mother used as a professional hair salon and heading for the bedroom she shared with her almost four-year-old sister Bridget. The gown was hanging from the closet door, the closet she shared with Bridget, although at the moment, three-quarters of it was taken up with Lisa's clothes.

It didn't take her long to put on the strapless floor-length dress. It was one of three Sam brought back from her recent trip to New York City. Lisa felt uncomfortable accepting the expensive gifts but hadn't been able to find a way to refuse. It truly made Sam happy, so she had accepted. Of course, she hadn't known then that she'd be wearing one almost immediately. The dark green satiny material was soft and fit her very well. Sam had a good eye for fit, that was for sure. Even in her ample bust area. Her mother said the dark color of the dress and Lisa's black hair contrasted nicely with her light winter complexion. And thank God she'd had some high heels to match. Sure, she was almost six feet tall, but what girl didn't like heels? Besides Marlee, that is.

With a stomach full of butterflies, Lisa checked her makeup and jewelry one last time and gave the mood ring a quick turn for luck. She glanced at the clock. Sam, Susie, and Marlee would be there any minute in the limousine they had rented. Lisa headed out to the living room. Her parents, her younger sisters Lynnie and Bridget, and her younger brother Lawrence Jr. oohed and aahed at her for several minutes. Bridget stared up at her over-tall sister with her mouth hanging open.

"Are you okay, Sweetpea?" Lisa said.

"You look so pretty, Weesa," Bridget said. "Just wike Princess Tiana."

"So that makes Sam your frog, eh?" Lisa's father quipped. He wasn't her biological father but had adopted her when she was six years old, and she didn't really remember a time in her life without him.

"I won't tell her you said that. But you know what? I do feel like a princess." Lisa twirled, and her dress billowed out, much to Bridget's delight.

"Hey, I hear the limo," her father said. "C'mon, guys, let's look." He ushered the kids to the front window while her mother fussed with Lisa's hair.

"Mama?" Lisa fell back into her childhood name for her mother. "I'm nervous."

Her mother nodded. "It's your first big dance." Her face had that all-knowing expression that Lisa had come to depend on. "Papa and I are a little nervous for you, too, but it's good to see that Reverend Rinaldi didn't scare you into hiding. Your friends have good heads on their shoulders, so I know they'll take care of you. Your father and I have firmly decided not to worry."

"Yeah, right."

"Well, not too much."

"Mom, my life might change after tonight, you know?" Lisa furrowed her brow. "And it may not be a good change."

"Stop scowling. You'll ruin your makeup. You know our family motto. 'Today is the day the Lord has made—'"

"Let us rejoice and be glad in it," Lisa finished the psalm.

"Honey, let yourself have fun tonight." Her mother kissed her on the forehead. "Okay?"

"Okay." Lisa had no idea how she was going to accomplish it, but she'd try.

The front door opened, and Sam, Marlee, and Susie hustled in from the cold.

"Sam," Susie said, "your mouth is open."

Lisa turned from her mother to see Sam standing near the front door open-mouthed much like Bridget had been. Sam looked gorgeous with her hair done up in a bun, a few loose strands dangling against her neck. And her makeup was so tastefully done that Lisa wanted everyone to go away so she could kiss those soft, lipstick-covered lips. The look of longing on Sam's face probably matched her own. Sam cleared her throat, obviously struggling to find her voice.

"Oh, this should be good," Susie said sarcastically.

Before Sam could speak, Bridget threw herself at her. "Hi, Samtha."

"Hi, Sweetpea," Sam said. "How's my best girl?"

"I'm not your best girl." Bridget giggled. "Lisa is."

The room grew still; Lisa's eyes were as wide as Sam's. "Did you hear that?" Sam whispered as if she didn't want to break the spell.

Lisa nodded. "She said Lisa. With an L. Lee-sa." Lisa glanced over at her parents. Her mother had a hand over her mouth and looked on the verge of tears. They had been waiting for this day forever.

Sam cleared her throat. "Um, you got that right, Sweetpea. Lisa *is* my best girl, but *you* are my other best girl." Sam looked up and said, "That Yves Fornier Roux looks stunning on you. Just like I knew it would."

Lisa's mouth dropped open. "This is a designer dress?" Lisa was used to getting her clothes at the local Walmart or sometimes the thrift store.

Sam nodded as if it were an everyday thing. "Do you like mine?" Sam took off her coat and revealed a knee-length dress of similar design but in a complementing lighter green color.

"I love it," Lisa said. "No wonder you asked me which one I was wearing."

"We had to match, didn't we?"

"Of course, you did." Susie made a gagging sound, but everyone knew she was teasing. "Should we take some pictures?"

They set up for pictures in front of the closed living room curtains. The gold curtains made a nice backdrop for Lisa and Sam's gowns and Marlee's dove-gray pants suit, which complemented Susie's form-fitting charcoal, white, and black knit dress.

Lisa's father took most of the pictures, but Lisa took a few of her friends with her own camera. Susie reached for Lisa's camera and said, "How about a family picture?"

"Get in here, Samantha Rose," Lisa's father said. "You're part of the family now, aren't you?"

Lisa smiled at how red Sam's cheeks became as she stood by Lisa's side in the Brown family picture.

"Samtha," Bridget tugged the hem of Sam's dress, "are you and Lisa getting married?"

Lisa snorted in a most unladylike fashion, but before anyone could answer, Lisa's six-year-old brother blurted, "Two girls can't get married, stupid."

"Lawrence Jr.," Lisa's mother boomed, "do not call your sister 'stupid.' Do you understand me, young man?"

"Yes, Mama." Lawrence Jr. hung his head.

"And, for your information, girls can marry girls if they want to. They can marry boys, too. And boys can marry boys."

"No, they can't," Lawrence Jr. said defiantly to his mother. He was clearly taking his life into his own hands.

"Yes, they can," Lisa's nine-year-old sister Lynnie said calmly. She was the bookworm and official smarty-pants of the family. "It happens all the time."

Lawrence Jr. scowled, unhappy at being told he was wrong.

Lisa's mother bit down a smile. "But Lisa is too young to be getting married anytime soon, so you can stop worrying about it, okay?"

Lawrence Jr. nodded but continued to scowl. It looked like he was trying to make sense of things. Lisa figured it might be time for her to have a talk with her little brother. The sooner, the better. He was already in the first grade, after all.

Lisa pulled on her silk wrap, and then they all put on their winter coats. She and her friends said their goodbyes and braved the cold for the limousine parked in front of the house. Cassie, the limo driver, opened the door for them, looking every bit the part of a chauffeur with her white gloves, dark pea coat, and black cap.

"You look fabulous, Lisa." Cassie held out a hand to help her in

33

the limo. Lisa had met Cassie the weekend before when she chauffeured Marlee and Susie to the Clarksonville Winter Formal.

"Thank you." Lisa tried to take a deep breath for courage without anyone noticing. Getting into the limousine was making this whole thing absolutely real, and her heart was racing.

As soon as Cassie pulled away from the house, Sam grabbed Lisa's hands in both of hers. "You are more beautiful in that dress than I ever imagined. I swear to God, if I had a ring, I'd ask you to marry me right now."

Lisa felt the flush start somewhere in her chest and radiate upward. "And I would probably accept."

Susie and Marlee snuggled on the seat across from them, obviously letting them have their moment. But, as usual, it didn't last long.

Susie cleared her throat. "You two kids done?"

"Shut up, Sus," Sam said with a grin. "Oh, my God, I can't believe you're here with us," she said to Lisa.

"Yeah, man," Marlee said. "I'm glad you found the courage."

"Me, too. I didn't want to miss this with you guys. You're all graduating in the spring and leaving me."

"But we have each other now," Marlee said, "and we're gonna have a good time tonight." She showed off some cheesy dance moves in her seat, making everyone laugh. Lisa was glad for the diversion.

"You know," Sam said, "Daddy wanted Roland to drive us in the Town Car and have his bodyguard go with us. How wonderfully comfortable would that have been? Excuse me, Bruno, but can you look away while I properly kiss the love of my life?"

"Gag me." Susie coughed into her hand but then winked at Lisa. Probably to let her know she was only teasing. Lisa knew.

"It's true," Sam defended. "She is the love of my life."

Lisa felt heat run up her cheeks again.

The forty-five-minute trip to East Valley flew by, and it wasn't long before they were at Sam's estate. Apparently, Sam's mother also wanted to have some pictures taken of the girls on their big night. The gate to the fenced-in grounds finally opened after what seemed like an hour, and Cassie pulled the limo up and around the circular driveway stopping right in front of the marble steps.

Sam's mother whisked them into the music room, which she called the conservatory, where a professional photographer was set up. Lisa froze. Who was this guy? He could plaster her picture all over the Internet, and then everyone would know her secret. Oh, God, she shouldn't have done this. She shouldn't have let her stupid jealousy over Alivia get in the way of her rational brain. What was it her father always said? "You can't fix stupid." Yeah, she had been stupid, and now she was paying the price.

"Why, Mother," Sam said carefully, "you've hired a photographer." The muted surprise in Sam's voice was unmistakable. Clearly, Sam hadn't known.

"We have to do this right, Samantha Rose. This is your first school dance."

When Sam's mother rushed away to direct the photographer, Sam turned toward her friends and mouthed, "Sorry."

"*Aay*, it's okay," Susie said. "So, we won't get to the dance until midnight. *No problema*."

Sam tried to smile but didn't seem to be able to muster up the strength.

Trying not to look scared out of her mind, Lisa smiled for the pictures. She was happy to be sharing something with Sam and her friends, but she was experiencing the whole thing outside herself.

They wrapped up the photo shoot because it couldn't be called anything else and headed for their coats.

"Are you okay?" Sam asked, shrugging on her black woolen overcoat. "You seem a little, I don't know, deer in the headlights?"

"I'm okay." It took all of Lisa's strength to keep the panic from showing on her face. "I just, I uh…where's the bathroom again?" Of course, at the mansion, they probably called it something fancy like the *chamber de toilette* or something. It didn't matter; she needed a moment by herself.

Sam led her to the bathroom down the hall. Once the door clicked shut, Lisa leaned back against it and started crying. She caught herself after a few moments, mainly so she wouldn't ruin her makeup, and took a few deep breaths. She had to get herself together so she could go out and make the biggest mistake of her life.

Chapter Five

"I can do all things through him who strengthens me." — Philippians 4:13

Lisa's eyes grew wide as the limousine pulled into the East Valley High School parking lot. There were a million cars, and that meant a lot of people.

"It's okay." Sam's whisper was barely audible against the heartbeat pounding in Lisa's ears. Lisa could only nod. Words were stuck in her throat. Sam's eyes and the smile that took over her face sent Lisa the message that Sam knew how nervous she was.

The limo pulled up to the curb, and everyone got out, except for Lisa.

"You coming, baby?" Sam held her hand out for Lisa to take.

"One second." Lisa closed her eyes and took a deep breath. She usually only did this at night, right before bed, but desperate times called for it. She mumbled, "God, please give me the strength to get through this. I don't usually ask for help but please help me and everybody else not lose their ever-lovin' minds over our queer invasion. In your name, I pray. Amen." She opened her eyes and grabbed Sam's still outstretched hand. Lisa pulled her coat tight against the cold. And her nerves.

Sam leaned close and whispered, "Whenever you want to leave, say the word, and we're gone. Okay?"

"Okay," Lisa said. "I'm okay." *I think.*

The four friends turned to head into the school building. Sam stopped short and groaned.

"What's the matter?" Lisa asked.

Sam pointed to several uniformed police officers milling about inside the gym lobby. One, in particular, was pointing right at Sam and talking into some kind of two-way radio. The kind you see on TV cop shows.

"Looks like Daddy's protecting what's his." Sam groaned. "Whatever. C'mon, you guys. Ronnie and everybody are already inside. They saved seats for us at their table."

Once they checked their coats and had their pictures taken by the official photographer, they entered the gym looking for Ronnie, Jordan, Alivia, and Karl.

Marlee and Susie held hands, and Lisa wondered if Susie was nervous, too. This was her school, after all, and she was coming out officially in front of her classmates for the first time. Rumors had gotten around about Susie going to the Clarksonville dance with a girl, so holding hands with Marlee would instantly turn those rumors into fact. Knowing that Susie might also be nervous made Lisa relax a little for some weird reason.

"Oh, man." Marlee pointed out the decorations. "Obviously, you guys have a much bigger budget than Clarksonville."

The oversized gym had been decorated with sparkling stars, spinning disco balls, and lifelike snowballs of different sizes. The DJ was already pumping music, and a bunch of kids were already crowded around his booth.

"There they are," Sam said and led the way to a table near the refreshment igloo.

Lisa had to laugh. It really did look like an igloo. Okay, it was made out of cardboard, but still, it was fitting for a winter dance.

"Hello, women." Ronnie stood when they approached. Jordan and Karl also stood, and everyone exchanged hugs. Except for Alivia, who stayed seated and didn't hug anybody. Good. That meant she wouldn't be hugging Sam.

It felt good to be surrounded by people she could call friends. Even her summer teammates, Abby and Rachel, came by to say hello. Their table was on the other side of the gym, but at least they were allies. And so far, no one else in the gym seemed to be paying them any attention. Maybe no one would notice her after all. Yeah, right, she thought. She was over six feet tall in heels, and she was Samantha Rose Payton's girlfriend. She was going to get noticed, all right.

Lisa smiled. She couldn't help it. That's right, bee-otches, she was Sam's girlfriend, so get over it, already.

"What's so funny?" Sam said as she sat between Lisa and Ronnie.

"Nothing, really," Lisa said. "Just that everybody's going to check out who Samantha Rose Payton's girlfriend is."

Marlee plopped down on the other side of Lisa. "And they'll be so jealous, they won't be able to see straight."

"Straight!" Susie said with a laugh. "Good one, Marlee."

Marlee made a buck-tooth face which made everyone laugh. "Hey, you know what else is funny?"

"What?" Susie asked.

"I was just thinking how East Valley is, like, our arch-rivals." Marlee tapped Lisa on the arm. "But we came here willingly. What's up with that?"

"Yeah, we're crazy, all right." Lisa cringed. "We're sitting right in the lion's den."

Before Sam or Susie could respond, Jordan tapped the table in front of him and said, "I have a question." His naturally auburn hair was more on the redhead side of the spectrum, whereas Susie's was more on the darker brownish side. Of course, Jordan wore his hair spiked while Susie wore hers in a simple ponytail pulled low on her neck. He gestured to Lisa and Marlee but spoke to Sam and Susie. "Are these guys any good at softball?"

Sam and Susie burst out laughing.

"First of all, *amigo*," Susie said, "try sliding into home with Lisa blocking the plate. Uh, uh. Not gonna happen."

"And don't even think about stealing second base," Sam added. "Lisa can throw you out and still have time to do her nails. Make a muscle, baby."

Lisa, in her full-length designer gown, flexed a bicep muscle. She smiled when Alivia laughed, too.

"And Marlee?" Sam said. "I travel the interstate when I bat against her."

"Okay, I'll bite," Alivia said. "What is 'the interstate?'"

Lisa answered first. "Basically, it's a batting average under 0.200. Like interstate eighty-one through Syracuse. It's I-81 which looks like 0.181. Sam bats about one eighty-one against Marlee." Lisa barely held back her laugh at everyone's confused faces. "It means she gets a hit, like, eighteen point one percent of the time."

"Oh," Jordan said, dragging out the word. "So, you're saying that Marlee gets her out about eighty-two percent of the time."

Sam shrugged. "Yeah, pretty much."

The entire table, including Alivia, burst out laughing.

"Sam, how many golden sombreros have you gotten from Marlee?" Susie asked.

"Hey." Sam pouted, and Lisa looked at her, one eyebrow raised. One thing she knew well was Marlee's pitching, and not many people could hit it. Sam included. "Okay, okay, fine," Sam acquiesced. "And before you ask, a golden sombrero is when you strike out four times in one game. I guess I do have a few to my name." She turned toward Marlee. "Just wait till we play you this season." Sam's attempt at a fierce face made everyone laugh.

"Why does no one take me seriously?" Sam joked. "Okay, who's up for punch?"

Sam, Susie, Ronnie, and Karl stood and headed to the refreshment igloo to get punch and cookies for the table.

Alivia put her elbows on the table and leaned forward, giving Lisa a birds-eye view of her muffin-top cleavage. "Lisa, your dress is stunning. That silk wrap is perfect, and I love, absolutely love, your hair. You are quite beautiful."

Lisa felt her neck and face get warm. "Thank you. It's always nice to have an occasion to get dressed up. And I love your dress, too." Alivia wore a cornflower blue A-line chiffon dress. "I love the lace bodice." She wanted to make a comment about the plunging neckline but didn't quite know how to phrase it.

"Thanks. I'd like to say that Karl helped pick it out, but he knows nothing about fashion." Alivia flipped her banana curls behind her shoulder. "Samantha Rose bought that dress for you, didn't she?"

The question was innocent enough, but Lisa heard a tinge of something behind it. Jealousy maybe?

41

Before Lisa could answer, Marlee said, "Like Karl, I don't know anything about fashion, but you guys look fantastic in your dresses. On me, a dress just wouldn't look right."

Alivia seemed a little miffed at having her question derailed, and Lisa wondered if Marlee had changed the subject on purpose. Marlee was pretty smart, and it felt good knowing she had her back.

Alivia recovered quickly. "I love that gray suit on you, Marlee. Especially with the black highlights in your hair."

"Yeah?"

"It makes you look, I don't know, cool. Like you're a badass." Alivia smiled and then raised an admiring eyebrow.

Lisa remained polite but wanted to roll her eyes in the worst way. Alivia was flirting with Marlee. Alivia was a flirt, plain and simple.

While Marlee and Alivia continued discussing fashion, Lisa powered up her digital camera and checked the light setting and the automatic focus. Jordan sat up tall and gave her a cheesy smile, so she took his picture. After showing it to him, she took a few more of the gym and of her friends coming back with the goodies.

She zoomed in on Sam walking back, holding two plastic cups of punch. Geez, why did they serve red punch at a formal? Spilling even the smallest amount would ruin her dress. Lisa zoomed her camera in further, focusing on Sam's easy smile as she talked with Ronnie.

"Here you go, baby." Sam put the drinks down on the table carefully.

"Cookies for all." Susie placed a plastic plate of assorted cookies on the table. Lisa laughed when Marlee's eyes grew wide. Everyone knew that chocolate chip cookies were her weakness.

Marlee reached for the plate and grabbed two. Before she finished the first, she shoved the second one in her mouth. She looked so happy, like a seven-year-old kid.

"Hey, dyke," some jerk said to Marlee. "Got room for this in there?" He grabbed his crotch. His friends smacked him on the arm and laughed.

"Shut up, Ryan. You're being an asshole," Susie shouted back at him.

He laughed even louder, but Lisa was grateful when he and his friends kept walking.

"Sorry about that, you guys," Sam said to Marlee and Lisa. "This is a usual occurrence at lunch."

Ronnie nodded, and Jordan took his hand. "Welcome to our world, girls," Ronnie put an arm around Sam's shoulder. "That's what we've had to put up with here at wonderfully progressive East Valley High School, home of the homophobes."

Sam laughed. "Ronnie's sending around a petition to change the mascot from the Panthers to the Homophobes."

Lisa sneaked a peek at Marlee. Her face was drained of color, and the half-eaten cookies, what was left of them, were wadded up in a napkin. She seemed a little lost. Of all of them, Marlee was still kind of innocent and sensitive. And it hurt Lisa's heart deeply that some random kid could dampen her spirit that quickly. Susie, on the other hand, was uncharacteristically quiet. Her face was bright red with fury, and her arm was tight around Marlee's shoulders as if to shield her from any more hurt.

Lisa patted her friend on the back. "It's okay. He's a jerk, and you've got us."

"Yep," came Marlee's one-word response.

"Hey, let's get up and dance," Alivia suggested, reaching for Karl's hand.

"Great idea," Ronnie echoed. "C'mon, Jordan, let's show 'em how it's done." He stood and pulled out the chair for his boyfriend.

Before anyone else could get up, four couples walked purposefully toward them. Each boy had a protective arm around his female date's shoulders. Lisa didn't know what was about to happen, but she made sure her camera was on and turned the shutter to silent mode. As inconspicuously as possible, she pointed the lens toward the couples and took silent pictures of them. Two couples headed to the right of their table, the other two to the left.

It wasn't until they got closer that she saw the crosses hanging around their necks. Here we go again, she thought. Reverend Rinaldi times eight.

"God made man and woman for each other," the girl with the yellow taffeta dress said. The dress may have been pretty, but her expression was not.

"God made Adam and Eve, not Adam and Steve," another girl said.

"Hey, don't discriminate," Susie said. "What about Ana and Eve?" Everyone at their table laughed, Lisa included.

Lisa continued to click the shutter button on her camera as they walked by. She couldn't help it when she asked, "How can love be wrong if it comes from God?"

"It isn't love," a tall boy with freckles spat out. His eyes locked onto Lisa's. It was scary how angry he was. "This love of yours? These disgusting acts you call 'love' aren't love at all. It's lust, and you know as well as I do that it doesn't come from God." He smacked the table with his open palm. "It comes from the devil, from Satan himself."

"C'mon, Freddie." The girl in the yellow dress pulled on his arm. "We gotta go. Now." She glanced at one of the police officers, who seemed interested in what was going on at their table.

"John 3:16," Freddie hissed.

The others in Freddie's group didn't say anything as they walked by but instead glared contemptuously at them. They even glared at Alivia and Karl, the straight couple at the table.

"Man, I'm glad we didn't have to deal with anything like this at Clarksonville last weekend," Marlee said quietly to Susie. "Is this what you go through every day?"

"Not every day," Susie said. "It's calmed down a lot."

Alivia pounded her fist on the table. "But it shouldn't be happening at all. What gives them the right to talk to you guys like that? Stupid jerks." She buried her face into Karl's shoulder.

"You're right, honey," Karl said as he stroked her hair. "You're right."

"Freddie?" Ronnie pointed toward the tall, freckled kid. "He's a little out there. He and his family spend the weekends picketing Planned Parenthood on Main Street. Apparently, Planned Parenthood has pamphlets with the word abortion in them."

"Jerk," Sam said simply, which garnered a table full of amens from her friends.

Lisa was stunned. Those kids and their hate were exactly the kind of thing she was trying desperately to avoid. That was why she hadn't wanted to go to the dance in the first place. And here, in the first ten minutes, they had been verbally attacked by a few different kids. Sam reached for her hand and gave it a reassuring squeeze. Lisa was seconds away from asking Sam to take her home.

45

"I feel really stupid," Marlee said, "but what's John 3:16?"

Ronnie and Jordan sat down since it was obvious the group wouldn't be dancing just yet. Ronnie said, "It's a way for the Bible thumpers, the holy rollers, the holier-than-thou righteous assholes to let you know they're better than you are and that you'd better accept Jesus as your personal savior, or else."

"Or else what?" Marlee's face was priceless. She truly was innocent in most things.

"Or else you'll burn in hell for all eternity," Jordan said.

"Why?"

"They think that if you're a homosexual," Lisa put a distasteful slant on the word, "then you're a sinner who is going straight to hell. The only way to go to heaven is to become straight, accept Jesus, and apparently walk around condemning others." The last part was said a little too sarcastically, even to her own ears.

Lisa sat back in her chair and folded her arms. Her sermon was over.

Sam caressed her arm. "Baby, you know those kids are just jerks, right?"

Earlier, Marlee had been reduced to one-word answers, but Lisa couldn't even come up with that. She simply nodded.

One of the younger police officers on duty strode toward Sam. Lisa smiled appreciatively at the cute young blonde, her hair pulled back into a tight ponytail. The uniform definitely gave her a look of authority, and Lisa didn't want to get on the wrong side of her.

Sam gave the officer a quick shake of her head to let her know they didn't need her help. It looked to Lisa like that kind of thing wasn't new to Sam. The officer's job was probably on the line if anything happened to Sam.

Sam said, "We're okay, officer. Really."

The officer hesitated for a moment. "My name's Christie. Call me over immediately if there's any more trouble." She smiled and reluctantly retreated after Sam thanked her again and gave her a thumbs-up.

"Hey, you know what?" Jordan said. "Those jerks are entitled to their opinion."

"*Mierda*, I wish they would keep it to themselves," Susie said.

"Amen," Lisa agreed.

"There are those, not me, but there are those who believe that gay people are inherently evil," Alivia said. Figures she was looking right at Lisa when she said it.

With a twinkle in his eye, Ronnie teased, "Well, it's true. Being a homo is a sin, you know. It says it right there in the Bible. Leviticus or something."

"Leviticus 18:22," Lisa said. She knew the verse well. She'd read it in the Bible when she was twelve years old after discovering that she liked girls instead of boys. That part, liking girls, had never bothered her. The Bible passage did, though, and she still hadn't come to terms with it. She quoted, "You shall not lie with a male as with a woman; it is an abomination."

"Not a problem for me," Susie said with a laugh.

Ronnie laughed. "Sounds like you lesbos have it made!"

"Ha!" Jordan said. "I don't think you're ever gonna convince *them* of that." He pointed over his shoulder at the holy-roller table.

Lisa smiled half-heartedly. Maybe it was time to go back and re-read the bible verses about homosexuality. Maybe she'd read the pew Bible in church tomorrow if she went. She might not go. Ever again.

"Anne Foster is the adult sponsor of the Rainbow Youth

Alliance," Jordan said. "You guys met her at the Pride event last October. I think. Anyway, she says most people can't see past their own upbringing."

"Hey," Ronnie said, "you guys have to come to the youth alliance. Marlee, they have cookies."

"Uh, thanks, Ronnie." Marlee made a face. "I think I'm swearing off cookies after tonight."

"I don't blame you." He laughed and added, "We're meeting on Tuesday. You have to come because we're starting this video series on treating people with respect. Jordan is going to be the star. I'm directing."

The others got excited about the youth alliance meeting, but Lisa couldn't find much energy for it. That idiot who insulted Marlee and the jerks at the other table had completely unnerved her. They would never see past their own ignorance and probably didn't care about the hurt they caused. She picked up her camera and scanned through the pictures one by one.

Her breath caught in her throat when a picture of the freckled-faced kid named Freddie came up. His eyes shot fury toward her camera lens. His face was contorted in pure rage. His fists were clenched tight. Never in her life had she seen such hatred. And it had been directed at her and her friends. She turned the camera for Sam to see.

Sam shot her a look of concern and then whipped around toward the police officer she'd shooed away before. She was there in a flash, and Sam showed her the picture. It wasn't long before a big burly officer who looked like he could bench press any one of them was posted near the holy-rollers' table.

"Hey, let's lighten the mood." Ronnie held up his glass of

punch. "Here's to the queers." Lisa half-heartedly raised her glass.

Susie said, "If people see us treating each other well, and if we lead by example, then they'll see we're not monsters. We're just people. We're just us. And we are going to have fun tonight."

For the second time that evening, Lisa wanted to ask Sam to take her home. But something shifted inside her as she watched the burly police officer stare down the holy-roller table he guarded. It was the same thing that flashed inside her at the end of Reverend Rinaldi's sermon. She wanted to knock those jerks into next Tuesday. She wanted to stand up for herself and her friends. Not one to back down from a challenge, Lisa stood, draped her silk wrap over her chair, and said, "Screw it. Let's go dance. I'm here to have fun."

Chapter Six

*"Your words have supported those who
were stumbling, and you have made
firm the feeble knees."* — Job 4:4

At first, Lisa and her friends danced together as one big group. They were all a little shell-shocked after their visitation from Ryan the jerk and then Freddie and his holy rollers. Ronnie was making jokes about that being a great band name, "And now put your hands together for Freddie and The Holy Rollers!"

Everyone laughed, but it was disturbing to Lisa that people she didn't know thought they had the right to judge her and her friends. Lisa stopped thinking when the DJ played Seal's "Kiss from a Rose." Sam let out a whoop, and when she reached over, Lisa was ready to waltz to the song in three-four time.

Sam had such good rhythm that she was able to lead them artfully around the dance floor. Lisa loved the feel of her gown flowing behind her as she and Sam moved together. Soon Susie and Marlee were waltzing with them. Not as expertly, but they had gotten the hang of it soon enough. Marlee was leading.

"What are we doing?" Marlee called over to Lisa and Sam when they caught up.

"Waltzing," Sam said.

"All the cool kids are doing it," Lisa called back, hoping they were still within earshot as Sam surged around a couple of kids still doing freestyle.

Ronnie and Jordan were trying to waltz but soon gave up and turned it into a comical G-rated tango, Ronnie leading, of course. Alivia and Karl fell flat trying to waltz, mainly because each one kept trying to lead, so they simply joined Ronnie and Jordan and did a completely unsexy comical tango. Before long, most of the kids were doing the mock tango, and Lisa and her friends had to give up their waltzing, but it didn't matter. Lisa could finally say she was having fun.

Freestyle dancing was favored by most during the next song, a rap, and then something incredible happened after that. The DJ put on a song with a Spanish rhythm causing Susie to yell, "Let's salsa!" The floor basically cleared out except for Susie and Marlee. Always up for a challenge, Lisa watched them for a while and mimicked the smooth Latin movements. Before long, Sam and the rest of their friends joined in, Alivia and Karl included. Susie and Marlee clasped hands and danced around the floor, twirling and moving together expertly. It was breathtaking, actually, and was like watching a dance competition; they were that good.

Eventually, a few East Valley kids got brave enough to join them, and once the song moved on, a rousing round of applause broke out.

"Having fun is kind of fun," Lisa said to Sam, "but, geez, I need a break."

"No kidding." Sam started to lead the way toward their table, but Lisa wanted to freshen up.

"Restroom?" Lisa smiled.

51

"C'mon, I'll take you." Sam led the way, and Lisa, not sure what possessed her, reached forward and took hold of Sam's hand.

Sam pulled Lisa closer, and they headed toward a side door leading to a well-lit hallway.

"Hey, wait up," Susie called after them. "We're coming with you." She and Marlee followed behind.

Just as they opened the door, they heard a commotion in the hallway.

"Freddie, what are you doing?" the girl in the yellow taffeta dress screeched.

Thinking it might be Holy Roller Freddie picking on somebody, Lisa let go of Sam's hand and pushed her way through a group of kids. He could pick on her, but enough was enough. Instead of finding Freddie fighting, he was on the floor writhing.

"Oh, shit. He's having a seizure." Lisa pulled off her high heels, barely cognizant of doing so, and fell to her knees. She put her hands under his head. "You," she pointed to some jock wearing a letterman's jacket, "give me that jacket."

When he hesitated, Lisa barked, "Now! I have to cushion his head."

The kid sprang into action and tossed Lisa his coat. The first rule of seizures was to make sure the victim didn't hurt himself on anything in the environment. Freddie would crack his head on that cement floor if she didn't get something under it quickly. She carefully stuffed the jacket underneath his head and shoulders as gently as possible. His eyes rolled back in his head as his body seized.

Feeling the press of the other kids around her, Lisa looked up and said to the first person that made eye contact, "You, there, in the blue dress. Use that cell phone in your hand and call 911. Tell them he's having a seizure."

"Okay, okay," the girl said in a shaky voice and did as she was told.

"You! Tuxedo boy, go get some teachers." Good Lord, somebody be friggin' useful already.

"What can I do?" Sam bent down next to Lisa.

"Get these kids back into the gym. They're in the way and starting to piss me off royally." Lisa's growl was low but effective. Sam leaped up and enlisted Susie in her efforts to move the gawking crowd away from the action.

"Cell phone girl stays," Lisa said, pointing to the girl in the blue dress.

Sam nodded and continued herding the other kids back to the gym.

Cell-phone girl pulled the phone away from her mouth, "They said they're on their way."

"Excellent." Lisa nodded her approval.

"They told me stuff to do for him, but you're already doing it." She gestured to the jacket under his head.

"How long till they're here?"

"Ten minutes, maybe." Cell-phone girl held up her finger and turned away from Lisa, "Yes, I'm still here." She listened for a moment and said, "Okay, I'll meet you on the sidewalk outside the gym." She gestured to Lisa that she was heading outside, and Lisa gave her a thumbs-up.

Lisa put what she hoped was a calming hand on Freddie's shoulders and said, "You're okay, Freddie. You're safe. Don't worry. You're okay." She repeated the soothing message several times.

The girl in the yellow dress who had hurled insults at them

earlier kneeled next to Lisa, "What's happening to him?" Her voice was high and tight.

"You're his girlfriend?"

"Yes."

"Is he on drugs? Tell the truth." Lisa's eyes bored into the other girl's.

"No. No way. We don't do drugs."

"Are you sure?"

Freddie's girlfriend didn't answer. She kept staring at him and then started to cry.

"What's your name?" Lisa asked. She had to get more information.

"Rebekah."

Lisa heard the edge of hysteria in the girl's voice and tried to derail it with the question. "Rebecca with two *c*'s or Rebekah with a *k*?"

"One *k*."

"Okay, Rebekah with one *k*, tell me what happened."

"We were heading toward the restrooms, and then he just stopped and reached his arm out to, like, steady himself, you know? And then he crumpled to the floor. And that's when you came out. That's all I know. What's happening to him?"

"He's having a seizure."

Rebekah sat back on her heels, panic growing in her eyes. Lisa hoped the girl would keep it together. She didn't need two patients on her hands.

Freddie's tremors seemed to be lessening. Hopefully, the worst part was over.

Sam and Susie were effective in herding their classmates back into the gym. Lisa hoped they'd clear out fast because she had another problem to take care of and had to do something about it fast. A quick look around gave her nothing useful.

She saw Marlee out of the corner of her eye. Thank God. "Marlee?"

She was at Lisa's side in an instant. "Yeah?"

"I need you. Go get my wrap off the back of my chair. Hurry. Fast, fast, fast." Marlee took off without asking why, bumping into a few kids as she went.

Geez, where were those teachers? Or those police officers? Or any grown-up person?

Freddie's arms and legs continued to twitch intermittently, but not at the same magnitude. Thankfully, his head and torso had stilled. Lisa leaned her ear over his mouth.

"What are you doing?" Rebekah screeched.

"I'm making sure he's breathing." There was a lot of commotion inside the gym, and she had difficulty hearing. "Give me your mirror." Lisa pointed to the girl's clutch purse.

"What?"

"Mirror." Lisa pointed again. Every girl had at least two things in her purse, a mirror and a cell phone.

Rebekah pulled out her compact, and Lisa opened it. She put it next to Freddie's mouth, and it fogged up immediately. "He's breathing. Thank God," Lisa mumbled to herself.

Marlee made it back in record time, sprinting past the two teachers rushing toward Freddie. "Here you go." Marlee was out of breath as she handed Lisa the wrap.

"Awesome." Lisa placed the silk wrap carefully over Freddie's groin area.

"Now what are you doing?" Rebekah was clearly appalled.

"He wet himself," Lisa whispered so that only Rebekah could hear. "He deserves some dignity, don't you think?"

Rebekah's face and voice softened. "Thank you."

Lisa nodded and went back to reassuring Freddie that he was okay and that help was on the way.

Marlee explained to the middle-aged female teacher what had happened, while the younger nerdy male teacher kneeled and then leaned over Freddie, clearly not sure what to do.

Lisa told the kneeling teacher about Freddie's seizure and what she had done to help him.

"Thank you, young lady." The teacher looked relieved. "And someone called for an ambulance?"

Just as Lisa nodded, they heard the distant sound of sirens getting closer. In a matter of moments, the rescue squad burst through the doors, aided by the cute police officer named Christie, who had finally worked her way through the mob of kids. Lisa backed away when two of the paramedics asked her to.

She answered their questions as a good-looking paramedic in her late twenties took down the information. The woman's hair was as short as Marlee's. Was she family, maybe? To hide her blush, Lisa reached down and picked up the letterman's jacket that had been under Freddie's head.

Finished with the questions, the cute paramedic tucked the notebook into her back pocket. "Because you acted so quickly, you may have saved his life. If he had hit his head on this floor," she stomped down twice on the concrete with her boot, "he could have gotten seriously hurt."

"Where are you taking him?" Lisa asked.

56

"East Valley Hospital."

"Do you know if someone called his parents?"

"The teachers said they'd take care of that."

While Lisa was giving her statement, Freddie had been checked out by the other paramedics and loaded onto a stretcher. He had regained consciousness, and Rebekah was by his side, reassuring him. Good, at least somebody he knew would be with him.

The kid who had given up his letterman's jacket stood to the side, waiting for Lisa to finish her interview.

"We have all of your information, and if we need anything else, we'll give you a call," the paramedic said.

"Let's go, Erin," one of the other paramedics called.

"Gotta go." The cute paramedic winked at Lisa and then turned on her heels to follow the rest of her team out the door and into the waiting ambulance.

Lisa took a step toward the kid and handed him his jacket. "Thanks for this. You were the first one I saw that had something useful."

"Glad I could help. Freddie's a whacko, but you can't kick somebody when they're down, right?"

"Guess not," Lisa said.

"See ya." He turned and headed back in the gym.

Lisa took a step back, closed her eyes, and blew out a sigh. She was suddenly exhausted.

Sam was at her side in an instant. She held Lisa's shoes in one hand. "You were amazing, baby." She reached for Lisa's hand.

Lisa ignored the hand and wrapped Sam up in a quick but solid hug. "That whole thing was crazy. God, I hope he's okay."

"You were incredible, Lisa," Marlee said. "The way you got

everybody moving and helping. That was awesome."

"I really didn't do anything."

"Where is she?" Ronnie pushed his way toward Lisa, with Jordan, Alivia, and Karl following behind him. Ronnie pulled up short in front of her. He looked her straight in the eye and then bowed deeply in front of her. "My lady. It is an honor to be in your presence."

"Ronnie, stand up." Lisa shook her head. "I swear I didn't do anything. I just knelt by him until the paramedics got here."

Alivia moved closer. She was frowning. "You did a lot more than nothing, from what I hear. And how could you?"

"Huh?"

"Seriously." Alivia looked around at all her friends. They looked as confused as Lisa felt. "How could you help him? He condemned you. He judged you. He thought he was better than you, so why would you help him?"

Lisa's circle of friends was stone quiet. They collectively turned to look at her. What was she supposed to say? Why wouldn't she help him? Wouldn't they?

She hadn't formulated a response yet when a bunch of kids raced by them and out the door to the parking lot. They were Freddie's holy roller friends. "They must be scared, too. Not knowing how he is."

"See what I mean?" Alivia said. "Why do you give a flying f-bomb about them? I just don't get it."

Sam came to Lisa's rescue. "Because that's who she is, and that's why I love her."

Lisa hugged Sam and whispered in her ear, "Thank you."

"Love you, baby."

When Sam and Lisa separated, Lisa was just about to suggest they get out of there, maybe go back to Sam's or Susie's house or anywhere else but the East Valley High School gym. Sam beat her to it.

"Guys, we're gonna head outta here," Sam said. "Is that okay with you, baby?"

Lisa rolled her eyes as she nodded.

"It's been a blast and all, but I think we're all worn out." Sam put a protective arm around Lisa's waist.

"I've had enough drama for one night," Lisa said, this time out loud.

"For a lifetime," Marlee muttered under her breath, but everyone heard it and chuckled.

"Yeah, I think we're going to head out, too. Go somewhere nice and quiet." Ronnie raised a suggestive eyebrow at Jordan.

"Ah, boys in love," Sam said.

"Hey," Ronnie blurted, "I just got an idea."

"Uh, oh," Karl said.

Ronnie stuck his tongue out at Karl. "I just decided I'm having a New Year's Eve party. My parents always go out, so we'll have the place to ourselves. Everyone's invited!"

"Sounds like fun," Sam said. "I'm flying home from Switzerland that day, and I'll be jetlagged to beat the band, but I'll be there. Okay, then, have a fun night, everybody, what's left of it. We're outta here."

After the circle of friends hugged their goodbyes, Sam texted Cassie to bring the limousine around to pick them up. They collected their coats from the coat room, and just as Lisa was about to put her coat on, she realized that she had forgotten to get her silk wrap from the paramedics. Oh, well. It was Freddie's now.

"There's our ride," Marlee said, shuffling back and forth on the sidewalk where she, Susie, Sam, and Lisa huddled together to keep warm. The temperature seemed to have dropped since they'd gone in.

"Hey, tall girl," somebody said from behind them.

They turned around to see who had addressed Lisa. Oh, no. It was that jerk, Ryan.

"That was pretty cool what you did for Freddie back there. I mean, I still think you're a bunch of queers, but that was good." His friends didn't say a word. He smacked one of them on the chest. "C'mon, let's go find some beer."

Chapter Seven

*"How very good and pleasant it is when
kindred live together in unity!"* — Psalm
133:1

"Lisa Anne Brown, get out of bed this instant. You will not make us late for church," her mother boomed into Lisa's room.

"I'm not going, Mom." Lisa rolled over to face the wall. "I'm not going to that stupid church ever again."

"Oh, yes, you are, young lady." Lisa's mother threw open the closet door. She pulled out a thick wool skirt and a shirt to match. "There were conditions on going to that dance last night. We are going to church, and when we get home, you are studying for your exams. If I'm not mistaken, you have two tests tomorrow."

"English and Spanish. Let me stay home, Mom. I'll study. I promise."

"Get up, missy. I'm not fooling around." The volume in her mother's voice reached a level Lisa had never heard before. Her mother threw the skirt and blouse on Bridget's bed and huffed out of the room.

"Geez. Fine," Lisa mumbled. "Whatever." She sat up with a yawn. There were some things you did not push her mother about.

Going to church was one of them.

Even though she dressed in record time, there was no time for breakfast. She checked her siblings' seatbelts and then flung her own on. She stared out the window fuming about having to go back to that church.

About a half mile into the trip, Lisa felt an uncharacteristic quiet in the family van. Lynnie was reading in the farthest backseat as usual, so that wasn't anything new. But although Lawrence Jr. played with his Captain America action figure, he was doing it quietly in his seat next to Lynnie. And even Bridget wasn't asking a thousand questions or singing or fussing. It was the quietest car trip the Brown family had ever made to church or anywhere.

You would've thought they had made a vow of silence the way they entered their family pew, heads down, not making eye contact. Once the service started, and the kids stood to go to Sunday school, Bridget whispered, "Lisa?"

"What's up, Sweetpea?" Lisa whispered back.

"Did Mama put you in time out?"

Lisa simply nodded and put a finger to her lip to shush any further questions. She nudged her sister toward the aisle where Lynnie was waiting to take her hand. Lisa sat back against the pew and stewed. How could her mother make her go back to this place that had so openly condemned her? And her father? He hadn't stepped in at all. Hadn't they heard Reverend Rinaldi denounce her last week? Why should she have to sit there and listen to more stupidity? And the congregation, how could she look at them? Word had probably gotten around about the six-foot-tall, dark-haired gay girl from Clarksonville that had gone to the East Valley Snowball Dance last night. There weren't too many girls that fit that description, and she hadn't just gone to the dance and sat at the gay table, oh, no. She had gone to the dance with Samantha Rose Payton, daughter of the wealthiest people in Clarksonville County, who everybody knew. And now everyone would know that she, Lisa Anne Brown, was Sam's girlfriend. She kept her eyes down.

Thank God Reverend Owens was back. Maybe he'd say something about Reverend Rinaldi's sermon. Lisa brightened. Yeah, maybe he'd apologize for Reverend Rinaldi's rudeness and ignorance and un-guestlike demeanor. But as the service wore on, nothing like that happened. Not even close.

Discouraged, Lisa looked down and picked at her nails. When Mr. Petrov got up to read scripture, Lisa decided she would read scripture, too. But she wouldn't read what he was reading. She picked up the pew Bible and flipped to the beginning of the book. The good ole Old Testament. She positioned the Bible so no one, not even her mother, could see what she was reading.

She turned the pages until she found what she was looking for. Leviticus 18:22. She read silently to herself. "You shall not lie with a male as with a woman; it is an abomination."

Yep, she had remembered it correctly. It seemed pretty straightforward. Being gay was an abomination. It said so in the Bible, right there in black and white. Of course, the verse didn't say anything about two women, did it? Lisa chuckled silently, although she knew that wasn't a valid loophole. Not that she was looking for loopholes; she was just trying to understand. Why did the book of Leviticus mention anything about gays in the first place? Apparently, gay people had been around for a long, long time. She turned back to the first chapter of Leviticus and read silently as the service went on without her.

Holy crap. In Leviticus chapter one, God speaks to Moses about the proper way to slaughter animals. Gross. Apparently, there were right and wrong ways to make your "burnt offerings" to God. Moses was supposed to relay all of this to the Israelites. Lisa cringed as she skimmed the passage. It talked in detail about the different ways to slaughter bulls and sheep and goats and pigeons and turtledoves. Gross to infinity. This was in the Bible? It even specified what side of the altar you should smear the blood on. Clearly, this stuff was written when the world was a very different place. When did the book of Leviticus take place, anyway? She knew all about the parting of the Red Sea and everything, but did Moses do that before or after the Leviticus chapter? And, seriously, what was up with all the sacrifices?

She turned back to the table of contents. Leviticus was the third book of the Old Testament. Genesis was the first, of course, and Exodus was the second. She had read parts of Genesis before, but not that thoroughly. She set her chin, determined to figure this out. She flipped back to Genesis, chapter one. "In the beginning when God created the heavens and the earth—"

"Lisa," her mother hissed.

Lisa looked up to see the entire congregation standing. Oh, geez. She stood and smoothed out her skirt, a finger tucked in the book of Genesis. Wow. Was it time for the affirmation of faith already? She didn't need to affirm her faith. She had faith. Faith in God. Faith in herself. She just wasn't sure she had faith in her church or the people around her anymore.

Once the service was over, Lisa thought her torture was also over, but, no, of course not. Her mother sprang the news that she had made an appointment for Lisa with Reverend Owens immediately following the coffee reception. This was the second meeting her mother had set up. The first was in the spring when she found out Lisa was gay. This new one must be because of Reverend Rinaldi. Lisa knew her mother simply wanted her to check in and make sure everything was okay on both sides.

Reluctantly, Lisa followed her family through the side door of the sanctuary to a hallway leading past the Sunday school to the reception hall. Bridget skipped ahead with Lawrence Jr. right behind her. Oddly, Lynnie walked side by side with Lisa and didn't have her nose in a book like she usually did.

It was basically Lisa's job to keep the kids in line whenever they stayed for coffee receptions, so Lisa quickly corralled Bridget and Lawrence Jr. into the unofficial kids' corner of the hall. She grabbed a wooden fold-up chair, hung her coat over the back, and plopped down in it. Lynnie scraped another chair across the floor and had her book open before she'd sat down. Bridget and Lawrence Jr. ran around playing tag with a couple of the other kids. All Lisa wanted to do was go home and pretend to study in her room while she texted with Sam and then took a nap. She would have texted Sam then, but her mother had strict rules about cell phone use in church.

Geez, she was tired. She hadn't gotten home from Sam's until midnight. After they left the dance, they'd all gone back to Sam's house and slow danced in the living room of Sam's suite. Way too soon, it was time for Lisa and Marlee to head back to Clarksonville.

Feeling eyes burning into her, Lisa looked up and saw her mother and Mrs. Maynard looking right at her. Her mother had the oddest look on her face. Oh, geez, Lisa thought. Mrs. Maynard must have heard about the dance, the gay table, and the fact that Lisa had gone with a girl. Crap.

Lisa swallowed hard against the lump in her throat and looked away. After forever, she dared to look up again and watched as her mother said something to Mrs. Maynard, tapped her arm, and headed toward her in the kids' corner. Oh, geez, now what?

Just then, Reverend Owens appeared from out of nowhere. "Are you ready, Lisa?"

Lisa bolted out of her seat and threw her winter coat on. "Absolutely." She motioned to her mother that she was going to Reverend Owens's office. Her mother nodded and headed back to the coffee station.

Lisa followed Reverend Owens out the back door of the rec hall to the main administration building of the church, where he had his office. The last meeting Lisa had in his office was in mid-July, after her mother found out her relationship with Sam was more than friendship. That meeting had gone okay. It was obvious at the time that neither of them wanted to be there, and Reverend Owens had basically told her to pray for guidance and to make good choices. That was good advice for any occasion.

Lisa couldn't help thinking that this time would be different.

"Let me take your coat, Lisa." Lisa would have preferred to keep it on, almost like armor against the judgment she was sure she'd be receiving but handed it to the reverend and sat down in the same chair she'd sat in the last time.

His desk was piled high with papers and books. Dust covered the old-fashioned computer monitor and the overflowing bookshelves.

"So your mother—"

Lisa didn't let him finish. "Can you tell me about Leviticus, Reverend?" She wanted to steer this conversation because once

Reverend Owns got talking, it was hard to derail him. "It's about the Levites, right? One of the twelve tribes of Israel?"

"You're curious about the Old Testament, are you?" He sat down behind his desk in an ancient office chair. It looked as old as he was.

"Yeah, I mean Genesis was all about creation. Adam and Eve eat from the tree of knowledge, Cain kills his brother Abel, Noah builds the ark, and all that, but—"

"Lisa, you can't forget about the stories of Abraham and Isaac and Jacob and Joseph and the valuable lessons we learn from the sinful cities of Sodom and Gomorrah—"

"I know, I know. I learned most of that through Sunday school." She didn't mean to be rude by interrupting him, but she had to grab the reins back, otherwise, she'd be there until Christmas morning discussing the meaning of every chapter and verse of the Old Testament. Except that the reverend would probably keep talking his way into the New Testament, and she'd be there through Easter. She pressed on. "In Exodus, Moses leads the Israelites out of Egypt, parts the Red Sea, gets the Ten Commandments from God, but how does that lead to the next book Leviticus?"

"Well, remember that in Exodus, Moses delivered the Israelites to Mount Sinai, and all along their journey, Moses relays the laws that God wants them to obey and the traditions He wants them to follow."

"Yeah?" Lisa scooted forward on the chair. Now they were getting somewhere. "Leviticus starts with burnt offerings, and disgustingly, how to do them."

"Exactly. Leviticus is basically a detailed list from God to the Israelites about Jewish ceremonial laws that He wants them to carry out. Leviticus is mainly in God's voice. Did you know that? Back in my seminary days, we studied –"

"Why all the rules in Leviticus, though?" *Stay on track, Reverend, stay on track.* The last time she had a meeting with Reverend Owens like this, she heard way too many stories about his time in seminary. A time he obviously looked back on fondly, but today she didn't have time to hear about how every Sunday, they were issued one cloth napkin that they had to use for the entire week of meals. "It seems like a lot of rules. It must have been hard for the Israelites to follow them all."

Reverend Owens nodded. He leaned back in his ancient chair and put his fingertips together. "God's rules for the Israelites were strict. Infractions often meant death. God sent fire down to kill two priests who didn't use the proper procedure for approaching the altar."

"That seems pretty harsh."

"God's not fooling around in Leviticus. If anyone cursed God's name, ate meat with blood still in it, or performed sexual sins, they were punishable by death."

"You shall not lie with a male as with a woman; it is an abomination," Lisa quoted and sat back in the chair. She stared at the faded carpet under her feet. It was one of God's laws. Directly from Him.

"Leviticus 18:22."

The grandfather clock clicked off the seconds in the uncharacteristically quiet office. Lisa choked back the emotion building up inside. The old carpet blurred in her vision as tears took over. She reached up and wiped at her eyes. She didn't want to cry in front of Reverend Owens. Why didn't he say something? Anything.

"Lisa, look at this."

She looked up to see him stand and take a plaque off a bookshelf.

"Here, read it out loud." He handed her the plaque.

"'Love conquers hate.' This is from the Human Rights Campaign?" She pointed to the tiny blue and yellow square under the words. "Isn't that a gay and lesbian group?"

Reverend Owens nodded. "A parishioner gave this to me a few years ago. I can't say his name, but he was in the same predicament you're in."

"Predicament?" she mumbled under her breath. Is that what it was?

He put the plaque back on the shelf. "I keep it there to remind me that we have to deal with God's plan for each of us in our own way. We must each have our own personal relationship with God. We must each deal with the temptations of the devil in our own ways, as well. Beware the tools of the devil, Lisa, for he is quite crafty." He stood up. Their session was apparently over.

"Perhaps you simply haven't met the right young man yet, Lisa. Perhaps this is a test of your faith. God hasn't given up on you." He turned away from her and looked out the window to the prayer garden covered with snow. "Go with God, Lisa."

Lisa wasn't sure what to make of his final statement, but it was obvious that she had been dismissed. Remembering her manners, she said, "Thank you, Reverend. I appreciate you taking the time to talk with me today."

He nodded once but did not turn around.

She stood, shrugged on her coat, and left with more questions than she went in with.

Chapter Eight

"Discipline yourselves, keep alert. Like a roaring lion your adversary the devil prowls around, looking for someone to devour." — 1 Peter 5:8

Lisa had intended to spend most of her time after church studying for her English and Spanish exams, but she couldn't concentrate and lay on her bed trying to make sense of life. In her head, Reverend Owens kept saying, "Beware the tools of the devil," and "Go with God." Sitting up with a start, her unread English notebook hit the floor with a bang as she realized what he had been trying to tell her. He thought the devil had coerced her into the abomination of homosexuality. In other words, "Go with God, Lisa, not the devil."

Unsettled, she texted Sam and told her about her visit with the reverend. Sam helped her understand that the reverend wasn't perfect. He was human just like they were and a product of the generation he'd grown up in. Lisa wished she could have talked to Sam on the phone instead of texting, but if her mother caught her on the phone, she would be in time out for real and wouldn't be able to see Sam at the youth alliance meeting on Tuesday. There was no way she was going to take a chance on that.

After a grueling marathon of three exams in two days, Tuesday evening finally came. Lisa was free and clear until Thursday morning's U.S. History and Government exam. Ugh. That one was going to fry her no matter how much she studied. Mrs. B's exams were legendary for causing the brainiest of brainiacs to cry. Thank God Friday's Anatomy exam would be a cakewalk. She had an A+ in that class and didn't expect that to change.

Lisa heard the crunch of tires on the snow in the driveway. She peeked out the front window.

"Mom, Marlee's here. I'm going now." Lisa threw on her coat and scarf and opened the front door.

Her mother came out of the kitchen, Bridget in tow. "Have a good time but be back here by nine at the latest."

"Yes, Mom. Thanks for letting me go. I think…" she swallowed against the sudden lump in her throat. "I think maybe this youth alliance will be good for me."

"I know, honey. I know. Have a good time. But I want you in your room at nine to study for at least an hour."

Lisa nodded, gave her mother and Bridget one giant hug, and headed out into the cold. Honestly, she had expected her mother to forbid her from attending the youth alliance meeting. It was exam week, after all, but miracles did happen in the Brown household now and then.

She kicked the snow off her shoes and hopped into the passenger seat of Marlee's van.

"Hey, catcher," Marlee said from the driver's seat. "Look what I found on the side of the road." She pointed to Julie and Marcus in the back seat.

"Hey, you guys." Lisa put her seat belt on. "Are you ready to see

71

what this youth alliance is all about?"

"Yeah," Julie said. "Are you sure it's okay for us to be there? Being of the straight persuasion and all?"

"Ronnie and Jordan said the group was for anybody," Marlee said. She pulled the van onto C.R. 62, heading for Clarksonville Community College. "And, hey, if we hate it, we don't have to stay, right?"

"I hope we don't hate it, though," Marcus said. "It would be nice to have a place to hang out. A place without judgment." He smiled at Julie and reached for her hand. She smiled back. They were obviously smitten with each other.

Lisa smiled. A happy feeling bubbled up inside. She was going to see Sam and be surrounded by her friends. One dark spot marred her happy bubble, though. Alivia was probably going to be there, too.

Marlee pulled the van onto the college campus. Using the GPS on her phone, Lisa gave Marlee directions to the Student Union building.

"Hey, I forgot to ask," Marlee said. "How was your Algebra 2 exam this morning?" Marlee was the resident math nerd.

"Great!" Lisa said. "I can factor n^{th}-degree polynomials with the best of them."

"Yeah," Julie added, "it wasn't too bad, but I'm not looking forward to U.S. History and Government on Thursday."

Marcus chimed in. "I still have two more chapters to read. Thank God we don't have any exams tomorrow."

"No exams tomorrow was the only reason my mom let me go to this thing tonight," Lisa said.

"Mrs. B assigns more reading than anyone can humanly

handle." Marlee pulled the van into a parking spot. "I got heartburn studying for her exam. Hey, look, Susie and Sam are here already." She pointed to Sam's Sebring a few spots away.

"Yay." Lisa bounced in her seat, clapping joyously. "I know it's only been three days since the dance, but it seems like forever."

"You've got it bad, Lisa," Julie teased.

Lisa snorted. "So do you." She winked at Marcus, who blushed to the roots of his short blond surfer-dude hair.

They quickly found the meeting room on the first floor of the Student Union, and as soon as Lisa spotted Sam, she flung herself into her arms. "I missed you." A quick kiss and a healing hug were all the fuel Lisa needed to feel better. Marlee and Susie were exchanging a similar greeting.

"Enough nookie nookie," Ronnie said with a smile from the back of the room. He introduced Lisa and her friends to the other members of the youth alliance. In addition to Ronnie and Jordan, there were three guys and one girl from Southbridge High School, where Jordan went to school.

Anne, the adult leader of the group, finished fussing with the video camera and looked up. Lisa and her friends had met her a few months before at the gay pride event on campus. A smile filled Anne's face. "Wow. This is such a great turnout."

"I know," Ronnie squealed like a little girl. "I'm so excited."

"Stash your coats on the table in the back," Anne said, "and then have a seat so our director can tell us what we're in for tonight."

With the addition of Lisa, Sam, Marlee, Susie, Julie, and Marcus, the size of the group had doubled. Lisa relaxed a little bit. Alivia and Karl were nowhere to be seen. Maybe a gay group was a little too much for Alivia.

No sooner had the thought entered her head when the door opened, and Alivia floated in with Karl trailing behind her. They said hello to everybody, but Alivia's hello to Lisa was cold and perfunctory. Alivia undid her coat, and Lisa was amazed at how tight her peasant blouse was. There was no mistaking her intent; she was putting her best perky assets forward, just like she'd done at the dance. Lisa looked down at her own tight lemon-colored sweater. Hmm, the battle of the boobs was on. Lisa wrapped her arm around Sam's and pulled her closer. She was rewarded with a flirtatious smile that curled her toes. Ronnie was rambling on about the *Respect* video they would be filming that evening, but all Lisa wanted to do was ditch the meeting and find a place to let Sam explore the assets under her sweater.

Lisa reluctantly turned her attention back to Ronnie when she heard him say, "So each of you will get a part in the *Respect* video if you want one, that is." Ronnie flicked his head to toss a lock of his dark, meticulously styled bedhead hair out of his eyes. "The more diversity we have, the better." This time he was looking straight at Julie, their resident person of color. "This is not necessarily a gay/straight thing. It's a people thing. And the lovely Jordan will be our host and narrator."

Jordan bowed, and Lisa found herself clapping along with everyone else. Jordan was a good-looking guy, handsome even. He had tamed his ginger hair for the video instead of wearing it in his usual spiked doo. He wore it more like Ronnie's style, professional bedhead.

"Thank you, thank you." Jordan put up his hands to stop the applause. He leaned back against the whiteboard in the front of the

74

room, the heels of his hands resting on the marker tray. "We have a lot of work to do tonight. Our goal is to make a short video of a diverse group of kids stating our obvious and sometimes not-so-obvious differences. We want to somehow, and I'm not sure how we do this, but we want to convey the idea that everyone needs respect. You know what I mean?"

"Like, we're all different, but we're all the same," Lisa offered.

"Yes!" Jordan pushed off the board and pointed a finger at Lisa. "That's exactly it! We're all different in one way or another, but then again, we're all the same."

"I love it." Ronnie put on an imaginary director's hat. "I had some ideas, but now I see a whole new video playing out in front of my eyes. Here's want I want us to do. Everybody grab one of these board markers and write a word that might describe our differences. Anything goes, but keep it appropriate for kids. We want this video to be seen, not censored." He picked up a marker and wrote the words GAY, LESBIAN, STRAIGHT, BI, ACE, TRANSGENDERED, and QUESTIONING in all different places on the board.

"Go, go, go," Ronnie urged. "What're you waiting for?"

Lisa leaped up and followed her friends to the board. She wrote, "TALL."

Sam copied the theme and wrote, "SHORT."

"Baby, you're not short," Lisa said and then rested her elbow on top of Sam's head.

Sam chuckled and ducked out from under the elbow. "I'm the shortest one here. I always am, but that's okay. I've got you, and together we're perfect."

"Yep."

Lisa leaned down for a hug when Ronnie snapped, "Writey,

writey. No nookie, nookie."

Lisa stuck her tongue out at Ronnie and turned away before seeing what mature gesture he responded with.

The whiteboard was quickly filling with words. Some handwriting was neat, others not so much. Even Anne threw in the words "OLD" and "YOUNG."

"One more minute, you guys. Find your seats when you're done." Ronnie set the timer on his phone and went back to frantically writing a script on the whiteboard in the back of the room.

Once everyone was seated, Ronnie went through his script, and they collectively made adjustments until everyone was satisfied with it. They moved the long tables out of the way so they could move around freely. Anne moved behind the video camera that was perched on top of a tripod. It definitely wasn't a professional camera, but it looked expensive. Lisa wondered if Sam had anything to do with it.

"Places, please," Ronnie said. "Let's try to get this scene in one take."

Lisa moved to the far left of the whiteboard with the words written all over it in colorful ink. Sam moved to the far right, and everyone else squatted in height order between them but below camera range.

Ronnie looked at Lisa and Sam and said, "Action."

Lisa looked right at the camera lens as Ronnie had directed. "Some of us are tall."

"Some of us are short," Sam said.

One by one, the others stood until everyone was standing, and collectively they said, "and some of us are in between."

"Cut!" Ronnie called. "Excellent. Okay, onto the next scene."

Scene by scene, the camera captured their differences. Lisa particularly liked the one where they got in order by skin color. Ronnie decided to use forearm shots to focus on skin color only. Lisa ended up next to Marcus at the lighter end of the color scale, and it was funny to see Julie blow Marcus a kiss from way down the line. Lisa had never truly noticed how vastly different everyone's skin color was. Somehow it suddenly seemed wrong to think of Julie and Susie as people of color when it was so glaringly obvious that they all had color in varying degrees. God, she hated labels.

For the gay angle, Ronnie didn't want people to out themselves. "People can be assholes," he said. Was he thinking about the holy rollers at the dance?

He directed them to stand in one group. Lisa wasn't surprised when Alivia ditched Karl to snuggle up close to Sam. By some miracle, Lisa was able to keep her temper from boiling over and resigned herself to stand next to Karl in the back.

"Action," Ronnie said.

"Some of us are straight, and some of us are gay," they said collectively.

Jordan took up the lines solo. "I know you're wondering who is who, but it's not for me to say." Jordan's voice was so calm and smooth that he could have been a radio announcer for that smooth jazz station from Montréal that Lisa's father sometimes played on Sundays.

"Cut! That was beautiful, baby," Ronnie gushed, causing Jordan to blush.

"Now, I want all of you to turn your backs to the camera while Jordan wraps up our message." He gave them stage directions as to when to hold up their numbers, when to turn around, and when to throw the confetti they held in their hands.

Lisa said to Karl, "I can't wait to see how this whole *Respect* video comes out."

"Me, too," he said.

Alivia must have heard Lisa's comment because she said, "Ronnie and Jordan came up with such a great idea."

"This is going on YouTube?"

"Yeah," Alivia said.

"That's incredible," Lisa said, trying to remain cordial to Alivia. "I wonder how many hits we'll get." Lisa was about to ask Sam if she needed to get her parents' permission when Ronnie asked for "Quiet on the set."

Jordan cleared his throat. He had a lot of dialogue ahead.

"Ready," Ronnie asked Jordan, who nodded. "Okay then. Action!"

"If we were all the same, we'd be a number in the crowd." Still facing away from the camera, everyone held a number over their heads. "We're tall. We're short. We're everything in between. We're different genders, different ages, different colors. We have a splattering of this and a spattering of that, but despite all these splatters, we're the same in all that matters."

Lisa was riveted. Ronnie had written an amazing script. The words were lyrical, like the Dr. Seuss stories she read to Bridget, yet they were as powerful as any sermon she'd heard in church. Sermon. Shoot. They hadn't written down any religious stuff on the board. Too late. They had to wrap this up soon, or she'd be late getting home.

"We're all human," Jordan said simply. "From top to bottom

and side to side; we live and love and laugh and cry. No one's better or superior; no one's lesser or inferior. To live is to love, to love is to live; so let's live and let live, let's love and let love."

Jordan paused for a moment, and this was their cue. Everyone turned around to face the camera, sporting smiles as Jordan finished. He said the words slowly to get the most effect. "Each of us is different, and yet we're all the same."

Ronnie motioned for them to toss the confetti and cheer.

"Yay!" Lisa cheered and threw her bits of white paper in the air.

They cheered and congratulated each other until Ronnie yelled, "Cut!"

Lisa blew out a sigh. "Geez, that was fun."

Sam grinned and smashed Lisa with a hug. It was nice to be free to be who she was with Sam.

"Well done, everybody," Anne said. She turned off the video camera and walked to the front of the room. "I have waivers for those of you who are under eighteen." She pointed to a pile of papers on a table near the door. "Bring them back or mail me the signed copies. Ronnie, Jordan, and I will get busy editing this masterpiece, and we hope to have a finished product to show you at our next meeting."

"You know what, you guys?" Lisa said.

"What?" Ronnie asked.

"We didn't mention religion." Lisa gestured to the whiteboard that was still covered with their words.

"You're right," Anne said. "We didn't. Hmm. That's a big issue for many people, isn't it? Did you have something in mind, Lisa?"

"Not really. I know we can't redo this whole thing, but maybe we could make another video. You know, sometime."

Ronnie narrowed his eyes. "A debate." He stabbed his finger in the air.

"Debate?" Lisa cringed and looked over at Sam, who simply shrugged her shoulders.

By this time, a few of the others had gathered around, obviously interested.

"Maybe we should invite Freddie and his Holy Rollers," Jordan offered.

"No," Lisa said quickly. The very idea made her incredibly uncomfortable. Not only did she not want to see that kind of hatred directed at her ever again, but she'd learned that Freddie's seizure at the dance had been brought on by epilepsy, and since seizures could be triggered by stress, a heated debate could bring on another one. She had no desire to go through that again, and she was sure Freddie wouldn't want to either. "You guys are all actors." Lisa swept her hand around the room and made sure she included Alivia. "We can cast the holy rollers from you guys."

Ronnie pursed his lips as he nodded thoughtfully. "And you'll be on the other side denouncing religion altogether?"

Lisa inhaled sharply. "No, no. I, uh…" She struggled to find the right words. "I want to defend it."

"Defend the fanatics?" Jordan scrunched up his forehead. He was clearly confused.

"No, I want to defend religion. Defend the Bible."

"Whoa." Jordan's laugh said he didn't think it was possible. "Good luck with that one."

"C'mon, why not?" Lisa said. "The holy rollers always use the Bible against us. Maybe we can find a way to use it against them."

"Brilliant," Ronnie said, his eyes big. "I have no idea how we'll pull this off, but this is just brilliant."

"If not impossible," Anne murmured, but the grin on her face said she approved of the project.

"It's worth a shot," Marlee said. "I don't know anything about the Bible, but I'm willing to help out any way I can." Her cheeks were tinged red.

"Count us in, too," Marcus said and reached for Julie's hand. She smiled back at him and nodded to Lisa.

"Thanks, guys," Lisa said. "It sounds like we're gonna have a debate."

Anne looked at the clock and said it was time to clean up and head out.

Lisa picked up one end of a table while Ronnie picked up the other, and they moved it back into place. Lisa said, "I guess we shouldn't take any one religion's point of view, eh?"

"Right. But if you're going to use both the Old and New Testaments of the Bible, then the debate will have to be from a Christian standpoint."

"I hate to exclude people, but maybe this is where we have to start." They walked over to get their coats.

Ronnie nodded. "Give me your cell phone number, dearie, I have ideas, and we have tons to talk about."

"Oh, geez," Lisa said, "this is the first time a boy has asked me for my phone number."

"Really?"

"No, it isn't," Marcus interjected from across the room. "I asked you for it last spring."

"That's right. You'll always be my first, Marcus." She turned back to Ronnie. "And you'll be my second."

They laughed their way toward the door, and Lisa was surprised to see that Sam wasn't waiting for her. She turned fully around to double-check the room. No Sam. She must be in the hallway.

"Goodnight, Anne," Lisa said. "This was a lot of fun."

"Goodnight, Lisa. We'll see you next time."

"You bet."

Lisa headed out the meeting room door and stopped short. Sam and Alivia looked a little too cozy, leaning back against the wall deep in conversation. Alivia's cleavage was so close to Sam's arm that Lisa wanted to run over there and drop-kick Alivia to the next county. Lisa cleared her throat to let them know she was there. The smile that lit up Sam's face made Lisa think she must have imagined things, but then Alivia's smirk made it real. Game on, Alivia. Game on.

Chapter Nine

"My brothers and sisters, whenever you
face trials of any kind, consider it
nothing but joy, because you know that
the testing of your faith produces
endurance; and let endurance have its
full effect, so that you may be mature
and complete, lacking in nothing." —
James 1:2-4

When Lisa woke up early Saturday morning, it was uber dark. She tiptoed to the bathroom so she wouldn't wake anyone up. It was the first full day of Christmas vacation for the entire Brown family, and she wanted to steal a few moments for herself before the mayhem that was her family began. After using the bathroom, she slunk back to her room and eased open the closet door, hoping it wouldn't squeak and wake up her sister. She reached up on her tippy-toes to get the journal she'd hidden under a stack of sweaters. She climbed back in her bed, propped the pillows behind her, and pulled the covers up as far as they would go. Using a mini-flashlight to see, she wrote in her journal.

December 22
Sorry I haven't written in, like, forever, but life

has a way of intruding. Anyway, I'm sad because Sam left for Switzerland this morning, and Christmas is three days away, and I won't get to see her. I didn't even get to see her last night. She hung out with Helene. Sam texted me, though, and said they sat up late watching ice hockey and drinking hot tea. I feel bad. Helene will be completely moved out by the time Sam gets back. That's going to be hard for Sam, losing somebody that's been like a second mother to her.

Change of subject needed.

The U.S. History and Gov't exam was so hard that a few kids were crying at the end. Missy Matthews was throwing a fit, saying how unfair it was. She threw a tantrum like the ones Bridget used to throw. Foot stomping and all. It was kind of ridiculous, but I'm sure her daddy will call the school and give Mrs. B a piece of his mind. How dare a teacher upset his precious princess. Mrs. B will probably tell him to take a long walk off a short pier. On the other hand, I think I aced my Anatomy exam. I had all the vocab down pat but was bummed there weren't any questions on the limbic system of the brain. I thought for sure Ms. Lye was going to test us on that. Whatev. Doesn't matter. I aced it and can't wait for the second semester. Maybe I should talk to her about what

courses I should take senior year if I want to apply
to medical school.

I used to want to be a paramedic, you know? Ride
in the ambulance, take care of people in car
crashes or people like Freddie who need help. But
now I'm thinking bigger. I want to be a doctor.
What kind? Who knows.

Lisa waited for a moment to look out the window. Light was just
beginning to tinge the sky. Maybe it would be a sunny day, but that
usually meant it would be frigidly cold. She knew her mother was
going to make her take her sisters and brother outside to build a
snowman or a fort or something, but all she really wanted to do was
be with Sam who was probably somewhere over the Atlantic Ocean
at that point.

She stretched out her right hand. You'd think all that writing
during exam week would have built up her writing muscles, but no.

So speaking of holy rollers. LOL. Ronnie has been
texting me constantly! He says that the next time
the youth alliance meets, we're going to outline
and maybe even start videotaping our debates. He
and Alivia (of course, it would have to be her)…

Lisa paused from her writing to draw a bunch of frowny faces
around Alivia's name. Feeling childish, she scribbled them out and
then drew hearts around Sam's name to atone for her juvenile

behavior. But Alivia did make her frown. She didn't know what her deal with Sam was. The fact that Alivia went to school with Sam and got to see her every day was positively nerve-wracking.

Lisa groaned. There was no sense worrying about Alivia. Sam was on her way to ski in the Swiss Alps, far far away from Alivia.

Okay, where was I? Oh, yeah. Ronnie and Alivia are going to head up the "Homosexuality is a Sin" side of the debate. He said I need to pick people to help me on my side. Marlee said she'd help, but I don't know. I need somebody who knows the Bible. Maybe Susie. She's Catholic, and they're pretty strict about gay people, so maybe she has a clue where we can get started.

Ronnie told me some of the Bible verses he and Alivia plan on throwing at us. The Sodom and Gomorrah story in Genesis, to start off. I don't know how in the world I'm going to interpret that one in my favor, but I have to figure it out somehow. I've always left it up to my parents, Reverend Owens, and others to interpret the Bible for me, but I have to think for myself now. Ronnie said they're looking at stuff from the books of Genesis, Ezekiel, Deuteronomy, and Leviticus. At first, I thought they were sticking with the Old Testament, but then he sent a whole bunch of new texts yesterday saying Alivia found ammunition

in the books of Jude, Matthew, and Timothy. I'm
really really bummed that they found something
in Matthew. He's my favorite apostle. {BIG SIGH}
I have my work cut out for me, don't I?

Lisa jumped when Bridget stirred in her bed. Lisa had been so lost in thought that she forgot where she was. She scribbled a few more lines in her journal and then stashed it in her bedside stand.

"Morning, Sweetpea," Lisa said as Bridget sat up.

"Morning, Weesa." Bridget rubbed the sleep from her eyes and then leaped out of bed only to launch herself onto Lisa's bed.

Lisa moved over just in time so she wouldn't get flattened by the almost four-year-old. Lisa wrapped her arms around her sister and blew a zerbert on her neck.

Bridget's giggles were more than enough to pull Lisa out of her worries and back into a happy place.

"You know what we should do, Sweetpea?" Lisa sat up, taking Bridget with her.

Bridget caught her breath and said, "What?"

"We should make pancakes for everybody."

Lisa almost laughed at how Bridget's face lit up. "Okay." She leaped off the bed and headed for the door.

"Wait for me." Lisa threw her robe on and raced after her sprinting sister.

They made so much noise trying to throw together a surprise pancake breakfast for their family of six that by the time Lisa got ready to pour the pancake batter into the pan, the entire family was up and sitting at the table. In the past, when she and Bridget made surprise pancakes for the family, Lisa spent a good part of the time cleaning up Bridget's various messes, but not today. Today, Bridget actually set the table all by herself. Of course, Lisa had to get the dishes and juice glasses from the cupboard, but Bridget managed to get the silverware and napkins by herself.

"What a nice surprise," Lisa's mother said as she moved in to help.

"No, Mom. I've got this," Lisa said and flipped a pancake. "Go sit and enjoy some downtime, okay?"

"I'll just bring out the syrup."

Lisa rolled up a dishtowel and snapped it at her mother. "Git."

Her mother raised an eyebrow and nodded. "I guess I will. Thank you."

Lisa smiled and got back into production. She had to make quite a mound of pancakes to feed all six hungry members of the Brown family.

Lisa laughed when she heard her mother say to Lisa's father, "Apparently, I've been kicked out of my own kitchen."

"Take it when you can get it, eh?" Her father laughed his big, infectious belly laugh, and soon everyone was giggling and telling funny jokes.

"Breakfast is served," Lisa said, carrying a tray filled with the family breakfast.

Meals at the Brown house were always a noisy affair. The clanking of silverware on dishes and happy conversation filled the house. Oddly it made Lisa miss Sam. Sam always commented that she liked eating over at Lisa's. Sam was an only child whose family rarely sat down to eat together. That always made Lisa a little sad.

Lisa's mother cleared her throat.

Uh, oh. Lisa recognized the sound. Something unpleasant was

about to be said. Who would get it this time? Lynnie maybe? For not cleaning out the dishwasher? Lawrence Jr. for not putting away his action figures? Bridget for not being cute enough? Her mother turned toward Lisa. Darn. It was for her.

"So, Mrs. Maynard told me something interesting last Sunday," Lisa's mother said.

"What was that?" Oh, geez, Mrs. Maynard had probably heard about Lisa being a big old gay girl. And since Mrs. Maynard was the biggest gossip on the planet, the entire North Country probably knew she was gay by now.

"She heard something about you performing CPR on a boy at the dance last weekend?"

Lisa had taken the wrong moment to sip her orange juice and promptly started choking. She coughed it out and, when she could breathe again, said, "What? CPR? It's crazy how rumors get spread around in this town. He had a seizure, Mom and I helped him. That's all."

"What's a see-zer?" Bridget asked.

Lisa wiped Bridget's syrupy hands with the wet rag they always kept on the table during pancake breakfasts. "A seizure is when somebody's muscles tighten and loosen uncontrollably."

"Does it hurt?"

"I don't really know, but I tried to make sure he didn't bang his head on the floor." Lisa looked at her mother. "And that's about the extent of it, Mom."

Her mother reached over and patted her on the forearm. "Well, I'm glad you were able to help that young man." She chuckled and added, "I may not correct Mrs. Maynard. She was quite impressed with you."

Lisa laughed and felt her cheeks get warm. Mrs. Maynard wouldn't be too impressed if she knew Lisa was a flaming queer girl.

"Mom?" Lisa found herself saying. "I don't want to go to church tomorrow."

The sudden silence at the table startled her. Lisa stared down at her now-empty plate. "I think I want to give our church a break."

"And do what?"

"I don't know." Geez, she should have thought it out more. "Maybe I can check out another church. Maybe find one that's more accepting." She barely choked out the last words as tears closed her throat.

Afraid she would embarrass herself in front of her family, Lisa excused herself and bolted from the table. Once alone in her room, she plopped on her bed and let herself cry until she was cried out.

Lisa wiped at her eyes when there was a gentle knock at her door. "Can I come in?" her mother asked.

"Sure, Mom." Lisa sat up and reached for a tissue from her bedside stand. "Sorry about the theatrics. I didn't want to upset the kids."

"I understand." She patted Lisa's knee. "Make room for your old mother."

"Mom, you're not old." Lisa scooched up on the bed and pulled her long legs up to her chest.

Her mother sat down. "Tell me what you're thinking."

Lisa was surprised. She had fully expected her mother to tell her in no uncertain terms that she would be going to church with them the next morning without question. Her mother's reaction was puzzling, but like her father had said earlier, she had to take it when she could get it.

"I don't know, Mom. The reason I go to the Presbyterian Church of Clarksonville is because you and Papa bring me there."

"You were going there for six years before Papa came into the picture."

"That's 'cuz you brought me there when I was a baby. That must have been hard for you. Being a teen mom and still showing your face at church. I don't know if I can be as brave as you were. The Bible isn't very understanding about unwed mothers, is it?"

"No, it's not. Somewhere in Genesis, there's a passage about a woman named Tamar. She isn't married but gets pregnant. The man who got her pregnant called her a whore and said she should be burned."

Lisa's eyes grew wide. She didn't remember that passage in the Bible. "What about *him*? He's an unwed father. I guess that doesn't matter, eh?" Lisa was disgusted at the inequity.

"But Psalm 127:3 says, 'Behold, children are a heritage from the Lord, the fruit of the womb a reward.' You were my first reward, Lisa, and I have been blessed with three more. As far as church goes, I had the support of my parents and refused to be ashamed of the beautiful baby girl I brought into the world." She reached up and pinched Lisa's cheek.

Lisa's heart swelled. Her mother had gone through so much.

They both stayed silent for a moment until her mother asked, "So did you have another church in mind?"

"You'd be okay with me going to other churches?"

"I think you'd resent Papa and me if we don't let you explore your options. It'll be good for you."

Lisa thought about her biological father, William, who lived in East Valley. "Maybe I can go to William and Evelyn's church with them. They wouldn't mind. Do you think?"

"The only way to find out is to call him. I think they go to the Unitarian Universalist Church in East Valley."

Lisa nodded. She hadn't really thought the idea through, but it might be a great experience to get a different perspective.

"Maybe Marlee can drive me."

"Marlee?"

"Yeah, she wants to help me with that debate project I told you about. Oh, did you sign the waiver thingy?"

"Yes, it's on the table by the front door." She narrowed her eyes and said with a sigh. "I'll okay your church-search venture on two conditions."

"Okay."

"One. If it's snowing tomorrow, you come to church with us because I don't want you out on the roads in the snow with a new driver."

"Okay, I can do that." Lisa was perking up. Her mother was actually going to let her do this. "And, two?" She cringed for her mother's benefit.

"You will, absolutely will, go to church with us on Christmas Day."

Lisa smiled, relieved. "Of course, Mom. No one is going to keep me from having Christmas with my family." Not even a bigoted, self-righteous congregation.

Chapter Ten

"Ask, and it will be given you;
search, and you will find; knock,
and the door will be opened for
you." — Matthew 7:7

William held open the door to the Unitarian Universalist Church so that Evelyn, Lisa, and Marlee could pass through. After church, they would be heading back to William and Evelyn's house for a pot roast dinner.

The pointed arches and the stained glass windows of the church were spectacular, and the clean white wood of the building itself added a quiet reverence to the snowy grounds. But wait. There were two days until Christmas. Where was the manger scene? Where were the shepherds and the baby Jesus? Maybe they had set that up inside. Lisa had seen the church before, driving around with Sam, but she had no idea it had been founded in the 1820s. The lobby itself wasn't anything to write home about, but neither was the lobby in her church—her former church, Lisa corrected herself.

Evelyn turned to Lisa and said, "We're so glad you called about going with us today. We don't get to see you enough."

"I know," Lisa said. "I thought it would be a good way to see you guys and to explore other churches."

"We're glad you did," Evelyn said. "And, if I might add, that dress looks lovely on you."

"Thanks." Lisa wore one of her newer knee-length dresses because she wasn't sure how strict the dress code was at this church. She needn't have worried, though, because a lot of people had on jeans and sneakers. That seemed a little disrespectful, but who was she to judge? She was a visitor in their world.

Marlee was typically a jeans and t-shirt girl, but today she was dressed up in a loose-fitting silk blouse, black dress pants, and dress shoes. Marlee was an incredibly good sport for helping her out this way.

As they headed into the sanctuary of the main church, William took four pamphlets from the ushers at the door and handed one to each of them. "Are you questioning your faith, Lisa?"

"No, not really. Just the delivery of the faith."

"Then you're in the right place." He turned to Marlee and asked, "Do you also go to the Presbyterian Church of Clarksonville?"

Marlee blushed. It was so cute on her. "No, no. I don't go to church, like, ever. My parents used to take me to Lisa's church when I was a baby, but they stopped going for some reason." She lowered her voice and said, "You know, I feel so ignorant about all of this." She gestured around her. "Please don't let me make a mistake, like standing when we're supposed to be kneeling or something."

William laughed. "I think you've got our church mixed up with the Catholic Church. We don't do much kneeling around here."

"See? I don't even know stuff like that." Marlee sent Lisa a pleading look.

"Don't worry," Lisa said. "I'll help you through it. Well, William and Evelyn will, anyway."

"Girls," Evelyn said, "we'll sit in this row here, okay? The big guy and I need to sign up for some volunteer work. We'll be right back."

William smiled at Marlee with a twinkle in his eye. "Now, don't go kneeling willy-nilly all over the place while we're gone, okay?"

"Yes, sir." Marlee saluted him as he and Evelyn headed to the back of the church.

Lisa and Marlee sat in the pew, and Lisa drank in the atmosphere. There was definitely a lighter feel there. The casual way many of the people dressed set a different tone than she was used to. As the sanctuary filled, people spoke in full voice, unlike in her church where most casual conversations happened in hushed and respectful tones. Yes, this church had a definite easy-going feel. She liked it.

Marlee leaned closer and whispered, "I like William and Evelyn. They seem so cool."

"Thanks. I like them, too."

"So, William is your, uh, real father?"

"Yep. I think of him as my bio-dad, but I don't call him that to his face. I just call him William." Lisa gave Marlee a reassuring smile to let her know it was okay for her to ask. Lisa had only met her bio-dad six months before, so it was all new to her, too. She had always known that the man she called 'Papa' at home wasn't her biological father, but she loved him just as much as if he was.

"And Evelyn is your stepmom?"

"I guess so. I haven't really thought about it. It's all kind of confusing."

"What's confusing?" William asked from behind her.

95

Lisa chuckled. "Life. Life is confusing."

"I hear that." William entered the row and sat next to Lisa while Evelyn sat in the aisle seat.

"So, please excuse my extreme ignorance," Marlee said, leaning over Lisa, "but I assume the Unitarian Universalist Church is a Christian church, so—"

"Actually, the UU Church isn't Christian." William took a moment to gather his thoughts. "A UU Church is creedless." William laughed at Marlee's confused expression. "Other churches promote conformity among the members of the congregation." He looked at Lisa. "Like your church. The Presbyterians take pride in conformity, but UU churches don't. You *can* be a Christian to belong, but you don't have to be. You don't have to believe in heaven and hell. Heck, you don't even have to believe in God. Many people here do, of course, but others don't."

Lisa's jaw dropped open. How could you call it a church if some people don't believe in God?

Evelyn leaned over William to join in the conversation. "We're a church of diverse people. If there are a hundred UUs in a room, you'll probably have a hundred different views on the meaning of life and spirituality. But our church believes in the worth and dignity of every single person on the planet."

"Many call ours the liberal religion," William added. "Whatever your beliefs, you're welcome here. You're welcome here, whatever your station in life or whoever you love. We challenge you to be the best you that you can be through love and learning from others."

"Wow," Marlee sat back, "that's an amazing philosophy. I was going to ask why you chose this church, but I get it. It's no wonder you like coming here."

"Yeah, really," Lisa added, but it was all she could add at the moment. Respect for everyone, no matter who you were, sounded like a truly amazing way to live. But to not necessarily have a belief in God was confusing.

As she looked around the sanctuary, she realized there wasn't a single cross or depiction of Jesus anywhere. William wasn't kidding. This was not a Christian church. She wasn't sure if she was ready for such a big leap.

After a welcome from one of the church leaders, an obviously flaming gay guy got up and sang a song from one of those old Broadway musicals. The congregation clapped along, but Lisa couldn't help wondering what his performance had to do with church. It didn't make sense in her world. After that, a few children got up and shared their Skype experiences with a UU church in Kenya. That was amazing. She could totally see her sister Lynnie talking books with the kids there.

The congregation sat and sang a few songs, but then they stood and sang a few more. Lisa couldn't make sense of any of it but followed along out of respect. One of the religious leaders took the stage and cleared her throat. She stood about five-ten, looked to be in her early forties, and wore no make-up. Her buttoned-down white shirt tucked into a pair of chinos, resplendent with a wide brown belt, made her look strong and authoritative. Lisa's gaydar pinged. Marlee elbowed Lisa as if to say that her gaydar had gone off, too. Lisa smiled and nodded back.

The woman looked over the congregation, section by section. "We have a wonderful turnout here today and a few new guests. Should anyone want to introduce us to their guests, please feel free to do so at this time." She stepped back and smiled.

No, no, no, Lisa willed William with her mind. Don't make introductions. Lisa cringed when he stood up to his full six-foot-six-inch height. "I would like to introduce two young people here today with my wife and me. This is my daughter Lisa." A few excited murmurs ran through the crowd. Oh, geez. Nothing like being outed as his illegitimate daughter in front of the entire congregation. Lisa leaned forward and waved when the congregation clapped for her. It was so weird. She hoped her smile looked genuine and didn't betray how nervous she was. "And this is her friend Marlee." Marlee also waved.

Lisa willed her bio-dad to sit down, but he kept on. "They are Clarksonville High School students, and they are the pitcher and catcher from last year's state championship softball team." This last bit got wild cheers from the crowd, and Lisa felt her face flush even more. She smiled and nodded her thanks to the enthusiastic crowd.

William finally sat down and shut up. Thank God.

"I didn't know you were going to do that," Lisa hissed at William.

He chuckled and said, "I didn't want to make you nervous about it, but it's a tradition here. And if you didn't notice, I'm proud of you. Both of you." He reached around and managed to hug both of them with his long arm.

Lisa's heart felt full at that moment. Funny how that kept happening.

After a few more guest introductions, the religious leader resumed her command at the podium. "We are all in this together on this spinning planet. Sure we walk separate paths and have different experiences. We look different from one another, like different foods, enjoy different hobbies, work at different jobs, and speak with different accents. I tell you," she said with a laugh, "I still can't understand my father-in-law half the time. That's what I get for marrying a southerner."

Lisa laughed with the congregation, but she was disappointed. She thought the leader was going to say she was married to a woman. Maybe this was a place where even if people knew you were gay, they didn't talk about it.

The leader spoke about her northern New York upbringing and how she had to face her own prejudices when she fell in love with a southerner. She talked about meeting her future in-laws, sweating her butt off in Alabama in October, and eating weird southern food, but she had done it out of love. Soon enough, she learned that these things weren't weird; they were just different, and who was she to judge anyway?

"In fact," the leader said, "my wife makes the best grits and eggs in the entire North Country."

This also got a few laughs, but Lisa was ecstatic. Here was a charismatic church leader who was a lesbian and openly admitting it in front of her entire congregation. She couldn't imagine anything remotely resembling that at her church. No way. Not in a million years.

"If I had succumbed to the me-first phase or the what's-in-it-for-me movement, my heart may not have been opened enough to let that eggs-and-grits-making southerner into my life. Here at the UU of East Valley, we welcome new experiences into our lives. We want a world where we can help each other understand our differences and accept them as just that – differences. Not right. Not wrong. Just different. Variety is the spice of life, after all."

She wrapped up her sermon or speech or whatever it was called and then asked a few more people up to the podium to give announcements.

Once the service was over, they headed to the recreation room to share 'coffee and camaraderie.'

Lisa and Marlee stood off to one side of the crowded room while William and Evelyn went to get hot chocolate for all of them.

"So, what did you think?" Marlee asked. She leaned back against the paneled wall.

"Geez, I don't know. I'm still trying to wrap my head around it. I mean, it was like, okay people, let's have no judgey."

"Yeah, it was kind of like that *Respect* video we made at the youth alliance the other night. Live and let live, man."

Lisa nodded. The service had been a breath of fresh air. "It's like they're a society of people who think for themselves."

"Exactly," Marlee said. "I'm not a church-going person, but I kind of liked it. I bet Susie would like it, too, if her mother let her go."

"That would be cool."

"Uh, oh. Incoming," Marlee said.

"What?" Lisa turned to see where Marlee was focused. An overweight middle-aged man with a grizzly beard was headed their way. He wore stained jeans and a faded Buffalo Bills sweatshirt that looked like a second skin.

"First time here, girls?"

Lisa cringed at his onion breath. "Yes, my father is over there." Okay, that was lame, but she wanted him to know they weren't alone.

"Do you know anything about bees?" he asked.

Lisa exchanged a glance with Marlee. Where was this going?

"As much as the average person, I guess," Lisa said. "Why?"

"I'm a beekeeper. I sell honey to the co-op in town. You should check it out sometime. I'm Bernie." He stuck out his hand. "Bernie the Bee Man."

Marlee reached for his hand first. "Nice to meet you, Bernie the Bee Man. So, I have a question for you. Where do bees go in the winter? I mean, do they fly south like birds?" She took a couple of steps away from Lisa, and luckily, Bernie followed. No way. Marlee was taking one for the team. Marlee was intuitive about many things and must have known that the guy was making Lisa uneasy.

Lisa's phone vibrated in the pocket of her winter coat draped over her arm. She pulled it out and almost squealed out loud. It was a text from Sam wanting to know if she could call. "Marlee, it's Sam." She waved her phone back and forth. "I'm going to take this call, okay?" She grimaced at Marlee to convey that she was sorry for leaving her alone with the Bee Man. With relief, a glance told her that William and Evelyn were on their way back with the hot chocolates.

"Go for it. I'm learning about the competitive market for queen bees. There's a lot of money to be made." Marlee winked and turned her attention back to Bernie, the creepy Bee Man.

Lisa sent a quick text back to Sam that read, "Call me in two minutes." She had seen a library in a room off to one side of the recreation room. It was empty, so she went in and shut the door behind her. The room was small, about the size of her family's living room, and was crammed with books on the shelves lining the walls. It also had one rectangular table piled with pamphlets and magazines in the middle.

She answered her phone on the first ring. "I miss you," Lisa said.

"Me, too." Sam sounded like she was in the room next door.

"How's Switzerland?" Lisa looked out one of the many windows onto the packed parking lot behind the church.

"Cold," Sam said with a laugh. "We've all got jetlag, and Mother's a little cranky, but it'll be fine once we hit the slopes."

Lisa had never skied in her life, but the idea of skiing in a European country with Sam sounded romantic. Tears sprang to her eyes. "When are you coming home?" Her voice was choked with emotion.

"Oh, baby, are you okay? What has you so upset today?"

"Nothing. I'm just—" Lisa took a deep breath. Life really had gotten kind of confusing. "Marlee and I are here at William's church."

"Marlee went, too? Awesome."

"Yeah, she's a good sport. I mean, it was a good service, but it left me feeling kind of empty. Well, not completely, because the speaker was truly empowering. She is a lesbian, by the way, but the service didn't fill my…" By this time, she found herself in front of one of the bookshelves. Right in front of her was a Bible. So, they actually did have Bibles. Who knew? There were other sacred religious books, too, like the Muslim Koran, the Jewish Torah, and Buddhist Scriptures. There was even a book for atheists called, *Atheist Manifesto: The Case against Christianity, Judaism, and Islam.*

"What's up, baby?" Sam's voice was gentle.

"This church really makes room for every kind of belief or disbelief about God, but I don't know, the service didn't fill my void." Void might not have been the best word to use, but it was the best she could come up with. "I mean, they didn't quote the Bible at all."

"I'm sorry I'm not with you, but maybe next time, okay?"

"Okay." Lisa didn't think she'd be returning to the Unitarian Universalist Church any time soon, though.

"Guess what?" Sam said. The excitement in her voice was palpable.

"What?"

"Helene made it to Québec just in time because her sister had her baby girl yesterday, and Helene's going to help Chantal and her husband with the baby. I'm so excited for Helene. She finally has a niece."

"That's awesome. Speaking of nieces, Aunt Fran is due on Christmas day." Aunt Fran was William's sister and lived with her wife in Massachusetts.

"We're going to be overrun with babies." Sam's enthusiasm was catching.

"Maybe one day that'll be you and me."

"Absolutely. One day. Oh, hey, Alivia texted me. She said she's having fun getting ready for the big Bible debate."

More like the big Bible debacle, Lisa thought sarcastically. She had no idea how she was going to defend herself against its contents. "I'm looking forward to it," she said through gritted teeth.

Marlee stuck her head in the room. "Hey. William and Evelyn said they want to get going. Evelyn wants to check on her pot roast in the crock pot."

"Two minutes," Lisa said to Marlee. Marlee nodded and backed out of the library. "Hey, Sam, I have to go. Text me later about your skiing trip, okay?"

"I will. And I love you," Sam said. "I miss you, baby, but I'll be home soon."

They said her goodbyes, and Lisa headed back into the rec hall.

"Hey," Marlee said. She had been waiting right outside the library door. "Did you know that honeybees stay in their hives over the winter? It's so cool." She laughed at her unintentional pun. "They form this ball inside their colony where the center is really warm and vibrate their tiny wings to generate heat." They headed toward William and Evelyn, who were waiting for them by the door.

"Thank you, Marlee." Lisa was grateful that she had a friend like Marlee who could help her stop obsessing about the doom and gloom in her life, like a church that hated her, a girlfriend that was far away, and an upcoming Bible debate.

Marlee winked. Oh, yes. Marlee had known exactly what Lisa had needed at that moment.

Chapter Eleven

"She will bear a son, and you are to name him Jesus, for he will save his people from their sins." — Matthew 1:21

Christmas day, Lisa's favorite day of the year had finally arrived. Santa had put up an artificial Christmas tree overnight while the kids slept, and there were presents for everyone. This was Lisa's second year helping Santa put up the tree and stashing the presents underneath on Christmas Eve, and she loved her new role. Of course, they'd have to wait until after church to open most of them, but the kids were always allowed to open one gift from Santa before heading out to church.

Bridget sat on the floor in her pajamas with her new box of 64 Crayola crayons. She was coloring in her new Dora the Explorer coloring book. Lawrence Jr's Teenage Mutant Ninja Turtle action figures were fighting each other with his help while Lynnie ran her hands lovingly down the spine of a boxed set of Little House on the Prairie books.

"Go ahead and open yours, Lisa," her mother urged.

Lisa held a rectangular present in her hands that had been wrapped in Santa's special bright red paper. "Mom, aren't I too old for Santa gifts?" Even as she said the words, she clung tightly to the present.

"Never. Now open it." Her mother sat back on the couch and took a cup of freshly brewed coffee Lisa's father brought her.

Lisa wondered if she and Sam would ever play out a scene like this with their own children. She smiled at the thought. Maybe it would be in Switzerland.

Lisa carefully undid the tape in the middle and was about to ease the paper off when her father grunted in displeasure.

"Rip it off like you mean it, Lisa bear," he urged her. This got the kids' attention, and they gathered around to watch.

Lisa pulled at the paper from the middle and ripped it into pieces. She balled it up and tossed it at Lynnie, who let it hit her on the arm. She obviously would rather let it hit her than drop her precious box of books.

Lisa felt a wonderful calm take over her as she pulled the rest of the paper off. It was a Bible. Her parents, er, Santa, had brought her a New Revised Standard Version Bible. It was the Bible the Presbyterian Church used. The sleek black cover and silver-edged pages made the book seem so elegant. And it wasn't heavy. Probably because of the super-thin pages.

"Open it up and read the inscription," her mother said.

She opened it to one of the first inside pages. "Given to Lisa Anne Brown by Santa on this 25th day of December." Of course, it didn't really say Santa, it had her parents' names, but she had to pretend for the kids' sake.

"Santa knew you've been doing some searching, so he thought you might want a Bible of your own," her father said.

"Santa is a wise man." Lisa thumbed through the book until she found the book of Matthew in the New Testament and then read from it. "'The child conceived in her is from the Holy Spirit. She will bear a son, and you are to name him Jesus, for he will save his people from their sins.'" She smiled up at her parents. "Thank you, Mom. Thank you, Papa. Merry Christmas."

"Merry Christmas, Lisa," her mother said. "We hope you find what you're looking for."

"Or, in the least, what you need," her father added. "All right, Brown children, it is time to get ready for church." A collective groan came from the kids, but they each raced back to their rooms to get ready.

The church was packed with people, and they had to park the family minivan on the side street. Her father grumbled about twice-a-year Christians as they made their way to the church. Easter Sunday would have a similar crowd, but Lisa didn't mind. The excited energy inside the church always made Christmas and Easter special.

Even though he was kind of the enemy right now, Reverend Owens was bright and resplendent in his Christmas robes. His sermon and the scripture readings were all about the hope that the birth of Jesus would bring to the world. Jesus was God's son, the Messiah that would save mankind. God had been the god of the Israelites before then, but then Jesus came along to help people understand that they were all God's children.

The ride home was brimming with energy. After they changed clothes, the family ripped into their presents, and then Lisa helped her mother get the Christmas turkey and all the fixings on the table.

Heading into a food coma, Lisa pushed her plate away from her. "Everything was so good, Mom."

"You helped with most of it, so thank yourself." Her mother beamed at her and then wiped Bridget's hands.

"Can we go play, Mama?" Bridget asked, her eyes wide.

"Bring your plates into the kitchen first."

Her siblings pushed their chairs back so fast, it made Lisa laugh.

"Would you like some coffee, Lisa?" Her father asked.

"No thanks. I have no room, Papa, but thanks for asking." She hadn't acquired a taste for the nasty stuff, but it was nice that he had asked. It made her feel grown up.

He patted her on the shoulder and headed into the kitchen, partly to get the coffee and partly to check on the kids' progress.

"Mom?" Lisa said. She had been musing on something ever since the church service that morning.

"Yes, honey?"

"Do you think I can go to Marlee's tomorrow? I want to work on that Bible debate for the youth alliance."

"Can you be back in time to help me with dinner?"

"Yes, of course."

"And how about taking the kids outside to play in the snow today?"

"Sure, sure. I was planning on doing that anyway. But, I mean, I don't even know if Marlee's around tomorrow. She might be working or something or going out to see Susie."

She sent Marlee and Susie a text, and Marlee got back to her almost immediately, enthusiastic about getting together. They set a time for ten the next morning. After helping her mother clean up the kitchen from Christmas dinner, she bundled up the kids, and they headed outside to play in the snow. Bridget decided they needed to add a snow lady to the snowman they had made the day before. The snow was kind of icy and didn't hold together very well, so they placed a small snow mound near the feet of the snowman, and Lynnie said it looked like a baby. Bridget announced that the baby was Jesus and the snowman was Joseph. Maybe if it snowed again, they could build a Mary snow woman.

Since the snow was uncooperative, they set their sights on the playground at the end of their street. It wasn't exactly playground weather, but she knew her parents needed a break, and she was determined to keep the kids occupied for at least an hour outside. If they ran around enough, they could stay warm.

Lawrence Jr. took off running, and Bridget followed him. Lynnie kept stride with Lisa.

"It was really weird when we went to church without you last Sunday," Lynnie said. "Where did you go?"

"You remember William, right?"

"Yeah."

"I went to his church." Lisa held open the metal gate to the playground so Lynnie could pass through.

"Why?"

How much of the truth should she tell? Lynnie was growing up fast, but she was only nine years old. Sugar-coating it is.

"He invited me to go, so I thought I'd see how other people attend church." It was a small lie but a necessary one.

Lynnie was quiet for a moment. "Who is William, anyway? Is he your uncle? You look like him."

Oh, geez, this was uncharted territory. "No, he's not my uncle. If he were, he'd be your uncle, too, right?"

"I guess."

Lynnie sat on the last remaining swing. Lawrence Jr. had draped himself face down on the middle swing while Bridget struggled to get in the baby swing.

"Let me help you, Sweetpea." Lisa picked her littlest sister up and plunked her into the wrap-around seat.

"So, did you guys like your Christmas presents?"

"Yeah!" Lawrence Jr. said, pushing himself higher.

Lynnie nodded.

"So, Lynnie, I bet all you want to do is get inside so you can read some of those books you got, right?" Lisa teased.

Lynnie's face lit up as she nodded vigorously.

"How about you, Bridget? Did Santa bring you good stuff?" It had been a Dora the Explorer Christmas for Bridget with new pajamas and toys. "Do you like your new backpack?" Lisa guessed her mother was trying to get Bridget used to the idea of going to pre-school in the spring.

"Yeah. I can put all my new crayons and coloring books in it. Higher, Lisa, higher," Bridget commanded.

"Okay, okay." Lisa pushed her sister a little higher on the swing. She had no idea how the kids could stand the cold breeze the swings created, but they were kids, after all, and pretty resilient.

"Hey, thanks for my t-shirt, you guys," Lisa said. One of Lisa's gifts from her three siblings was a gray Yankees t-shirt with the team emblem across the front. "I love it."

"I picked it out," Lawrence Jr. said. "We bought it at Walmart."

"Think I should wear it to Marlee's house tomorrow? She's a Mets fan."

Lynnie chuckled. "Not unless you want to make her your enemy."

"Maybe I shouldn't then."

"Maybe not."

"Hey, Lynnie," Lisa said, "why don't you go push Bridget on the merry-go-round?" She pulled her littlest sister out of the swing.

"Okay." Lynnie leaped off the swing and said, "C'mon, Bridget, I'll push you on the round-and-round."

"Me, too," Lawrence Jr. said and was about to hit the ground running when Lisa reached out and grabbed him by the coat.

"Hey, hang out a minute, buddy. I wanna talk to you about something."

He seemed disappointed but sat back down on the swing, this time right side up. "What did you want to talk to me about?"

Lisa sat down on the swing that Lynnie had just vacated. "Well, uh…" Now that she had him alone, she wasn't sure what she wanted to say. She watched Lynnie grab one of the metal bars and run around the well-worn path pushing the merry-go-round faster and faster, much to the delighted squeals of her younger sister. "You know Sam, right?"

"Yeah, is she coming over?" He kicked his feet out to swing higher.

"I wish, but not today." Lisa cleared her throat. "Mama and Papa know about this, and I wanted you to know, too. Sam is my girlfriend."

"Your girlfriend? Like you kiss her and stuff?"

"Mm hmm. And we hold hands and hug, too."

"Does Lynnie know?"

"Yes. She's known for a little while."

He swung back and forth a few times and then said, "Does Bridget know?"

"No, the only thing she knows is Dora the Explorer."

"I know," he said with a laugh. "It's ridiculous."

"Not unlike somebody else's obsession with Teenage Mutant Ninja Turtles and Captain America, eh?"

"Or you, 'cuz you like softball so much."

"I do." Lisa silently wished for spring to come early. The Bible debate would be over, she'd have her driver's license, and softball would be in season. Life was always good when it was spring.

"You know what?" Lawrence Jr. said.

"What?"

"I like Sam."

"I'm glad. I like her, too."

"Duh, she wouldn't be your girlfriend if you didn't like her." Lisa laughed.

He stopped swinging and said, "Are you going to marry her?"

"I don't know. Maybe one day. I think I want to go to college first."

"So, girls really can marry other girls?"

"Of course."

"And boys can marry other boys?"

"Yep, girls can marry boys, and boys can marry girls."

He stayed quiet for a few moments as if digesting this news. "Okay," he said after an eternity. "Can I go on the merry-go-round now?"

"Yep, go." Lisa let out a long breath. That went way better than expected. It turned out to be a pretty good Christmas gift.

Lisa smiled at the sight of her three siblings playing. While the kids were occupied, Lisa took the time to muse on what approach she and Marlee and Susie should take to combat Alivia's planned assault. Thank God Ronnie leaked Alivia's battle plans to them.

They had a fighting chance now.

But why was Alivia so gung-ho? Maybe she was jealous that Lisa was Sam's girlfriend. But why? Alivia was straight. Lisa groaned. Whatever. This was a Bible debate, not a personal one.

Lisa leaped up and ran over to the merry-go-round. Lynnie squealed and jumped on when Lisa grabbed the metal bar.

"Hang on, you guys," Lisa called to her sisters and brother as she used her pent-up frustrations to give them the ride of their lives.

Lisa spent Christmas evening with her family, watching the kids play with their new toys. She went to bed when the kids did, but she didn't go to sleep. She wrote in her journal for a while and then tucked it in a drawer. Finally, it was time. She picked up the book she'd been waiting all day to read. The silver letters on the spine spelled out the words 'Holy Bible.' She ran her thumbs across the black leather and opened the book reverently.

The pages fell open to Psalms in the Old Testament. She read a few of the psalms, enjoying the lyrical quality of the words, and found one that stirred her heart.

"Hear the voice of my supplication, as I cry to you for help, as I lift up my hands toward your most holy sanctuary. – Psalm 28:2."

Supplication. That was just a fancy word for a plea. That's what praying felt like these days—pleas to God to help her make sense of being gay in a world that said she was a sinner. She read on and found another one to her liking. One she would have to remember as she tried desperately to find a way to take on Alivia and the rest of the world.

"The LORD is my strength and my shield; in him my heart trusts; so I am helped, and my heart exults, and with my song I give thanks to him. – Psalm 28:7."

Chapter Twelve
*"Happy are those who find wisdom,
and those who get understanding."—*
Proverbs 3:13

The day after Christmas, Lisa drove to Marlee's house. She
wished she had her license and not just a stupid learner's
permit. That way, her mother wouldn't have to be put out whenever
Lisa wanted to go somewhere. She pulled the family minivan down
Marlee's long gravel driveway and expertly, in her opinion, did a K
turn, so the van was pointed toward the street. After giving her
mother a quick hug and a promise to be home in time to help with
dinner, Lisa jumped out of the driver's seat and ran to the side door
of Marlee's house. She rang the bell and waited. The big farmhouse
had an awesome wraparound porch, and that's where the front door
was, but Marlee's family and friends never used it. They just used
the side door that led to the kitchen.

"C'mon in, Lisa." Marlee's mother opened the door. "Marlee
and Susie are in the basement."

"Thank you, Mrs. McAllister." Lisa wiped her wet boots on the
inside mat and then hung her coat on one of the hooks. "Did you
have a nice Christmas?"

"We did. It was nice and quiet."

"That's good. How's Marlee's grandfather?"

"Go ask him yourself. He's in the living room."

"Thanks. I think I will."

Lisa walked quietly into the living room, just in case Marlee's grandfather was napping. He and Marlee's grandmother had only intended to stay for Thanksgiving, but he had suffered a mild heart attack while trying to shovel the ever-falling North Country snow. She smiled when she saw him sitting up on the couch, reading a book. It was good to see that the hospital bed was gone. Marlee's grandmother was reading in an armchair next to the cozy crackling fire in the fireplace.

"Hello, Mr. McAllister. How are you feeling today?" Lisa gave him a hug. She'd only met him a couple of times, but he was such a personable and kind man that she felt like she'd known him her whole life.

"I'm feeling well, young lady. Another week or so, and we'll be out of my daughter-in-law's hair." He winked at her.

Lisa smiled. "Well, I'm sure you're not a bother. Your color is really good." His skin looked healthy and pink, and his eyes were bright and focused. "How's your energy level these days?"

He chuckled. "You sound like that doctor friend Marlee's mother keeps bringing home to check on me."

"Answer the girl's question, Will." Marlee's grandmother sat stone-faced, her large-print book open in her lap. There was no mirth to her voice and no smile on her face. It was almost as if the joy of life had left her.

"I'm feeling pretty good these days," he said. He smiled and added, "Have fun on your project. It sounds interesting."

"I hope it doesn't get the better of us." Lisa tapped the Bible in her hand.

Lisa wasn't sure, but it almost sounded like Marlee's grandmother made a disapproving grunt. Typically, not one to back down, Lisa turned to face her. "We hope to figure out what the Bible really says about being gay." Okay, it felt really weird speaking so out and openly to Marlee's grandparents, but she couldn't help it. Although Marlee's grandfather had been very supportive when Marlee came out, Marlee's grandmother was not. She hadn't shown any support at all. Maybe Lisa was being spiteful, but she hated to see Marlee hurting like that.

"That sounds like a lot of research," Marlee's grandmother said.

"It will be, Mrs. McAllister. It will be." It was also kind of weird having two Mrs. McAllisters in the house, but both Marlee's mother and Marlee's grandmother shared the same last name. Lisa wondered if she would change her last name if and when she married Sam. Lisa Ann Payton. She liked the ring to it, but then again, maybe not. Papa had always been a true father to her. She wanted to honor him by keeping her adopted last name. Maybe Sam would take her name. Samantha Brown. Hmm, that sounded a little too plain, and Sam was anything but plain. A pang of loneliness tickered across her chest. She missed Sam.

Lisa cleared her throat and said, "Well, if you'll excuse me, I should get downstairs."

"Of course." Marlee's grandmother went back to her book.

Lisa was about to turn and go, but something stopped her. Marlee's grandmother looked pale and had dark circles under her eyes. "Excuse me, Mrs. McAllister, I may be talking out of turn, but you look quite pale. Are you getting enough sleep?"

"No, she's not," Marlee's grandfather said. "She's been too busy

116

worrying about me."

"I'm fine."

Lisa had read ahead in her Anatomy textbook about blood disorders, and Marlee's grandmother fit all the symptoms. Including her irritability. "It might be a good idea to make sure you're getting enough iron, okay? You could have a slight deficiency."

"Yes, doctor," Marlee's grandmother said with a genuine smile which made Lisa's heart joyful. It was the first time she had ever seen the woman smile.

Lisa smiled back and then hustled down to the basement.

"Hey," Marlee said as she leaped away from Susie on the couch. "What took you so long?"

"Ha. I thought I'd give you two enough time to get hot and heavy with each other before we get hot and heavy into the Bible."

"*Aay*," Susie said, "if you had been any longer, the door would have been locked." She and Marlee exchanged a scandalous glance which made Lisa blush.

"Okay, then." Lisa cleared her throat. "Should I go home?" She took one step toward the stairs. She was kidding, but maybe she wasn't.

"No, no, no, no, no," Marlee said and steered Lisa to a fold-up chair. "I set up this card table so we'd have a place to work." She put a King James Bible in front of her own chair. "I don't know how helpful I'm going to be. I mean, isn't the Bible just a bunch of stories written a long time ago?"

"It's the word of God," Susie said, her face serious. She got up from the couch and sat at the table. "Supposedly."

Lisa held her gasp inside. She and her friends hadn't talked much about their beliefs in God. She hoped this project wouldn't drive a wedge between them. Lisa told herself to chill out. Marlee and Susie were there to help, not judge.

"Here's my Bible from home," Susie said.

"What version is that?" Lisa put her own brand new Bible on the table.

"It's a Catholic Bible." Susie picked the book up and examined the inside cover. "The New American Bible Revised Edition."

Marlee, who had been fussing about getting them bottled waters and cookies, stopped what she was doing, her mouth wide open. "Wait, wait, wait. Revised Bibles? Different versions?"

Lisa smiled. Marlee was naïve and innocent in so many things. "Yep, mine is the New Revised Standard Version. It's the one my Presbyterian Church uses."

"And my Catholic Church uses this one." Susie waved her Bible.

"How can that be?" Marlee sat down hard in her chair. Her look of confusion was priceless. "I thought the Bible was the Bible was the Bible. The word of God. How can you revise the word of God? How can the Catholics have a different Bible than the Presbyterians?" Before Lisa or Susie could answer, Marlee sat up board straight and didn't look at either of them. It was as if she were talking to herself. "And, now that I think about it, how can there be so many different religions? How do Buddhism, Judaism, Islam, and Hinduism fit in? And who are the Mormons? Are they Christians? And what about the ones that come to our door all the time, forcing us to pretend we're not home?" She snapped her fingers, trying to come up with the name.

"Jehovah's Witnesses?" Lisa offered.

"Yes!" Marlee stabbed a finger in the air at Lisa.

Lisa smiled at Marlee's enthusiasm. "Both the Mormons and the

Jehovah's Witnesses are Christian denominations."

"Okay, okay," Marlee said, clearly not done with her musings. "Methodists, Baptists, Episcopalians are all Christians, right?"

"Yep," Lisa said. "And Lutherans, Anglicans, Pentecostals, and so many more."

"And then there are the Unitarian Universalists from that church we went to on Sunday and Wiccans and Agnostics and Atheists." She sat back against her chair and blew out a sigh, clearly exhausted. "I am really, really confused."

"Are you done, *mi amor*?" Susie said with a laugh and reached for Marlee's hand.

"For now." Marlee shook her head slowly. "Teach me, okay?"

"You got it," Lisa said. "And to answer some of your questions, there are so many different religions because there are so many different beliefs. It was like William said on Sunday. If you have a hundred people in a room, you'll have a hundred different views about spirituality."

"Hmm," was all Marlee said.

"And about the different versions of the Bibles," Lisa continued, "maybe a better word to use is translation because the Bible is the Bible is the Bible like you said, but it wasn't originally written in English. The Old Testament was in Hebrew and the New Testament in Greek."

"That's another thing," Marlee rested her head in her hands, "why are there so many different languages?"

"You're full of questions, aren't you?" Lisa asked.

Marlee grimaced in apology.

"That's okay, though," Lisa said and meant it. "More people need to question the world around them instead of blindly accepting what they're told."

"Well said, *amiga*." Susie nodded approvingly. "Well said."

"Okay, women," Lisa took a deep breath, "we've got a big task ahead of us. We've got to find a way to defend ourselves using this book."

Susie opened a notebook. "I wrote down the list of Bible passages that Ronnie said he and Alivia are planning to use against us."

"Yeah, he texted them to me, too. So, since you're the only one who thought to bring a notebook, can you take notes?"

"*Sí, claro.*" Susie opened to a fresh page. "I guess we'd better start with Genesis."

Lisa nodded. "The story of the sinful city of Sodom."

"Sodom?" Marlee giggled. "Like as in sodomy?" She whispered the last word.

"Yep," Lisa said.

"Oh, man, I can't wait to hear about this city." Marlee was all ears.

Susie consulted her notes. "Ronnie said we should read Genesis 19:4-5."

"I'll read it out loud, and then we'll figure out how to handle it, okay?" Lisa opened her Bible to the passage.

Susie and Marlee nodded.

Lisa cleared her throat and quoted, "But before they lay down, the men of the city, the men of Sodom, both young and old, all the people to the last man, surrounded the house; and they called to Lot, 'Where are the men who came to you tonight? Bring them out to us so that we may know them.'" At Marlee's confused expression, Lisa added, "To 'know' someone is to, uh, have physical relations with them."

"All those men in the city wanted to have sex with the men in the house?"

Lisa nodded.

"Why?"

"That's the big question," Lisa said. "The one we have to figure out."

Susie added, "The men in the town didn't realize that the men in the house were angels sent by God to destroy the cities of Sodom and Gomorrah."

"Weren't there any women in the town?" Marlee asked.

"*Sí, sí.* Lot had a wife and two daughters. Right, Lisa?"

"Mm hmm." Lisa nodded.

"The whole thing sounds like intended rape to me," Marlee said matter-of-factly.

Lisa exchanged a glance with Susie and said, "That's how it reads. You know, I think we should read the chapter leading up to this one and then read all of chapter nineteen. Let's read silently, to ourselves, okay?"

Susie and Marlee nodded and flipped their Bibles back to Genesis chapter eighteen, and they read silently for a while, although Lisa had a little trouble concentrating because Marlee kept making weird little noises as she read. Reading the Bible was obviously new to her.

"What?" Marlee screeched. "Are you kidding me? First of all, this guy Lot has a really weird name, but he was going to send out his two daughters so the men could gang rape them? His own daughters? What kind of book is this? Why aren't we protesting this passage?"

"We should be, *mi vida*, we should be," Susie said, "but that's a fight for another day."

"Maybe not," Lisa said. "Maybe we can use this. I don't know how yet. Susie, can you write down the passage?"

"It's Genesis 19:8," Marlee said in disgust. "Let's keep reading."

This time Marlee read quietly, and Lisa was able to concentrate better. Marlee closed her Bible first, and Susie closed hers a few minutes later. It wasn't that Lisa was a slow reader; it was that she wanted to glean the essence of each passage.

"Okay," Marlee said, "you two have a lot of explaining to do."

"Genesis 19:32-36? Lot's daughters?" Susie said knowingly and exchanged a glance with Lisa.

"Yep." Marlee sat back and folded her arms. There was an accusing look on her face.

"It was a different time back then," Lisa offered lamely.

"Really? That's all you've got? His daughters get their father drunk, trick him into having sex with each of them so they can get pregnant to…" she paused for a second to find the passage, "quote 'preserve the seed of our father?'"

"To be honest, *mi vida*, I didn't know that passage was in the Bible."

"I'm guilty, too," Lisa said. "I let other people interpret these chapters for me. My understanding was that God hated the wickedness and evil ways of those towns and sent his angels to check it out. When the angels were almost raped, they decided to go ahead with the original plan and destroy Sodom and everyone in it."

"But they let Lot and his family go," Susie said.

"Because he was so *righteous*," Marlee said sarcastically. She made air quotes when she said the word righteous. "He wants to send his daughters out to be raped but then ends up knocking them up instead." She grunted. "Nice. That's really nice."

"Marlee, I know that part doesn't make sense," Susie said with a sigh, "but I think Lot's daughters thought the entire world had ended, and they panicked. They thought they were saving the human race."

"And maybe," Lisa added, "just maybe, it was a way to show that even the righteous aren't perfect and that Lot was capable of taking on the ways of Sodom, too."

They sat silently until Marlee said, "You know, in my Latin class, we learned about ancient wars. Sometimes the victors humiliated the leader of the losing side by raping him. After that, they probably cut his head off and put it on a stick or something."

"Yikes," Lisa said. "That's crazy."

"But maybe that's what those men in the town were up to. They weren't a bunch of gay guys," Marlee said the word gay with a high tight voice. "They simply wanted to show these angels that this was their town. Didn't they call Lot an outsider?"

Lisa nodded.

"See? They didn't want anybody just coming into their town and hanging with Lot, who wasn't a native of their town, either. They wanted to show their dominance."

"*Dios mio*," Susie said. "I just thought of something. When I was little, we had a dog that—"

"You had a dog?" Marlee sounded amazed that there was something about Susie she didn't know.

"*Sí, mi vida,* his name was Domingo. We had him when I was seven or something. *Mami* said he ran away, but I think she gave him away."

"Why?"

"He was a nice dog, but he was always humping your leg, especially if somebody came over to the house. *Papi* said he wasn't really having sex on your leg. He was showing his dominance."

"That's it." Lisa snapped her fingers. "Those men of Sodom wanted to show their superiority, their dominance, over the angels. The men of Sodom thought they were better than everyone else. Geez, we may have broken the code on this one."

"I think we did," Susie said.

They high-fived across the table and sat back, satisfied.

Susie leaned forward and flipped her notebook back to the first page. "Okay, one Bible passage down, only…" She used the tip of her pen to count the number of passages left to tackle. "Only eleven more to go."

Chapter Thirteen
*"And now faith, hope, and love abide,
these three; and the greatest of these is
love."* — 1 Corinthians 13:13

Lisa sat back against her pillows with a sigh. She was finally taking a moment for herself and let the unfolded laundry sit in a heap on her sister's bed. Lynnie was in her room reading, and Papa had taken Lawrence Jr. and Bridget to the playground. Her mother was in her hair salon giving Mrs. Winfred a perm. Everybody hated the smell, so that's why her father bailed with the kids. Lisa opened her journal and put pen to paper.

December 31
Sam! Sam! Sam! Samantha Rose Payton gets back from Switzerland tonight, and I am going to see her and kiss her until we both can't breathe! I almost want to ditch the New Year's Eve Party at Ronnie's and make Sam drive us somewhere private. I miss her so much. We texted every day and even FaceTimed a couple of times with our phones, but it is NOT THE SAME! I don't think I can do a long-distance relationship. It's too hard.

Lisa tapped her pen against the paper. When Sam went off to college the following year, they would be in a long-distance relationship. But by then, Lisa would have her license and could drive wherever Sam was, and hopefully, that would be Rockville University. That way, the year after that, they could go to the same college and play on the same softball team. And be roommates. That would be incredible. Fingers crossed. She went back to her journal to amend her last statement.

> Forget what I just wrote. I will do a long-distance relationship with Sam. My heart has been lonely with her gone.

> Okay, time for cheerier things. Aunt Fran had a baby boy on Saturday. I now officially have a first cousin. William was so happy when he called me about it, and I can't wait to see the baby. Maybe he and Evelyn will have a baby soon, and then…Oh, wow! I'll have another brother or sister. Oh, geez, I don't know how to handle that, so I'll think about it later.

> Sunday at church was okay. A few people heard about me saving Freddie's life (ha ha ha). People can be so crazy. I didn't "save his life." I just helped him out a little. I tried to tell people that, but they believe what they want to believe. It was nice having people at church thinking nice things

about me instead of abomination-type things.

Oh, we did great with the Genesis Bible passages about Sodom. And I've been making notes on the other books in the Old Testament: Exodus, Leviticus, Numbers, and Deuteronomy. Oh, it was really funny when Marlee saw the book called "Numbers." She thought there was math in the Bible but was disappointed when I told her that Numbers was about Moses counting his people to make sure they had enough for the inevitable wars they would have when they tried to move into their Promised Land.

Anyway, Marlee helped us figure out that Deuteronomy means second law or something like that. It's Greek, but she knows Latin and was able to figure it out. Marlee doesn't know the Bible, but sometimes I think she knows everything else. When I read Deuteronomy, I got the sense that it wasn't a second set of Laws but a rehashing of the ones from the previous books. Like a summary. Now, I mean, I knew about the Ten Commandments and all, but there are so many more laws that it's hard to figure out where to start. How can you live your life and obey all those things outlined in the Bible?

Lisa reached for her Bible lying at the foot of her bed. She thumbed through the pages of the Old Testament until she found the passage she wanted. She wondered if it would be sacrilegious to use post-it notes in a Bible. She chanced it and stuck a bright orange one on the page with Deuteronomy 22:11-12. She picked her pen back up.

> Here's a weird one from Deuteronomy. "You shall not wear clothes made of wool and linen woven together. You shall make tassels on the four corners of the cloak with which you cover yourself." I don't remember seeing any tassels on Freddie's cloak. I guess that makes him an abomination, eh? Ha ha ha.

> And there are these other crazy laws, like the one in Deuteronomy 22:20-21 that says something about an entire town getting together to stone to death a woman that is not a virgin on her wedding day. Wow. That is more than a little ridiculous. Not to mention extremely misogynistic.

> This one from Deuteronomy 23:2 hurts most of all. "No one born of a forbidden union may enter the assembly of the LORD." That's me—the bastard kid, born out of wedlock. Now I've got two big strikes against me.

> All these laws are about purging the evil from

Israel. The evil. Is that what I am? Evil? Some
people think so. Some think I'm under the
influence of the devil.

Lisa drew a frowny face on her paper and was about to draw
devil horns on one of the faces when there was a soft knock on her
bedroom door.

Lisa's mother said, "Can I come in?"

"Sure, Mom." Lisa tucked her journal under her comforter. She
was pretty sure her mother knew she kept a journal, but she really
didn't want to talk about what was in it. "Do you need me?"

"No, Mrs. Winfred's perm solution is doing its magic for a few
minutes, so I thought I'd get some fresh air." She sat on Bridget's
bed and started folding clothes. "Are you excited about your big
party tonight?"

"Yeah, Sam's coming home." Lisa couldn't help smiling.

"Won't she be tired from her trip? It's a long flight from
Switzerland."

"I don't think she cares, but if she falls asleep, Susie can drive
her home."

Her mother set down the socks she had paired and rolled into a
ball. There was a wistful look on her face.

"Are you okay, Mom?"

She nodded and took a slow breath as if resigning herself to
something. "You're growing up, aren't you? Right before my eyes."

"True. I'm almost six feet tall now," Lisa said playfully. Her
mother was getting all serious, and it was making her nervous.

Her mother smacked Lisa's knee playfully. "You know what I

mean."

"It was going to happen eventually, Mom."

"Yes, indeed." Lisa's mother took another slow breath and touched the Bible on Lisa's bed. "Some people's minds will never change, you know. No matter what you say or what you do. You know that, don't you, Lisa?"

Lisa felt her chest tighten. She did know it, and it kind of sucked, too. "Mm hmm."

Her mother picked up the Bible and thumbed through it until she found what she was looking for. "Here," she handed the open Bible to Lisa. "Read Psalm 46."

"Be still and know that I am God," Lisa read.

"Be still," her mother echoed. "That one got me through a lot of tough times."

Lisa pulled a post-it note off the pad and bookmarked the passage. "Thanks, Mom. I'll try to remember."

Her mother ran a loving hand down Lisa's cheek and then headed back to Mrs. Winfred, who had probably passed out from the fumes.

"Be still," Lisa repeated to herself.

After writing a few more thoughts in her journal, finishing the laundry, and making dinner for the family so her mother could have a few moments to herself after working on Mrs. Winfred all afternoon, Lisa was finally in Marlee's van on the way to the New Year's Eve party in East Valley. Julie and Marcus had also been invited and were in the back seat.

"There's the house," Lisa said. She couldn't keep the excitement out of her voice.

"Oh, man," Marlee said. "Look at all the cars. Ronnie outdid himself."

Once inside the house, Lisa was disappointed that Sam wasn't there yet. Hopefully, her flight hadn't been delayed. The party was in full swing. The living room furniture had been moved, the lights were low, and couples were slow dancing. She waved to Jordan, who was hanging by the back door with a bunch of kids from Southbridge. She recognized some of them from the youth alliance.

Ronnie showed them where to stash their coats in a back office on the first floor and then gave them a quick tour of the amenities available. As soon as Marlee saw Susie, she ran across the room and flew into her arms. Their kiss was kind of steamy and attracted a lot of attention. Susie dragged Marlee willingly into the kitchen, so Lisa, Julie, and Marcus headed to the dining room to check out the buffet.

"Where are your folks, Ronnie?" Lisa filled a plate with cut veggies and dip.

"I sent them away." He shooed away his imaginary parents with both hands, which made Lisa chuckle. "They're at my aunt's house in Plattsburgh for a few days. So we are free and clear, dearie. Drinks are in the kitchen. Special drinks are Karl's domain," he added with a wink.

Lisa shook her head. She was not interested in drinking alcohol, but they followed him back into the kitchen to get sodas. Marlee and Susie had staked a claim at the kitchen table and were already in a deep conversation with Alivia and Karl about the town of Sodom.

Lisa was surprised when Marlee blurted, "Have you guys wondered if God even exists? I mean, is there really some God overseeing everything?"

"I've wondered sometimes," Susie said. "But there are so many amazing things in this world that it can't be due to random events or chance." Much to Lisa's surprise, Susie was drinking a beer.

"I know what you mean," Alivia said. "It's like there's some cosmic force at work."

Lisa grabbed three root beers from the fridge, handed one to Julie and another to Marcus, and then all three joined their friends at the table.

"Honey," Alivia said to Karl, "what about you? Have you ever wondered if God exists?"

Lisa hid a smile at the surprised look on his face. Karl was usually reserved and quiet, letting Alivia do all the talking, but he'd actually been asked to speak. He cleared his throat. "Sometimes I think that when I pray, it's just me asking for stupid, selfish things. I mean, really? Is God going to drop everything just to help me pass a math test or score a touchdown? Doesn't God have better things to do?"

"And what if you don't pray?" Marlee's cheeks turned bright red. "What if I don't believe in all of that? God, the Bible, Jesus. I mean, there are so many sketchy things in the Bible, and, believe me, I've been trying to figure it out. Like the creation story in Genesis. God creates Eve, but she's an afterthought? Hmm, Adam needs a helper, so let's make a woman from his rib, but, of course, she's not equal to him in any way." The sarcasm in Marlee's voice was clear, and Lisa's heart went out to her. She looked so troubled. "I mean, am I going to hell if I don't believe all this stuff?"

"Do you believe in heaven and hell, Marlee?" Ronnie asked.

Marlee gathered her thoughts and said, "You know what? Not really. I don't want to offend anybody, but I can't wrap my head around all this God stuff. I'm more of a believer in math and science."

The table got quiet for a moment, and then Alivia said, "How about you, Lisa?"

"Hmm?"

"God? Ever doubt His existence?"

"Nope."

Alivia scoffed. "Never?" Her tone made it crystal clear that she didn't believe Lisa.

"Never. I get, geez, I don't know how to describe this, but I get a warm feeling when I'm in church or praying or whatever. It's like I get strength or empowerment. I feel hope. I feel love. It makes me feel like I can do anything."

"This youth alliance debate is gonna challenge your beliefs," Alivia stated matter-of-factly. Her eyes narrowed as her gaze bore down on Lisa. "There's no way you can handle what we've got planned."

Lisa recoiled as if struck by Alivia's words but then leaned forward across the table. "Is that a threat, Alivia?"

Lisa was secretly pleased when Julie pushed her chair back, seemingly ready to defend her friend if necessary.

"No, it wasn't a threat," Karl said to Lisa and put his arm around Alivia's shoulder to pull her away from the table. He sent Alivia a look as if to say she had overstepped. "We're all friends here."

"Yeah, right," Lisa mumbled and looked away.

"Hey, Lisa," Marlee said, "I've been meaning to ask you. Why the heck did you have to tell my grandmother the family needed to get more iron?" She was clearly changing the subject.

"Why? What d'ya mean?" Lisa said.

"We've had nothing but spinach this and spinach that with

dinner. Man, I had no idea spinach could be prepared in so many disgusting ways." She looked at Susie and said, "Except for that one dish with all the cheese. That one was almost palatable."

Susie and the rest laughed at Marlee's silliness, but Lisa couldn't. She'd lost her sense of humor for some reason. Maybe coming to this party was a bad idea. She should leave. She could text Sam to pick her up on that side street by Marlee's van.

She was just about to get up and find her coat when Ronnie said, "Speaking of debates, Anne wants us to record opening statements on Tuesday." He let Karl add rum to his plastic cup of Coke.

"Opening statements?" Lisa wasn't sure what he meant. She'd never been in a formal debate before.

Marcus said, "You basically start with the topic of debate—a statement that has potentially differing opinions." Marcus was on the debate team at school. Maybe he could be the one to argue for her side of the debate; they could use his experience.

"Here's what I think," Jordan said. He pulled a chair up to the table. "For the first session, both sides should trade one-liners. You know? Rapid fire. Back and forth. That'll set the tone of what's to come."

"Like what?" Lisa asked. She glanced at the kitchen clock. Where was Sam?

"Like, uh, Alivia or Ronnie can say, 'God hates gay people,' and then Lisa can come back with 'God made me in his own image, so how can he hate me?'"

"Oh, I get it," Ronnie narrowed his eyes at Jordan. "You are very clever."

"We should have three cameras," Jordan mused. "Hey, I just

made myself the director, didn't I?"

"Why not? It's your turn," Ronnie said, "but I don't know where you're going to get three cameras. Anne had trouble getting the one."

"Aww, we have to have three," Jordan whined. "We'll have one camera trained on the religious goody-goodies and the other on the heathen homosexuals, and the third will capture everything in wide angle. Oh, my God," he squealed. "I can't wait to get started."

"So back to the one-liners," Alivia said, clearly happy to get back to torturing Lisa. "What if I say—"

"Where are my people?" Sam burst into the kitchen.

Lisa stood up so fast that she knocked her chair over. Sam flew into her arms, and they melted together. Oblivious to everyone, Lisa whispered in Sam's ear. "I missed you so much. Don't you ever leave me like that again."

"I won't."

They kissed right there in the kitchen in front of everyone, much to Ronnie's delight, who shouted, "lesbo-a-go-go!" Jordan added a catcall whistle.

When the kiss ended, Sam didn't let go of Lisa but reached out with one hand and smacked Ronnie on the arm.

"Hey!" Ronnie rubbed the spot where she'd hit him.

"You deserved it," Sam said with a smile.

Sam's blonde hair was loose over her shoulders. Lisa wanted to run her hands through it but reluctantly stepped back so Sam could take off her coat.

"Hey, everybody," Sam said and hung her coat over the back of the chair Lisa had vacated. "It's so good to be back in the good old U. S. of A. You don't even know."

"Did you miss us, Samantha Rose?" Alivia asked, her voice soft, her eyes flirty, her breasts pushed up and out toward Sam as if saying hello to the world.

Oddly, at that moment, Lisa couldn't recall what the Bible said about murder.

Chapter Fourteen

"Be on your guard; stand firm in the faith; be men of courage; be strong." —
1 Corinthians 16:13

Lisa and Sam sneaked away from the New Year's party to drive to a quiet spot to reconnect. Lisa held Sam tight when Sam cried about getting home from the airport earlier that evening and walking into Helene's empty rooms. Helene, Sam's nanny, had moved out while the family spent Christmas in Switzerland. Sam knew Helene would be gone when they got back, but seeing the proof was hard for her to take. Lisa kissed away Sam's tears until the kisses developed into something more.

They kissed again at the stroke of midnight, and Lisa made two silent New Year's resolutions. The first one was to pass her driver's test on her birthday in February, and the second was to keep her head held high if and when the kids at school called her names or whispered about her when school started again. She was pretty sure that everyone would have found out by now that she'd gone to the Snowball Dance as Sam's girlfriend.

After her silent resolutions, Lisa and Sam restated their vows of commitment to each other. Feeling secure, Lisa mentioned her fears about Alivia trying to get in between them, but Sam reassured her that nothing and no one would ever break their bond. Ever. Satisfied, Lisa snuggled with Sam until it was time to go back to Ronnie's house so Marlee could drive them home.

~~~

The first day back at school after Christmas break was the longest day of the century. The news about her and Sam going to the dance together had made its way around Clarksonville over the break. Girls in the hallway and in her classes whispered behind their hands and then laughed. Even guys looked at her, which had never happened before. Some of it could have been her paranoid imagination, but she didn't think so. It was exactly the kind of attention she didn't want, the kind of thing she had been trying to avoid. Now that the unwanted attention was happening, she almost regretted going to the dance, but then again, that was ridiculous. She loved Sam and wanted to do things with her, like go to dances. She had to stop hiding. She had to come out once and for all and be herself. Remembering her resolution, she kept her head high and tried to let the stares and whispers roll off her back. It was a losing battle, though, and she felt like bolting out the front doors of the school and running home.

Julie and Marcus had come out of the closet, too, and held hands as they walked to classes together. Being open and honest must have been their New Year's resolution. A lot of kids whispered and laughed right in front of them. Lisa couldn't wrap her head around what was so fascinating about other people's lives that you had to whisper and laugh.

Both Lisa and Julie were relieved when they headed to the gym for their last class of the day. Lisa pulled the gym door open so Julie could go through first. With the new semester came a new elective. Lisa had requested a last period second semester PE class so that if softball games took her out of school early, it wouldn't affect any academic courses.

One section of the old bleachers was full of junior girls needing to fulfill their yearly physical education requirement.

"Geez," Lisa said, "this is going to be a huge PE class."

"No kidding, Brown girl," Julie said, using Lisa's nickname. "I hope we don't end up playing dodgeball every day."

Lisa grimaced for Julie's sake. "You ain't lying, White girl."

They sat on the lowest bleacher, the only bleacher left, and chatted until their teacher came in, wheeling a cart full of combination locks. Lisa was relieved that their softball coach would be their PE teacher.

Coach Spears surveyed the noisy crowd of girls. The instant the late bell rang, she blew her whistle. Many of the girls held their hands over their ears and looked offended that their uber-important conversations had been so rudely interrupted. Lisa bit down a smile. They would soon learn that this was not going to be a democracy. Coach Spears was easygoing, but she suffered no fools.

"When I call your name," Coach Spears said, "come up and get your lock. Then you will stand silently on this line until everyone's name has been called." A murmur of groans went through the bleachers.

Lisa exchanged a glance with Julie. Geez, did they think they wouldn't have to move on the first day of class? Lisa couldn't wait to see what Coach Spears had in store for them that semester.

Their coach motioned to them to help her give out the

combinations and locks. As Coach called the names out one by one, Lisa and Julie searched for the lock with the girl's name, locker, and combination attached to it.

"Missy Matthews," Coach Spears read.

Missy, a thin brunette, stood and picked her way down the bleachers. Her classmates parted the way for her as if Cleopatra were walking among them. Lisa tried not to roll her eyes as the self-appointed queen of the junior class made her way to the lock cart. Missy had a way of gathering followers, just like a royal court. It was kind of disgusting to watch the other girls fawn over her and subjugate themselves into her entourage. Missy was going out with Brad Potter, the best-looking guy in the junior class. Of course, she was.

There was a huge pile of locks, and neither Lisa nor Julie could find Missy's name at first. They started over, moving the locks one by one from the right side to the left.

Missy groaned impatiently as if she were surrounded by incompetent morons. At this point, Lisa had finally located Missy's lock but waited an extra beat or two before handing it to her. Missy didn't acknowledge her existence.

Whatever. Lisa would not be heartbroken because Missy Matthews had dissed her.

Once in the locker room, the girls scurried about finding their assigned lockers and making sure the combinations worked properly. There were four long rows of lockers stacked two high. Julie found her locker right away in the first row, but Lisa didn't find hers until she'd gotten to the far corner of the last row. Thank God it was a top locker. At almost six feet tall, it would suck to have to bend for a bottom one. Coach Spears most definitely had a hand in that selection.

Lisa groaned when she saw Missy coming down her row, head down, reading the numbers. Marnie and Collette, two of her ladies-in-waiting, tagged behind.

"Aha," Missy exclaimed, "here it is. Why do they have to make this so hard?"

This time Lisa couldn't hold back her laugh. She looked away to hide her grin and snapped the lock onto her locker.

"No way," Missy said.

Lisa turned around but stopped dead in her tracks when she realized Missy's comment was directed at her.

"No, no, no. There is no way I'm changing in front of her." Missy pointed a finger at Lisa.

Knowing no other person was standing unseen behind her, Lisa stood even taller. Sure that she was now six and a half feet tall, she took a step closer to Missy. Lisa tried to hold back her laugh when Missy and her maids took a step back.

"I'm not—no way," Missy said again. She looked at her ladies-in-waiting for confirmation. Each of them grimaced as if looking at something disgusting.

"Is there a problem here, girls?" Coach Spears turned the corner and positioned herself in between Lisa and Missy.

"None here, Coach," Lisa said. She tried to stay six and a half feet tall, but the day had worn on her nerves, and she was shrinking. The whispers, the judgmental looks, the nervous glances had nearly exhausted her.

"She's a…" Missy said. Disgust battled with fear on her face.

"She's a what? Junior? Tall girl? Softball player? Big sister?" Coach Spears suggested.

"She's a dyke."

Lisa inhaled sharply. She hadn't been called a name in so long that she was out of practice. Her armor must have thinned since her childhood days of being called a bastard.

"And what if she is? What does that have to do with your locker?"

"I'm not undressing in front of her." Missy's entourage shook their heads in disgust as if Lisa were the scum of the earth. Lower than low.

"And you don't have to," Coach Spears said evenly, surprising everyone.

"I don't?"

"No, of course not. You can drop PE, take a study hall, and then take two semesters of PE as a senior."

"No way. You can't make me do that," Missy said.

"I'll take this locker," a voice said from around the corner. Julie appeared and reached her hand out for Missy's lock.

No one moved until Coach Spears said, "That's an acceptable compromise."

"Why should I be the one to move?" Missy stomped her foot.

Lisa could not believe Missy had actually stomped her foot at Coach Spears.

"You're moving all right." Coach Spears took the lock from Missy and handed it to Julie. "You're moving right to Assistant Principal Braun's office."

"What? Why?"

"Why are you still here?" Coach Spears was only five foot four, but you would never have known it watching her stare down Missy Matthews.

"Fine. Whatever. Daddy is going to call, and you'll see what happens to you then." Missy's entourage scurried out of her way as she stormed out of the locker room.

Coach Spears turned to look at Lisa and rolled her eyes. "Are you okay?"

"I'll live," Lisa said. "I guess." She truly hadn't known the depths of homophobia some people had. "What's going to happen now?"

"Phht." Coach Spears waved her hand. "Mr. Matthews will call, but he won't call me directly. No, the coward will go right over my head to Assistant Principal Braun, who will say all the right words to make him go away. It'll be just like last year when I took her PE class out to the field to play soccer, and light rain started to fall, completely destroying her hairdo before we could get back inside. Or how 'bout the time—"

"No, I get it, Coach. I get it," Lisa said, her eyes wide. She exchanged a glance with Julie. She had no idea people like that existed. "I'm sorry if I caused you any trouble."

"You? Nah." Coach Spears winked at Lisa. "I want you to live your life. Let the Missy's of the world barely register on your radar. They are not important."

"Thanks, Coach. I'll try."

"Yeah," Julie said. "That's good advice."

Coach winked at them again and took out her whistle. Lisa and Julie flung their hands over their ears.

The whistle blew, and Coach Spears yelled to the locker room, "Be back in the bleachers in two minutes."

Coach Spears headed out of the locker room, but before Lisa and Julie followed, Julie turned to Lisa and said, "Brown girl, why does it always feel like us versus them?"

143

"Good question, White girl. And we're getting more of that tonight. You're still going, right?"

"Wouldn't miss it," Julie said. "C'mon, we can't be late for Coach Spears's countdown."

They hustled out of the locker room and made it to the bleachers with plenty of time to spare. Missy Matthews was nowhere in sight, but Lisa prayed that didn't mean trouble down the line.

~~~

The drive to Clarksonville Community College that evening was a short one. Lisa smiled when Julie reached for Marcus's hand as they got out of Marlee's van. It was nice to see them be open about their relationship. And it was even nicer that they were invested in the youth alliance, too. Having support when the world was full of people like Missy Matthews was a gift.

Lisa's heart did a flip-flop when she saw Sam's car in the parking lot. How can love that makes your heart sing like that be wrong? The Missy Matthews' of the world just didn't get it. They didn't take the time to understand. Lisa shrugged mentally. She had to let it go like Coach Spears said. The Missy Matthews' of the world were simply not important enough to waste time on.

Sam was in her arms before the door to the Student Union meeting room had closed. Their kiss didn't have a chance to heat up, though, because Anne called for their attention. A lot of the same kids from the last youth alliance meeting were there, but there were a few new faces, too, including some of the kids from Jordan's school who had been at Ronnie's party.

Lisa threw her coat onto the pile and sat with her friends.

Anne clapped her hands twice to get them to settle down. "You're all excited about this new project, aren't you?"

A chorus of hoots filled the room.

"Well, good, because I think if we do this right, we can help a lot of people." Anne reached up to flick a lock of her dark hair out of her eyes. "We must set some ground rules before we get started, though. The gentlemen to my right," she pointed to Jordan and Ronnie, "will outline the basic rules, but I want everyone to understand that enlightening others is behind the spirit of this debate. Religion can be extremely personal, and we are not here to judge anyone." She looked around at the faces in the room. "Okay?"

Everyone agreed, and then Ronnie and Jordan gave general outlines of the debate. Swearing and name-calling were not acceptable behaviors. And no matter what people's personal opinions, everything was to be polite and respectful.

"Before we get started," Ronnie said, "Jordan and I have a surprise for you."

Jordan hurried over to the wall switches and turned off the lights. Ronnie made a few clicks to his computer, and the *Respect* video they'd made at the last meeting started playing on the screen. The guys had added some smooth background music to the opening title page. It was cool.

The video had been edited well, and Jordan was a natural on the screen. Lisa hated looking at herself on camera. She thought she looked like a she-giant from the planet Gigantus. Whatever. It didn't matter what she looked like, though. That was the point of the video, wasn't it? Everyone was different, so get over yourselves and respect each other already. Lisa realized that it also applied when she looked at herself. She wondered how she could get Missy Matthews to watch the video. In less than a day, Missy had become Lisa's poster child for bigots.

Once the video was done playing, Jordan said they had a couple more edits to do, but it would go live on the college website and on YouTube by Friday evening. An excited buzz swept the room.

Channeling that excitement, the group moved on to their new project. Lisa and her friends gathered their thoughts and agreed that Lisa and Marcus should be the main spokespeople. Lisa had had the most experience with religion and the Bible, and Marcus was on the speech and debate team at school. Lisa welcomed the role, and her group went over their list of opening one-liner statements.

"Places," Jordan called. He was the director of the new video. "Remember this is for educational purposes, and the views expressed here may not necessarily represent those of the speakers." He winked at Ronnie. Clearly, Ronnie had made him say that since Ronnie was on the *Is-a-Sin* side of the debate. Jordan reminded them that Lisa and Marcus's *Not-a-Sin* side would start the crossfire. He reminded them not to use real names and that pauses could be edited out. Entire scenes could be reshot if necessary, too. He didn't want them to worry about those technical things.

Sam gave Lisa a quick kiss for luck, and Lisa stood beside Marcus behind their designated podium, which was turned slightly to face the opposition's identical podium. Alivia was probably chomping at the bit to sling trash at Lisa.

Lisa spread their notes out so they could read through them one more time. Funny thing, there was no actual script for this debate. Each side had to come up with its own arguments and defenses. That was Jordan's idea, seconded by Ronnie, and approved by Anne. Jordan wanted more spontaneity in the exchanges. He wanted realistic and emotional interactions. Lisa's nerves ratcheted up a notch when she saw the three video cameras that Anne had somehow rounded up. One was trained directly on her. She took a deep breath to calm her nerves.

"Ready, teams?" Jordan asked from his directorial position behind the cameras.

Lisa and Marcus nodded at Jordan. Lisa decided to attack this as if her softball team had taken the field against their arch-rivals East Valley. She knew her team matched up well against East Valley and could beat them on any given day. She set her chin. She was ready.

"And action," Jordan called.

Marcus said matter-of-factly, "Homosexuality is not a sin." There it was the main topic of debate.

Alivia responded. "Your decision to live as gay people is a sin against God's laws." It sounded like she meant every word. Maybe she did. The funny thing was, Marcus wasn't gay.

Lisa forced herself not to swallow the lump building in her throat. She felt the pressure of representing every gay person on the entire planet who had been told they were a sinner. She stood tall and said, "I didn't *decide* to be gay, just like I didn't *decide* to have brown eyes."

"God will heal you." Ronnie's voice took on a self-righteous tone.

Marcus answered, "There's nothing wrong with us that needs healing."

"You are blasphemers for questioning the holy words of the Bible." Alivia's eyes flashed.

"It's all in the interpretation," Lisa said, willing her voice not to shake, "because the Bible has been used to justify many terrible things like sexism, slavery, murder, wars." Lisa looked Alivia right in the eye.

Alivia looked ready to fly over the podium and take Lisa down. Geez, why was she so angry?

Ronnie answered, "You gay people ignore the Bible's teachings."

Marcus didn't miss a beat. "The Bible teaches many things if your heart is open." An excited twitter went up in the crowd. Lisa's spirits were lifting. She had come up with that line.

"You must atone to God and to us for what you are," Alivia snarled. She smacked the podium with her open hand.

"I will not apologize for who I am," Lisa roared, ignoring their notes. She jabbed a finger toward Alivia. "Least of all to you."

Chapter Fifteen

*"Please accept my gift that is brought
to you, because God has dealt
graciously with me, and because I have
everything I want." — Genesis 33:11*

"Samtha's here. Samtha's here," Bridget yelled and flew to the front door. She struggled to turn the knob, but even if she'd been successful, she wouldn't have been able to open the door. With an almost four-year-old in the house, her father had installed a deadbolt to make sure the younger kids wouldn't get curious and walk outside on their own.

"Thank you, Sweetpea," Lisa said. She undid the deadbolt and opened the door. Her heart swelled as it usually did when she saw Sam. "Stay here, Bridget," Lisa said. "Lynnie, come help Sam. It looks like she has a lot of boxes."

"Okay." Lynnie stood up from her usual spot on the couch. Uncharacteristically, she put her book down instead of carrying it with her.

Lisa and Lynnie threw on their coats and headed out the door and down the shoveled pathway to Sam's car parked in the street. Lisa wrapped Sam in a bear hug and kissed her right there in the front yard. She didn't care who saw them. She'd had a week at school with sly looks, whispered words, and wide berths in the hallways. You'd think she was Typhoid Mary or something. But Saturday had finally arrived, and Sam was there to exchange Christmas presents with her and her family. Life was good, so who cared that people knew she was gay?

"That was brave," Sam said. "Not that I minded. I just wasn't expecting it."

"It's cute," Lynnie said and smiled.

"Thanks, Lynnie," Sam said. "Okay, troops. Gather round. We've got a lot to bring in." The trunk of her Sebring was filled with boxes of wrapped Christmas gifts.

"Cleaned out your garage, eh?" Lisa bumped Sam with her hip.

"Ha ha." Sam bumped back. "Ooh, careful with that one, Lynnie. That's your present."

"What is it?" Lynnie held a large box in her arms and shook it gently. "It's not books."

Sam ran an imaginary zipper across her lips.

"I'll find out soon, won't I?" Lynnie headed back into the house, leaving Lisa and Sam to bring in the rest of Sam's packages.

"Sam," Lisa reproached, "you know you didn't have to do all of this." She gestured to the loot they carried.

"I know." There was a chipper lilt to Sam's voice. "I like to." As they headed toward the house, Sam added, "I have a church for us to go to tomorrow. I know you want to experience other points of view, so Marlee will pick you up, and Susie and I will meet you there. I mean, if you want."

"Of course, I want to go. If my parents will let me go. What church is it?" Lisa held the door open for Sam to pass through first.

"It's in East Valley. It's called the Church of God of Love."

Lisa's parents, hearing the conversation as the girls walked in, gave their permission heartily as long as Lisa would be home for Sunday dinner with the family. Sam assured them that would not be a problem. Lisa was secretly pleased that Sam was showing an interest. Their conversations rarely centered around church or God or much of anything religious.

Once the presents were set under the tree, and everyone had a cup of hot chocolate courtesy of Lisa's mother, Lisa's father said to Sam, "How's the youth alliance project going?"

"Good," Sam said. "Really good so far. Lisa has a calming presence."

"Pfft," Lisa said in disagreement. Didn't her nerves show Tuesday night?

"I know you don't believe it, Lisa," Sam said, "but I think a lot of people are going to learn from you. From the way you stand tall and say it like it is."

"Thanks, Sam." Lisa looked at her parents. "That's our hope, anyway."

Lisa's mother said, "Lisa showed us the *Respect* video you all put together. Very well done. I hope it enlightens some of the less-enlightened."

Sam nodded. "Ronnie and Jordan are the force behind that, and they're also the force behind the one we're doing now."

"Ronnie was the lead in Fiddler on the Roof, right?"

"Yes, and Jordan is his boyfriend."

It seemed weird to Lisa's ears to hear them talk so openly about gay people, but this was what she and the youth alliance were fighting for, wasn't it? To make being gay a non-issue.

"Okay, kids," Lisa's mother said. "I think it's time to give Sam her presents. Bridget, Lawrence Jr., will you do the honors?"

"Finally," Lawrence Jr. said and dove under the tree for the presents with Sam's name on it. Both he and Bridget wore red Santa hats. The tradition in the Brown household was that the ones who handed out the gifts got to wear Santa hats. Lisa had given hers up to Lawrence Jr. once he was old enough to help Lynnie.

"Lynnie," Sam said, "would you like to hand out my gifts to everyone?"

"Wait, wait," Lisa's father said. He got up and rummaged in the hall closet. "Here you go, Lynnie." He plunked a plush red and white Santa hat on her head.

"Thanks, Papa." Lynnie was most definitely a daddy's girl.

Lisa remembered a time when she was the apple of his eye. She still was, she supposed, but she had been in first grade when he came into her life. He hadn't watched her grow up from a baby. It had always dinged her a little bit that she didn't share real DNA with him.

"Thank you, Bridget." Sam held up a macaroni necklace. The curved noodles had been painted and covered with glitter. "I love it." Sam put the necklace over her head and admired it.

"I got one just like it," Lisa whispered.

The presents were opened in a fury. Lisa got a gold heart-shaped necklace and the latest iPhone from Sam. Lisa gushed over the gifts but also felt a little hollow in the pit of her stomach. The gifts Sam lavished on her family were so expensive. There was no way her family could ever give Sam things like that in kind. Sam had received hand-made gifts from the kids and a hat, glove, and scarf set from her parents. Lisa gave Sam a bracelet, but it wasn't gold like the necklace Sam had given her. It would probably turn Sam's wrist green in a week.

The first time Sam brought over expensive gifts for the family, Lisa's mother and father had reluctantly accepted them, saying that Sam didn't have to buy their affection. Sam said it wasn't anything like that, and she just wanted to make other people happy. That was all. It seemed true enough to Lisa, and after a while, her parents eased up on their protests, but not altogether.

Sam had gotten both Bridget and Lawrence Jr. LeapPad tablets already loaded with age-appropriate educational games. Lawrence Jr. was busy adding up numbers to shoot down aliens. Lisa wished she'd had one of those when she was little. Maybe geometry wouldn't have been such a chore.

Lynnie had two boxes from Sam. She'd already opened the smaller one with a Kindle Fire tablet loaded with apps and a dozen books that Sam thought Lynnie would like. Lynnie was sitting quietly, sliding her finger across the tablet to see what books Sam had given her.

"Lynnie," Sam said, "don't forget to open your other box. Sam reached for Lisa's hand. Whatever was in that box was going to be big.

"Okay." Lynnie reluctantly put her new Kindle device down and pulled the bigger box closer. Everyone in the room, even Lawrence Jr., stopped what they were doing to watch Lynnie open the gift.

She reached into the box and pulled out a gift wrapped in green paper with elegant white Christmas trees. The package, like all the rest, had been inexpertly wrapped. During one of their nightly phone conversations, Sam told Lisa she was wrapping each one of the gifts herself. And it showed, but Lisa loved Sam all the more for it.

Lynnie's face lit up in wonder as she ripped off part of the paper. No one else could see what was underneath. Lynnie looked up at Sam. "Really?"

"Really," Sam said. "And I will help you."

Lynnie leaped up, her present still in her hands, and ran over to hug Sam. Lisa scooted over on the couch so that Lynnie could sit between them. She knew when she'd been replaced.

"Open it up, so everyone else can see," Sam said.

Lynnie carefully unwrapped the rest of the box and pulled out a delicate violin. Lynnie cradled it gently in her hands.

"Santa told me you wanted to learn," Sam said, "and I'll teach you how to take care of it and how to play it. And the best part?" she looked at Lisa's parents. "It's electric as well as acoustic so that she can wear headphones while she practices."

"The Lord be praised," Lisa's father said, looking up to the heavens.

Lisa's mother shot him a look for his attempted humor, but she smiled back at Sam and said, "Thank you for all the gifts, Samantha Rose." Her eyes filled with tears, and she choked out, "I don't know if we can ever repay your kindness. We are truly blessed to have you in our lives." She stood and pulled Sam into a hug.

Sam's eyes were moist when she sat back down. "I'm also blessed, Mrs. Brown. I haven't really had people to share gifts with. And I will treasure these." She rubbed her fingers along the necklace Bridget made for her, the bookmark that Lawrence Jr. made with felt, glue, and cut-out magazine pictures, and the classical music CD Lynnie had bought for her. "These are really special."

"Oh, geez," Lisa said as she reached for the tissue box. She took one for herself and then sent the box around to Sam and her mother.

Her father pretended he hadn't been tearing up, but Lisa had seen the sheen in his eyes.

"Okay, family," Lisa's mother said. "It's time to thank Sam, so she and Lisa can be on their way."

Promising to be back by eleven o'clock, Sam and Lisa got in Sam's Sebring. When Sam suggested that Lisa drive, Lisa was ecstatic and grabbed the keys willingly.

"Where are we headed?"

"The heater's working great, so how about a little alone time at the college softball field?"

"You got it." Lisa pulled the Sebring away from the curb. She loved the feel of the leather steering wheel cover underneath her gloves. She only had her learner's permit and was a very careful driver, but they could get in trouble if a cop pulled them over. Sam wouldn't be eighteen for another three weeks. "Hey, what do you want to do for your birthday? Do you want me to throw you a surprise party like we did for Susie?"

Sam laughed and put her hand on Lisa's thigh. Although Lisa wore thick jeans against the winter cold and Sam had gloves on, the touch sent a warm signal to all the right places. "If you tell me about it, then it won't be a surprise."

"Oh, yeah. Duh," Lisa said with a chuckle. "I guess you could pretend you didn't know."

"Actually, I think I want to have a few friends over to the house. We can use Helene's apartment, you know? It has a kitchen and room for slow dancing." The hand on Lisa's leg moved slowly up and then back down. The movement sent a surge of desire through Lisa's body. God, how she had missed Sam. How can this feeling be wrong? How can this feeling be from the Devil? How could you be sent to hell for loving someone? It made no sense.

The college parking lot was empty, so Lisa parked Sam's car in the far corner of the lot, just beyond the reach of the street lights. A quick move to the back seat, and they were lost in desire for each other. Maybe it was true that absence made a person's heart and other places yearn for each other.

All good things had to end, and after a couple of hours, Lisa reluctantly drove them back to her house. Her father's pickup truck was in the road where Sam usually parked. "Okay, that's weird," she muttered.

"I guess you should park in the driveway," Sam said.

Lisa pulled the Sebring into the driveway next to the family minivan. She turned to face Sam. "I'm going to miss you."

"We'll see each other on Tuesday for the youth alliance."

"I know, but it's hard to leave you."

"Same." Sam's expression told Lisa everything she wanted to know. The physical closeness they had shared earlier in the backseat had been amazingly life-affirming.

They sat in silence for a few moments until Lisa reached over from the driver's seat and gave Sam a searing kiss. Sam's moan was music to her ears. "I should go in before things get too, you know."

"I know." Sam opened the passenger door and got out.

Lisa got out and waited for Sam by the driver's door of the idling car.

Lisa enfolded Sam in her arms, and they stood together for several minutes until Sam said, "You should turn your car off; you're wasting gas."

"What?" Lisa was really confused. Was Sam staying longer? She was even more confused at the grin growing on Sam's face.

Sam reached around Lisa and opened the driver's side door. She leaned in, twisted the ignition key, and turned the car off. She pulled the keys out, stood up, and handed them to Lisa.

Lisa took the keys but was more confused than ever. "What are you doing?"

Sam, still grinning, put both hands in her pockets. Her blue-gray eyes smiled.

"Hmm?" Lisa still held the keys in her hands.

"They're your keys now."

"Oh, cool. Thanks," Lisa said. "Now, I won't have to keep using your keys when you let me drive your car."

"Check out the keychain."

Hanging from Sam's keys was a gold medallion. It used to read "Samantha Rose," but now it read "Lisa" in ornate script. "Baby, this is awesome. Thank you."

"Do you like it?"

"I love it." Lisa wrapped her arms around Sam's shoulders and gave her a quick kiss. Not that she'd run out of steamy kisses, but she'd seen movement near the living room curtains. One or both of her parents must have heard them out front. She still had a few minutes to spare before her curfew, and she was going to use every last second.

"Thanks for letting me drive your car once in a while. I can use the practice."

"You're welcome." Sam checked her watch. "Two more minutes of snuggle time."

Lisa leaned back against the car and pulled Sam against her. Desire spiraled through her again. "I wish I didn't have a curfew. I wish I could just drive over to your house anytime I wanted. I wish…" Lisa squeezed Sam. "I wish for a lot of things." The air was cold, but not bitter cold like it could get in a North Country winter. She could handle a couple more minutes outside.

The familiar rumble of a particular Toyota disturbed the quiet of their snuggling. "What the heck is Susie doing here?" Lisa said, confused again. "Is everything okay?"

"Everything's fine. She's my ride home." There was no mistaking Sam's grin. Something was up. Sam pulled away from Lisa and motioned for Susie to park at the end of the driveway.

"What d'ya mean, Susie's your ride home?" Lisa asked. At this point, both of Lisa's parents were looking out the window. It looked like her curfew was definitely up.

Sam grabbed Lisa's hand and said, "It's yours."

"What's mine?" Lisa still wasn't sure what was happening.

Sam pointed to the Sebring. "The car. It's yours."

"The car?" Lisa looked at the car, her parents looking out the front window, Susie, and finally back at Sam. Realization dawned on her. "You're giving me your car?"

Sam nodded, her expression filled with love. "Your parents are in on it."

"They are?"

"Yeah. Truth be known, they wouldn't let me just give you the car, so they're making monthly payments for it."

"How much?"

Sam scrunched her face as if deciding whether to divulge her information but then shrugged and said, "Fifty."

"Maybe I can help with the payments, too."

"You Browns are so proud. I wish you'd just let me give you things."

"Sam, you give me you, and that's all I want." Something dawned on her. "Oh, geez, that's why you gave me my own set of keys. Baby!" Lisa picked Sam up and twirled her around just like she would Bridget. She kissed Sam's face over and over and finally set her back on the ground, dizzy. "Thank you, baby." She leaned down and said into Sam's ear. "Really? Are you sure?"

Sam laughed. "Yes, of course. Daddy bought me a convertible Mercedes for Christmas, and –"

"Your father got you a Mercedes?" Lisa's eyebrows shot up to the sky. She had never known anyone with such wealth. There seemed to be no end to it.

Susie shot Lisa a thumbs-up from where she sat in her idling car. Lisa shrugged back that she was overwhelmed.

"And," Sam continued, "Daddy loved the idea of me giving you the car. Well, he didn't want me just to give it away. He said that wasn't sound business practice or something, but he was happy that I could help you guys out. Of course, it's not brand new or anything."

Lisa playfully smacked Sam on the shoulder. "Who cares?" Lisa looked back at the car. "Wow, Sam. This is really going to help. My mother's going to make me drive the kids everywhere in this. I can't believe you did this. Are you sure?" Lisa asked again because she was still dazed by Sam and her family's generosity.

"Lisa, you're my life. I knew it before but coming home to an empty house made me realize it even more. 'Where you go, I will go; where you lodge, I will lodge; your people shall be my people and your God my God. Where you die, I will die—there will I be buried.'"

"The book of Ruth. You just quoted scripture to me."

"I know how important God and church are to you, Lisa, so I've been trying to learn more."

Lisa couldn't help it. She didn't mean to, but all the pent-up anxiety of being outed at school, the mind games with Alivia, and her church turning against her all came crashing in on the love Sam showered her with. She buried her face in Sam's shoulder and cried.

"Oh, my," Sam said, rubbing Lisa's back over her coat. "You're okay, baby. You're okay."

"I know," Lisa choked out. She pulled back and wiped at the tears in her eyes. "I have you, so I'm more than okay."

Chapter Sixteen

"He heals the broken hearted, and
binds up their wounds." — Psalm 147:3

Lisa used the GPS feature on her new iPhone and directed Marlee to The Church of God of Love on Trinity Street. Lisa had never heard of the church before, but Pentecostals, according to her mother, could be a little fanatical about feeling the Holy Spirit. She said they adhered to the infallibility of scripture and often translated the Bible literally. They were waiting for the imminent second coming of Jesus, she'd said. Lisa wasn't sure what Sam had gotten them into, but they'd all be together, so it would be okay no matter what.

The parking lot was full, and Marlee had to drive to the farthest part of the lot to find a space. "Too bad we couldn't have taken your new car," Marlee said as they got out of the van and started the hike to the church.

"I'm still in shock that Sam gave me her car," Lisa said. It's crazy. I can't even legally drive yet." Lisa had to find a way to make sure Sam honestly didn't think she needed to buy her attention or affection. Lisa also worried that the kids would get used to Sam bringing them things every time she came over. She wanted them to stay humble.

Except for the huge letters above the door reading CHURCH OF GOD OF LOVE, it looked like any other church. The brick walls stood sturdy in faith, the steeple stretched high toward God, and the entryway welcomed them with warmth. Sam and Susie weren't there yet, so Lisa texted Sam. A quick reply said they were two minutes away.

The people going into the church seemed friendly. Every single one of them smiled as they went past. A middle-aged, balding man greeted them. "Are you new to our church?" The giant cross hanging around his neck bounced off his ample belly.

Close-lipped, Marlee simply nodded, so Lisa answered, "Yes, we're expecting two more friends."

"You're going to love The Church of God of Love." He reached behind him to get two pamphlets. He handed one to each of them.

Lisa read the title, "Getting Acquainted with the Church of God of Love. Feel the Spirit with Us!" She tucked the brochure into her coat pocket. "Thank you."

An older woman with a similar dangling cross came over to them. The curious glint in her eye told Lisa that the woman was on the prowl for gossip. Lisa thought of Mrs. Maynard and the other gossipy ladies at her own church and vowed never to become one.

The woman held a couple of "Getting Acquainted" brochures in one hand, but upon seeing that Marlee already had one, she put her stack on the table. She sidled up next to the man and placed a hand possessively on his shoulder. Her polyester dress was long and cut at a weird, not-in-style hemline. The polyester woman tilted her head "Who do we have here, Joe?" She looked Marlee over from head to toe, looking mildly annoyed, presumably by Marlee's short hair and the fact that she was wearing pants to church. Lisa had noticed that

162

all the women and girls wore dresses or skirts.

"They're new," Joe said. "They're here to check out the incredible word of God." His sentence lifted at the end. It was a question Lisa supposed she should answer.

Lisa nodded. The lobby was getting warm, so she took off her winter coat and draped it over her arm.

"It's so nice to see young people answering the call of God so early," the woman said. "Isn't it, Joe?"

Joe probably nodded, but Lisa didn't know because she was smoothing out her dress, hoping it hadn't wrinkled too much on the way over. When she looked up, Joe was staring straight at her breasts.

"Pfft." Lisa rolled her eyes and grabbed Marlee by the arm. "I think our friends are here." Lisa spun them around and dragged Marlee toward the door. "Geez," Lisa said when they were out of earshot. "Are all men like that? Creeps?"

"He reminds me of Bernie the Bee Man," Marlee said. "Hey, there they are." She pointed to Sam and Susie running up the walkway. They slowed down when they made eye contact.

Lisa didn't dare take Sam's arm, although she desperately wanted to. Giving her a hello kiss was definitely out of the question, too. It was something her mother had warned her about before she left. She'd told Lisa to "feel out the water" before diving in head first. Even Marlee and Susie didn't embrace or hold hands. Lisa's stomach tightened. It sucked always having to be on your guard, never knowing how people would react.

"Ready to go in?" Sam said, a little out of breath.

"Still jetlagged, eh?"

Sam nodded.

Lisa led her friends through the door farthest from Joe the Jugs man. They found a pew toward the back of the church and settled in with their coats jammed up into the corner next to Marlee.

Parishioners milled about the room, reminding Lisa of the Unitarian Universalist Church service where everyone was free and comfortable. Maybe her church was the only church that was quiet and somber. Nah, she suspected Susie's Catholic Church was quiet, too. Different strokes for different folks.

"There's a band?" Susie pointed toward the raised platform in the front of the church.

They craned their necks so they could see. There was a drum set, four or five guitars, a few music stands, and several microphones scattered about. Lisa couldn't figure out where the preacher's pulpit was. Maybe he was going to use a music stand or something. It was weird.

"That's wild," Sam said, referring to the instruments. "I should have brought my violin."

A clock counted down on a giant screen behind the instruments. Several young men walked onto the platform, each dressed in a suit and tie. One by one, they picked up the instruments and tuned them silently. A group of women walked onto the platform and stood behind a microphone that sat center stage.

When the clock hit zero, one of the guitar players stepped up to a microphone and said, "Worship with us." The band started playing immediately.

Lisa knew the song instantly and leaped to her feet along with several other people in the congregation. This was not a traditional song she'd heard at her own church. Oh, no, it was a song on one of her CDs of praise songs. "Shake the Foundation" had to be one of her all-time favorites.

Lisa joined the other parishioners as they sang along. She smiled as Sam leaned over her to exchange a glance with Susie. Susie threw her a thumbs-up. Apparently, they were well-pleased that they had found a church for Lisa. Lisa moved from side to side in rhythm with the steady beat. Marlee stood up and grinned. She was obviously moved by the music, too. Sam and Susie stood and fell into the rhythm of the beat, although Susie's movements had a salsa flair. God, you had to be dead not to feel the energy in the room.

Marlee leaned across Susie and Lisa to say to Sam, "What is that instrument?" She pointed to the guy playing a guitar near the drums.

"It's a bass guitar."

"Bass guitar?" Marlee asked again. She probably couldn't hear because the music was getting louder and faster.

Sam nodded.

Lisa laughed when Marlee said, "I want to play the bass guitar. That is so cool." And it *was* cool. The bass groove rocked the church. You could feel it in the floorboards and the pews. The Church of God of Love was rocking.

Some people clapped to the music, while others threw their hands high over their heads and rocked back and forth. Although she couldn't see them, she knew many probably had their eyes closed. Lisa couldn't help it. She had to join them. She was feeling it, too. She put her hands up to feel the energy and was instantly rewarded with tingling hands. The Holy Spirit. It had to be. She swayed back and forth like the others and felt the energy rush straight into her heart. The only time she'd ever felt anything like it was when she was alone with Sam. She leaned to the side until her body pressed against Sam's. Knowing she was grounded, she drew in more energy as the music got even faster and louder. She was not surprised when a familiar ache clutched at her chest, and her eyes welled up with tears. She didn't even care if her friends saw her crying. She let the Holy Spirit flood her senses.

As the music slowed, she opened her eyes and stood up straighter. She hated to lose the warm contact she'd had with Sam, but she wasn't sure how accepting this church was. Many people still swayed with their hands raised, but a calmness overtook the church as the music softened. It almost felt like the calm peace that overtook her after she and Sam had their intimate time.

Sam reached for her hand and gave it a quick squeeze. Lisa smiled and was saddened when Sam's hand went away, but she understood.

A few people got up to speak, and there were a few more songs of praise. Lisa wasn't hit as hard by the energy during those songs, but they were powerful, nonetheless.

"Hey," Susie whispered to Sam, "isn't that Freddie?"

Lisa looked where Susie pointed with her chin. Sure enough, Freddie sat in a center pew. His girlfriend Rebekah, the girl who'd worn the yellow dress at the dance, sat by his side. As if feeling four sets of eyes on him, Freddie turned around, and his mouth fell open when he saw them.

Susie waved at him and smiled. Marlee pulled Susie's hand down and yelled at her silently with wide eyes. Freddie said something into Rebekah's ear, and then she turned around to look at them. She looked as shocked as Freddie at their presence. Lisa prayed that Freddie wouldn't do something like shout scripture at them the way he'd done at the dance. She breathed a sigh of relief when he and his girlfriend simply turned around and focused on the introduction to the preacher. One of the guitar players stepped up on stage and placed a small wooden table near a lone free-standing microphone

The preacher was good-looking in a middle-aged Brad Pitt kind of way. He stood quietly in the center of the stage, dunking a tea bag into a cup. He took a sip, seemed satisfied with it, and pulled the tea bag out. It was kind of odd. Maybe he was setting the mood, getting the worked-up crowd to calm down inside. It was working on Lisa. She felt quite content.

"Marriage," the preacher said quietly, "is like the perfect cup of tea. It's the careful and practiced balance of tea leaves, sugar or honey, cream if you like, but it takes time to perfect. As Jesus said in Mark 10:6-9, 'But from the beginning of creation, God made them male and female. For this reason, a man shall leave his father and mother and be joined to his wife, and the two shall become one flesh.' So they are no longer two, but one flesh. Therefore what God has joined together, let no one separate.'"

Lisa's heart sank. Here it comes. She should have known this church would be like every other. Condemn the gays. Don't let them get married. "Well, too bad," Lisa muttered under her breath. "Marriage is legal here, and one day I am going to marry this beautiful girl sitting next to me." She looked at Sam and was saddened by Sam's angry face. Sam must be feeling it, too.

Lisa wasn't the only one muttering to herself. Susie's steady stream of quiet but angry Spanish was almost comical. Marlee rubbed Susie's arm, and Susie closed her mouth but did not look at Marlee. Her glare was fixated on the preacher.

Unable to focus, Lisa half-listened to the sermon. She reached for the "Getting Acquainted" pamphlet that Sam still held in her hand. One section of the pamphlet gave an overview of the church's beliefs. She smirked when she read the lines stating that marriage was strictly between a man and a woman until death parted them. As the sermon went on, Lisa realized his sermon was about the evils of divorce. Lisa felt that divorce was a personal thing between the two people involved, and the church should back off in that regard. Not that Lisa ever planned on getting divorced.

She skimmed the rest of the pamphlet, knowing she would find the words she was looking for, and she did. Right there, in black and white, it read, "The Church of God of Love condemns homosexuality as a moral sin."

That was all it said on the subject. She showed the line to Sam, who yanked the pamphlet from Lisa's hands. She balled it up and tossed it on the floor at her feet. Sam mouthed the word, "Ready to go?"

Lisa shook her head. She didn't want to stand up in the middle of the sermon and walk out. That would draw too much attention. "Let's wait until it's over," she whispered. Sam nodded.

At the end of the service, parishioners were invited to the front to be anointed with oil.

"We'll just skip that, you guys," Lisa said sarcastically. "Come on. Let's get out of here."

Marlee passed the coats over one by one, and then they made their way out of the pew. Lisa, feeling positively deflated, let Sam lead their group into the lobby.

They were about to head out the door when a familiar voice called out, "Samantha Rose. Wait." It was Freddie.

Lisa's chest tightened up. She did not want a repeat of the scene at the dance, especially when they were clearly on enemy territory. If any of them had known this was Freddie's church, they would not have gone. Not in a million years.

"What do you want, Freddie?" Sam asked coldly.

"Hi. Sorry to bother you guys." He ran his fingers through his strawberry blonde hair. The freckles on his face got lost in his blush.

Lisa exchanged a glance with Sam. What was Freddie up to?

"You have two more seconds, Freddie," Sam said.

"Okay, okay. I just wanted to say thank you." He looked at Lisa for the first time. "Rebekah told me everything you did for me. Thank you for, um, helping me the other night. At the dance." By then, his girlfriend Rebekah had caught up and latched onto his arm.

"Yes, thank you so much." Rebekah's smile seemed genuine.

"I didn't really do anything, but you're welcome," Lisa said. "How are you feeling?"

"Good. I get those, uh, spells occasionally." He leaned closer and said, "I'm glad my parents haven't tried to cleanse me of a demon or something."

Lisa laughed politely, but Freddie seemed almost serious. She wasn't sure if Pentecostal churches did that sort of thing or not, and she didn't want to find out. No, this was not the right church for her.

"We gotta go," Sam said abruptly and steered Lisa and her friends toward the door.

"Okay, thanks again."

They were already out the door when Lisa heard Freddie say, "Crap, I forgot to ask what her name was."

Half-tempted to go back in, Lisa resisted and headed down the front steps with her friends. Dejected, she walked in silence. She wanted to be upbeat but couldn't find the energy. There didn't seem to be a church for her anywhere. Unless there was some uber-secret gay church or something, there was no place for her.

Chapter Seventeen

"But those who wait for the LORD shall renew their strength, they shall mount up with wings like eagles, they shall run and not be weary, they shall walk and not faint." — Isaiah 40:31

After the church of God of Love service, Lisa sat with her friends quietly in Marlee's basement, munching on cheese and crackers and drinking Cokes. Lisa had about an hour before she had to be home for Sunday dinner. She was happy because Sam was going to stay for dinner, but she was also sad because it was looking worse and worse for her to find any kind of salvation.

Lisa opened up. "I feel like giving up."

"*Dios mio, amiga,*" Susie said. "I'm so sorry I suggested that church to Sam."

"So, this was your idea, eh?" Lisa said with a grin so Susie would know she was teasing.

"Yep. Sorry. That service was crazy. Catholics are way more reserved."

"It was really cool to start with," Marlee said. "The singing, the dancing, and clapping. I was digging it until…"

"The sermon," Sam finished. "I only glanced at that stupid

brochure the creepy guy gave me. If I'd read it all the way through, I would have seen their stance on *sinners* like us." She said the word sinner with sarcasm. "And we would have left right away."

"I know it sucked at the end," Lisa said, "but I think we were supposed to stay for some reason. Somewhere in the Bible, Matthew I think, it says something like, 'Search and you shall find.'" Lisa sighed. "I'm searching. I'm just not finding."

Lisa rested her head on Sam's shoulder. Sam pulled her close. "You'll be all right, baby. You have a good heart. God knows that."

"Here, here," Marlee said. "And you know what? I'm glad we went because I want one of those bass guitars. Oh. My. God. I have to learn to play one."

"Road trip!" Sam announced.

"Where to, baby?" Lisa sat up. She was grateful once again that Marlee had found a way to turn a dark conversation to a better place.

"North Country Music. It's a great music store in Clarksonville. They have bass guitars, amps, and whatever else you'll need to learn. They might even give lessons there."

"*Mi amor*," Susie said to Marlee, "you'd be really good at it." To Lisa and Sam, she said, "She has really good rhythm."

"TMI, Sus. TMI," Sam teased. She tried to hide against Lisa because they all knew what was coming next.

Susie smacked Sam on the arm. "She has good rhythm on the dance floor, *gringa*. Dance floor."

Marlee stood up. "Yes, let's dance. We need to lighten this mood before you guys have to go." She ran over to the iPod still set up from Susie's surprise birthday party. Marlee hit a button, and a sexy smooth rhythm filled the room.

172

"Let's salsa," Marlee said, gyrating around the basement floor to the beat.

Lisa let herself smile. "Yes, let's." She jumped up and reached for Sam's hand. "Dance with me?"

"Yes." Sam took the offered hand. "Forever."

~~~

Sam stayed for Sunday dinner upon Lisa's parents' enthusiastic invitation. After eating, the kids left the table to play, and usually Lisa would get up to clear the table and do the dishes, but this time she didn't. This time she and Sam lingered at the table with her parents.

"Lisa Bear," her father said, "people interpret the Bible and Jesus's teachings differently. Sometimes they hone in on one part of the Bible and go with it. The Pentecostals, well, I don't think their beliefs line up with yours."

"So why did you let me go, Papa?"

Lisa's mother answered. "You needed to see for yourself."

"We saw it all right," Sam said. She took a sip of coffee Lisa's mother had offered her. It was weird seeing Sam drink coffee, just like it had been weird seeing Susie drink beer on New Year's Eve. Did Lisa not know her friends at all?

"The first part of the service was fun," Lisa said. "People were clapping, singing, dancing, and jumping all around. Lots of people shouted at the preacher when he was talking. Geez, Reverend Owens would faint if we did those things in our church."

"Yes, I believe he would," Lisa's mother said with a chuckle. "You were outsiders today, trying to decide if you fit in."

"We didn't," Sam said.

Lisa's mother smiled. "This country was founded on religious freedom. I think a lot of people forget that."

"Different churches have different founding beliefs," Lisa's father added. "And if the beliefs of that church don't jive with yours, then find another one."

"That's how many of these churches came into being, you know." Lisa's mother took a sip of coffee. "Like Pentecostals. They began in the early 1900s. I Googled it."

"You did?" Lisa was surprised. Her mother never used the family computer.

"Okay, Lynnie helped, but the website said that Pentecostalism was basically started by a faith healer."

"He must have been a charismatic guy." Lisa's father said. "A lot of people seemed to like what he had to say and jumped on his bandwagon."

"And now there are many different offshoots of Pentecostalism because even they all can't agree," Lisa's mother added.

"Lisa, your parents are wise," Sam said.

"Don't I know it."

Lisa's mother stood and said to Lisa, "Why don't you and Sam go drive that new car of yours around while Papa and I clean up after dinner."

"Really, Mom?" One thing that could bring Lisa out of a bad mood was alone time with Sam.

"Go, go, go before I change my mind. Be back by six to start your homework."

Lisa stood and hugged her mother. For good measure, she hugged her father, too.

~~~

At school on Monday, there was no sign of Missy Matthews in Lisa's PE class. Rumor had it that Missy's daddy called the school and demanded that his daughter's entire schedule be changed, or he would go to the Superintendent. All that fuss so she wouldn't have to be anywhere near Lisa. Lisa knew Missy's motives were done out of fear and ignorance. For whatever unknown reason, Missy had felt threatened. The only way Lisa could figure out how to convince the world she was not a threat was to channel all of her energy into their youth alliance debate.

On Tuesday evening, Marlee picked her up right on time. Julie and Marcus were already in the backseat, scheming strategies and reading Bible verses as they headed to the Student Union building at the college. By the time she and Marcus stood behind their team podium facing the opposition, Lisa felt good. She and her team were prepared. They had a lot of good arguments. The only trouble was they had no idea what the other team was going to throw at them.

Jordan stood in front of the two teams while the rest of the kids sat out of sight of the cameras. There seemed to be more people here than ever before. Maybe the *Respect* video had gotten some attention, and kids wanted to be part of the youth alliance. That was a good thing.

"Last week," Jordan said in his director's voice, "both teams outlined their stance on the theme of homosexuality and the Bible. We've got those on tape and have already started editing, and I have to tell you, it looks amazing so far. The emotion is real, and the arguments on both sides are compelling. So let's keep that up."

He turned to the onlookers. "The only thing that was distracting was the crowd noise. You guys have to stay quiet while they're debating because the cameras pick up everything. No cheering or jeering for either side, okay?" When only a few heads nodded, he said more loudly, "Okay?"

This time heads nodded more vigorously.

"Better. And thank you." He turned back around to face the debaters. "Each group will get two minutes to make its statements. The opposition can then take up to ten minutes to consult with their team and come up with counter-arguments, and then you have two minutes for your rebuttal." He pointed to Anne, who sat at a desk with an official-looking clock. "Anne will call time, so don't push this. We want this debate to look real. We have to keep up the drama."

"Drama queen," Ronnie coughed into his fist.

"Takes one to know one," Jordan quipped without missing a beat.

"*Touché*," Ronnie said and smiled.

Jordan addressed the debaters again, reminding them to use proper decorum and not use real names. "Alivia and Ronnie have the first go-'round this time since Lisa and Marcus opened last time."

The debaters nodded. It was right at this point that Lisa's nerves went into overdrive. Her knees got wobbly, and her stomach got tight. She felt like David taking on Goliath.

"Breathe," Marcus whispered.

She took a deep breath and then said, "You, too."

"Just did."

Jordan backed up behind the cameras. Alivia stood tall at her podium. Ronnie stood stiffly beside her. He was arguing for the exact opposite of his beliefs. Lisa wasn't so sure about Alivia.

"Debaters ready?" They nodded again. "And, action!"

Alivia spoke first. "Homosexuals choose sin over righteousness."

"Revelation 21:8," Ronnie said. "But as for the cowardly, the faithless, the polluted, the murderers, the fornicators, the sorcerers, the idolaters, and all the liars, their place will be in the lake that burns with fire and sulfur." He put a particularly disdainful tenor on the words 'fornicators.' "Other versions of the Bible we looked at add the words 'sexually immoral' to the list. Its omission from this version of the Bible makes it crystal clear why our opposition asked us to use it."

Lisa ignored Ronnie's last comment and wrote down the Bible verse they'd quoted. Marcus scribbled notes beside it. Their team in the audience was busy finding the verse and reading the paragraphs around it to see if there was anything they could use.

"God's vengeance is great to those that try to tear apart the fabric of society." Alivia rambled on for a while, sounding like a real preacher. It was kind of scary. "Turn away from your evil ways, sinners. You can be healed of your sins if you turn away from the devil's temptations. Turn away so that you can be normal. You gotta turn, or you'll burn," she added smugly.

Marlee was gesturing wildly in the crowd at Lisa and Marcus. She must have had an idea. She frantically wrote something down on paper and then whispered something in Susie's ear. Susie then whipped out her phone and started tapping buttons.

"In Jesus' name," Ronnie said, putting it on thick, "amen!"

"Time," Anne called.

Thank God. That had been the longest two minutes in the history of two minutes.

"Debaters," Jordan said, "you have ten minutes to plan and then two minutes to rebut."

"You said, 'butt,'" Ronnie joked.

Lisa barely heard Jordan and Ronnie's banter because she and Marcus were scrambling to put their thoughts together. Debating was way tougher than she imagined, especially because she thought Alivia and Ronnie were going to open with the story of Sodom in Genesis. If not that, then at least they'd open with Leviticus. But they didn't. In a surprise move, they'd gone with the New Testament.

"Ronnie tricked us," Lisa said. "He made us think they were going a different direction." She vowed not to get fooled again. It was on.

Julie cleared her throat. "I'm not supposed to pass this along, but I have to. Apparently, Alivia found out that he shared their strategy with us and then changed it up. Jordan told me."

Lisa took a deep breath. What the heck was Alivia up to?

Marlee was still in her seat, frantically writing. It looked like Susie was dictating something to her from her phone. They must be doing some fast research.

"Okay, expert," Marcus said, "what's Revelation all about?"

Lisa drew a blank. Oh, God. Everything depended on her at this moment. She tried to block out the noisy room, but it was becoming harder and harder as her nerves ratcheted up.

"Bases loaded," Sam called from the crowd. "Hit a long fly ball, and you win! Easy. Come on, Lisa, you've got this."

Lisa smiled. In her own way, Sam was trying to tell her to calm the hell down. She took a deep breath and tried to ignore the imaginary ticking of the clock.

"Revelation is the very last book in the Bible. It was John's Revelation. He was in prison or something when he wrote it." She tapped the podium with her fingers. "What else? What else? Oh, he was giving Christians a pep talk. He was telling them to watch for the return of Jesus. And, yeah, duh, he warned about the final judgment that nonbelievers and sinners would endure. Ronnie read that long list of people who wouldn't make it to the kingdom of heaven."

"Ronnie added in the words 'sexually immoral,'" Marcus said. "He's obviously implying that gay people are sexually immoral."

"Yes," Lisa said. "But what exactly is sexual immorality? Rape, incest, and adultery, for sure. Bestiality certainly. But sexual relations between consenting adults? What's the problem if no one gets hurt? Oh, God, what if they bring up S & M or something?"

"Listen, I don't know from experience," Marcus said in a low voice, "but I'm pretty sure whips and chains cross over all lines— straight, gay, bi, whatever. So that's not a valid argument from their side. It's gays having sex. That's their issue." Marcus's blush swept from underneath his shirt collar all the way to the roots of his ultra-blond hair.

Lisa knew she was blushing, too, but she didn't have time to worry about it. She had an idea. "Sam, notebook." She waved for Sam to bring it to her quickly.

Sam scurried over with the spiral Lisa had used to take research notes for the debate. She thumbed through page after page, well aware that the clock was ticking down. She took a deep breath as she skimmed each page until she found it. "Here it is. Sex is basic biology, right? Animals have sex all the time, and there's no moral stigma attached to it. It's just biology. It's nature."

"But do animals have gay sex?" Marcus sounded doubtful.

"Yes," Lisa and Sam said together. Lisa continued, "Marlee researched it this summer when Susie's mother called Susie unnatural. Animals have un-procreative same-sex sex all the time. It's perfectly natural. Dolphins, monkeys, giraffes, even worms."

"Worms?"

"Worms."

"Okay, I like it. We can go with that." Marcus made some fresh notes on blank index cards.

Just then, Marlee came running up to the front, followed by Susie and one of the girls from Southbridge. "Here." She handed Lisa a piece of paper with mathematical graphs and computations on it. "Alivia used the word 'normal.' Susie looked it up on her phone, and normal is defined as 'conforming to a standard,' or 'usual,' 'typical,' 'average.'" Lisa blinked at Marlee. "C'mon, don't you see?" The excitement in Marlee's voice was growing. "These are all words used in statistics. Here's the normal curve." She pointed to the graph at the top of the paper. "Most people call it a bell curve."

"Yeah, I've heard of that," Lisa said. "Go on."

"Let's say you get the heights of a whole bunch of people. The average height for women is five feet four. That would be right here in the middle of the curve representing the high peak. Some people are a little taller than that, and others are shorter. This is where the curve dips a little lower on each side. Lisa would probably be way out on the far end of the curve because she's so tall."

"Marlee, how does this help?"

"I'm getting to that. See this far end of the curve? In statistics, we typically use a five percent rule to show that something is

significantly different than the mean. Out here in this little bit of the curve, far away from the mean, would be your outliers or people that are way different than average. Lisa, you might be out here regarding height, and we'd call you an outlier. Since gay people make up ten percent of the world—"

"According to Kinsey studies," Lisa said in response to Marcus's confused look.

"Since we make up ten percent," Marlee continued, "that's a lot closer to the mean than the alpha-level of five percent way out here. See? Statistically, the top five percent are so far from the middle that we can legitimately call them different, but the ten percent isn't. We're *not* different than the norm. Do you see?"

Lisa put a finger up as she digested Marlee's hurried statistics lesson. "Not enough to explain it."

"But I do," Marcus said. "Amazingly, I do. We use a lot of statistics in our debates."

"Awesome." Lisa high-fived Marcus and then Marlee. "Thanks, Marlee." Lisa turned back to Marcus and said, "We've got this. I'll do all the sexually immoral stuff—"

Her friends burst out laughing.

"Shut up, you guys. I didn't mean it that way." Lisa rolled her eyes but then laughed in spite of herself when she replayed the words in her mind. "I'll do the Revelation part, and you do the math."

"Deal."

"Time," Anne called from her spot behind the clock.

"Phew," Lisa said. "We figured that one out just in time."

"Podiums, please," Jordan called.

Lisa and Marcus high-fived each other as they officially stepped behind their podium. She reviewed Marcus's notes and scribbled a few of her own. Out of the corner of her eye, she saw Jordan stand up behind the cameras. This was it.

She took a deep breath and rehearsed her opening line quietly.

"Debaters ready?" Everyone nodded.

"And action!"

Lisa stood tall. "In Revelation 21:8, we are presented with the term 'sexually immoral,' but what exactly did the disciple John mean when he wrote that?" She looked down at the index cards carefully placed on the podium and found the words she needed. "Rape—"

"Cut!" Jordan called out. He beckoned to some people who were hovering just outside the room. "Come in. Come in," he said to them. To Lisa, he said, "I'm afraid you'll have to start over."

Lisa nodded. That was fine. She welcomed the few extra seconds to look over her notes. She looked up when she heard Sam gasp. Walking through the door were Freddie and his girlfriend Rebekah.

"Is this the youth alliance for homosexuals?" Freddie asked.

Lisa gripped the edges of the podium. This whole thing just got really real.

Chapter Eighteen

"I hereby command you: Be strong and courageous; Do not be frightened or dismayed, for the LORD your God is with you wherever you go." — Joshua 1:9

The fact that Freddie and Rebekah crashed the debate made Lisa more nervous than she already was. How could she and Marcus make their arguments in front of people who really hated them? Lisa figured that the members of the youth alliance outnumbered Freddie and Rebekah, so if the two pulled any shenanigans, they would be shut down and escorted off the premises easily. Unless they had guns or something. Then that would be a completely different story. Lisa tried not to let her mind go there.

Despite their ratcheted-up nerves, Lisa and Marcus's rebuttal arguments went well. Even Marlee's normal graph thing was well-received. By some miracle, Freddie and Rebekah were well-behaved. There was no mudslinging, Bible-quoting, or angry looks. In fact, they both seemed pretty calm, which was almost scarier. Why were they there? How did they find out about the youth alliance meeting?

Although it was late, the lobby was bustling with college students and teachers coming and going. They moved to a far corner of the lobby and stood in uncomfortable silence, not knowing why Freddie asked to talk to them after the meeting.

"I finally learned your name, Lisa," Freddie said. "These guys wouldn't tell me." He gestured at Sam and Susie.

"Why do you want to know my name?" Lisa took a step closer and fumbled for Sam's hand. She needed to feel comforted. Marcus and Julie flanked Lisa as well. It was nice to know her friends were there for her. "And why are you here? Are you stalking us? Stalking me?"

"No, no." Freddie's face turned red. "Nothing like that. I just wanted to thank you again for, uh…"

"For preserving his dignity," Rebekah said. "Everyone knows he had a seizure at the dance, but no one knew…" Rebekah had a loss for words.

"Do you have the thing?" Freddie asked Rebekah.

"Yeah." She pulled Lisa's silk wrap out of her purse and handed it to Lisa. "Thank you for its use."

Now Lisa understood. They wanted to say thank you for keeping the secret of his incontinence. No one, no matter who you were, would ever be able to live down wetting your pants in school, even if it was during a life-threatening seizure.

"It's been dry-cleaned and pressed," Freddie said. "I wanted to make sure it wasn't ruined."

"Thanks," Lisa said, "but how did you know we'd be here tonight?"

"That took a little detective work, but my social studies teacher showed your YouTube video in class on Monday, you know, the one about respect? It was awesome, by the way. I saw you in the video, and when it said the Rainbow Youth Alliance of Clarksonville created it, I looked up when your next meeting was, and *voilà,* I found you."

"That's kind of scary how easily you did that," Sam said. "Returning her wrap—are you sure that's the only reason you came here?"

Freddie crossed his heart and put his right hand in the air. "Promise. Although…"

"Although, what?" Sam exchanged a glance with Lisa.

"I wanted to ask why you four were at my church on Sunday. I thought maybe you were going to protest the service or something. But you didn't, so I'm really confused."

Lisa answered, "It's hard to be a gay person and find a church that accepts you, to help you connect with God. My own church, the one I was baptized in and have gone to since I was born, told me I was a sinner. I've been going to different churches lately to find one that might be a better fit. We loved your church."

Sam, Marlee, and Susie agreed and chimed in that they liked the music and the energy.

"But then we read in one of the brochures that your church does not condone same-sex relationships." Lisa frowned.

"My church tends to take the Bible literally," Freddie said quietly. "Homosexuals are not viewed in a good light there."

"Dude," Julie said, "you've gotta tone down the word 'homosexual.' It makes it sound so clinical. Just like when people call me 'negro.' It's archaic and more than a little insulting."

"It is?" Freddie's eyes grew wide as he exchanged a glance with Rebekah. "What do your people like to be called?"

"Human," Marcus answered first, even though he was as straight as they come.

185

"Exactly," Lisa said. "Don't separate us by our differences. Don't make the fact that I'm going out with Sam into some big thing. You don't have to get angry. We're not hurting you. Should I point at you two and say, 'Look at that heterosexual couple?'"

"Breeders," Susie added, pointing an accusing finger at them. The tone in her voice let everyone know she was kidding and was just furthering the point.

"I see what you're saying," Rebekah said. "The word 'homosexual' makes it sound like a label. Like a one size fits all thing."

"And it isn't," Freddie added. "Our church teaches that homo— excuse me, gay people were influenced by the devil and turned away from God."

"A lot of churches teach that," Lisa said. "So that's why it's so hard for me to find a way to reach God without persecution. And you know what? God made me, and God made you. He made all of us. Hey, Sam, can you look up a Psalm for me? It's one of the last ones, in the 130s or 140s, I think. Look up the one about God forming us."

"Got it." Sam opened Lisa's Bible she was carrying.

"God made us in his own image," Lisa continued. "So, who are we to judge His work? Who are we to judge God? That sounds a little blasphemous, don't you think?"

"Here it is." Sam handed the Bible to Lisa, her finger pointing to a particular passage.

"Thanks, baby," Lisa felt weird using the term of endearment for Sam in front of Freddie and Rebekah, but she wanted them to know that they were a couple just like them and shouldn't be treated any differently. "Let me read it out loud, okay?"

Everyone nodded, and Lisa cleared her throat. "Psalm 139, verses thirteen through sixteen. 'For it was you who formed my inward parts; you knit me together in my mother's womb. I praise you, for I am fearfully and wonderfully made. Wonderful are your works; that I know very well. My frame was not hidden from you, when I was being made in secret, intricately woven in the depths of the earth. Your eyes beheld my unformed substance. In your book were written all the days that were formed for me, when none of them as yet existed.'"

"I like the line 'Wonderful are your works,'" Freddie said.

"Me, too," Sam chimed in. "And I like the part about all the days being written for you. That kind of means that God knows what our lives would hold for us. He knows the challenges we have now and in the future. He knew we'd struggle with being different than the accepted norm."

"To make us strong, maybe?" Susie offered.

"Maybe," Lisa said.

"That is definitely something to think about," Freddie said. "Rebekah and I came here tonight to thank you again and give you your wrap back, but you've given us a lot more to think about in return."

"Eh?" Lisa said.

"I've always blindly accepted my church's teaching about homo— " He groaned. "Sorry. I'm going to have to break myself of that habit. What I'm trying to say is that I need to figure out some things for myself and not accept everything that's told to me."

Rebekah reached for his hand. "Me, too."

"And I know the perfect way to do that," Freddie said, excitement growing in his voice.

"How?" Lisa asked him.

"By joining your side of the debate."

The air got sucked out of the lobby as everyone gasped.

"For real?" Marcus said.

"Yeah, why not? I want to understand all of this. I've met you guys, and you're all really cool and nice and not demons at all."

They all laughed, but Lisa's laugh was guarded. She knew that some people truly did think gay people were possessed by the devil.

After lingering in the frigid parking lot of the college, discussing their blown minds over Freddie's announcement, it was time to go home. Lisa pulled Sam into a tight embrace and seared her with a kiss to last until Friday, when they'd be able to see each other again.

In the van on the way home, Marlee, Julie, and Marcus talked a thousand miles an hour about Freddie and Rebekah, the debate, and Alivia and Ronnie's arguments. Lisa threw in the appropriate responses at the right times, but she was happy to be going home. She was wiped out and had a mountain of homework ahead of her.

Lisa said her goodbyes to her friends and hurried to the front door. Her mother greeted her with a cup of hot chocolate.

"Thanks, Mom." Lisa hung her coat on the hook with her name on it and took the hot mug. "Winter's here to stay, eh?"

"Sure feels like it. Oh, good. You found your wrap." Lisa's mother pointed to the silk wrap that Lisa had placed on the bench by the front door.

"Yeah, Sam brought it to me." It was a little white lie, but she didn't want to tell her mother about Freddie and Rebekah. She hadn't told them how Freddie and his friends had harassed them at the dance. She didn't want her parents to worry.

"You'd better put that away before it gets ruined."

"Good idea."

"Come back out and sit at the table with me when you're done." Lisa's mother went over and sat at the kitchen table where a fresh plate of family-made sugar cookies lay on a Santa Claus plate.

"What's the occasion, Mom?" Lisa set her hot chocolate on the table and grabbed a cookie. Debating the Bible sure made her hungry, but everything made her hungry these days. Crap, was she in another growth spurt?

"Papa's getting the kids ready for bed, and I want to touch base with my daughter to find out how the debate's going."

"Okay, I'll be right out." Lisa hurried to her room, threw the silk wrap in a drawer, and kissed Bridget goodnight. "Where's Papa? I thought he'd be helping you with your prayers."

"He's making sure Lawrence Jr. brushes his teeth," Bridget said. "Did you have fun at your bate?"

"My bate?" Lisa's mind whirled. "Ah, yes, I had fun at my debate. I saw Sam and Susie and Marlee and Julie—"

"I like Julie. She's brown."

Lisa laughed. She had to have Julie over more often, so her brown skin wasn't the only thing Bridget remembered. Hmm, Lisa thought, just like being gay was the only thing Freddie had known about her and her friends.

Lisa gave Bridget another hug and headed out to the kitchen table. Her mother wanted details, but Lisa didn't quite know where to start. "The debate's going fine. Marcus is really good at teaching me about delivery and stuff. Marlee even gave us some math to use." Lisa's mother's eyebrows shot to the ceiling. "Mom, if I were close to understanding it, I'd tell you. I let Marcus explain that part."

"They quoted Leviticus, didn't they?" Her mother sat back and

189

took a sip of her coffee.

"No, and that was surprising. Ronnie kept texting me about Leviticus this and Leviticus that, but then they didn't use it, the stinkers. I think they're holding it back so they can slam us with it later." Lisa smiled when she heard Bridget in their room saying her prayers and her father trying to get her to talk in her "inside voice" because God could hear her no matter what, even if she whispered.

"How about Sodom and Gomorrah? Did they spring that one?" her mother asked.

"Not even that one. They used something from Revelation about sexual immorals not getting into heaven."

"Wow," Lisa's mother said, "this debate is truly getting serious."

Lisa nodded and took a slow sip of her hot chocolate. She filled her mother in on the details of the debate, all except the parts about Freddie and Rebekah.

"Eventually, you know they'll use the story of Sodom in Genesis and that passage in Leviticus," her mother said. "Somewhere in Matthew, Jesus tells the disciples to go into the world to heal the sick and spread the good news. He told them that any town that did not welcome them would suffer a worse fate than that of Sodom and Gomorrah."

"Just because they didn't welcome the disciples of Jesus? Because they weren't friendly?"

"Yes, because they were not hospitable. They wouldn't welcome strangers into their homes and help them out by providing food, water, and a place to sleep."

Lisa put her cup down. Forget the hot chocolate; she had to digest what her mother was saying. "So was that the issue God had with Sodom and Gomorrah? They were unfriendly and downright rude to strangers and travelers?"

Her mother nodded. "That was definitely part of it. I think you should try to find other Bible verses that mention Sodom. Look in Ezekiel in the Old Testament. The people of Sodom were unfriendly, unkind, unwelcoming, rude people, and God didn't like that. You can play up that angle."

Lisa sat back and sighed. "It's all about playing angles, isn't it? The interpretation? But I want to know what those passages really mean."

"I don't think we'll ever truly know. That's why there are so many different churches and different beliefs."

"What about non-beliefs? Atheists? I think Marlee might be one."

"That kind of makes me sad for Marlee, but she's a good and kind person. God knows where her heart is."

"I guess you're right, so how do you know so much about that Matthew passage?"

"When I was pregnant with you, my parents thought it would be a good idea if I joined a Bible study group. I was the only high school student. We studied the New Testament, the book of Matthew."

"Maybe that's why Matthew's my favorite."

"If you were a boy, I was going to name you Matthew."

"Really? Why did you name me Lisa?"

"I had one friend in high school who stuck by me. Everybody else flew to the hills. It wasn't as if they could catch pregnancy. My friend's name was Lisa, so I named you for her."

"Mom, that's sweet. How come I've never met her?"

"Her father got a transfer right after you were born, and they moved overseas. Denmark, I think. We lost touch." Her mother got a far-off look in her eye, so Lisa didn't intrude for a few moments.

"Mom, thanks for letting me join the youth alliance and do this debate."

"You're going to help a lot of people."

"I hope so." Lisa jumped up and hugged her mother.

"You're a kind and loving young woman, Lisa. That's all that matters in God's eyes."

Chapter Nineteen

"For God did not give us a spirit of cowardice, but rather a spirit of power and of love and of self-discipline." — 2 Timothy 1:7

Lisa sat in her usual seat by the windows in her Anatomy class. She'd stayed up a little later than usual to review her notes, hoping the extra studying would pay off on the endocrine system quiz. This was the one class in which she wanted to excel. In fact, she'd kind of gotten a reputation in the class as a brainiac. Okay, that had never happened before, but she'd take it. For one period a day, she got to feel the way Marlee probably felt every day of her life.

Lisa had her head down, scouring her notes on the pituitary, adrenal, and thyroid glands for the thousandth time. She barely noticed the other kids in the room or Ms. Lye until someone in the back muttered, "Oh, shit."

Lisa looked up and muttered the same sentiment because Missy Matthews was standing in the front of the room. She handed Ms. Lye an official-looking document.

"So, Miss Matthews, you're transferring from third-period Anatomy to second period?"

Missy nodded.

Ms. Lye scribbled something on the paper and said, "You'll have to take the only open seat we have." She pointed to the seat next to Lisa.

Lisa groaned silently to herself, but Missy groaned out loud. "Really?" The whine in her voice was clear to all with ears. "I have to sit there?"

"Unless you want to sit on the floor, I suggest you get moving."

With the hugest of sighs, Missy picked up her backpack and muttered, "I change my schedule three times, and I still can't get away from her."

Lisa ignored her. If Missy wanted to be an ignorant jerk, she could do that on her own. Without waiting for Missy to be seated, Ms. Lye said, "Put your notes away and take out a pen. Following this twenty-minute quiz, you'll start reading chapter ten in your textbooks. We finally get to learn about blood."

"Yay," one of the nerdy kids in the front row cheered, earning him a smile from Ms. Lye.

Ms. Lye was tough but fair. She was somewhere in her mid-thirties. Not a new teacher, but not one of those hanging-on-until-retirement teachers either. She was reasonably easygoing like Coach Spears, but if you crossed her or did something stupid like copy homework or cheat on a test, then she was all business. She always told the class she expected her students to be sincere and honest. She said she had more respect for a student who honestly earned an F over a student who cheated to get an A. That made sense.

Lisa reached down and slid her notebook gently past her Bible. Not that she usually brought a Bible to school but being part of the youth alliance debate was keeping her on her toes. You never knew when a Bible verse would come to her, and she'd have to look it up. She and her friends had spent a lot of time over the past couple of weeks thumbing through their Bibles at the lunch table, looking for scripture to use. She'd never thought in a million years she'd be reading the Bible with her friends at school, but life had a way of being weird. Especially lately.

Lisa stared out the window onto the softball field and felt a deep yearning. Having to wait all winter to play was pure torture. Speaking of torture, she should start doing squats now. That way, she'd be in better shape when inside practices started with Marlee in February.

"Lisa," the kid in front of her hissed.

Lisa looked up to see a stack of quizzes come crashing down onto her desk. Geez, she must have been lost in thought. She grabbed one for herself and handed the rest to Caroline, the girl who sat behind her. She took a deep breath to shake the cobwebs out. Maybe she shouldn't have stayed up so late studying.

Lisa was sailing through the quiz and was on the final question, an essay about the pancreas, when her pen slipped out of her hand and tumbled to the floor. Caroline stifled a giggle, and Lisa tried hard not to laugh at her own clumsiness. She reached down to pick up her pen, but it had rolled underneath the footrest of the kid in front of her. She had to get out of her seat to retrieve it. Luckily, she hadn't lost her train of thought and went right back to her description of digestive enzymes.

"Two more minutes," Ms. Lye called from her desk in the front of the classroom.

A collective, anxious groan came from just about everyone, Lisa included. Except for Missy. That was weird. Maybe Missy was a super-fast writer and had already finished. Whatever. Lisa returned and finished her last few sentences about how insulin and glucagon worked to maintain a steady glucose level in the blood.

Lisa finished her last sentence just as Ms. Lye called time.

"Pens down, people," Ms. Lye said, hands on her hips. "Please make sure your names are on your quizzes and then pass them up your row to the front."

"How do you think you did, Lisa?" Caroline asked from behind her.

"I thought it was pretty easy. How about you?" They chatted quietly for a few minutes until Ms. Lye directed them to open their books and silently read and take notes on their next section.

As the day plodded along, Lisa got more and more tired. Whose idea was it to have PE at the end of the day? Oh, yeah. It was hers. She'd rather take a nap than play basketball.

For three days in a row, Lisa had gotten changed for her PE class without incident. Missy's ladies-in-waiting were still in the class, but they hadn't caused a fuss or made any problems. Thank God.

Coach Spears set them up into four ability groups for basketball, one group at each basket, where they played five-on-five half-court games. Lisa was in the highest ability group with Julie and some of the other athletes in the school. In fact, a couple of the girls dinged her gaydar, but they weren't that friendly to her. Jessica Myers, in particular, hadn't passed her the ball once, even though Lisa was taller than everyone else and could probably score easily.

Everybody in the creation of the world seemed to know that she was gay. The Missys of the world were both repulsed and afraid of her, and the closeted gay girls didn't want to be near her. Guilt by association, maybe? If you were friends with Lisa, then you must be gay, too. Life sucked sometimes. Thank God Julie was still her friend. And the girls on the softball team? They were still cool.

Lisa was hard at work trying to get somebody, anybody, to pass her the ball when Coach Spears came up to their group. "Lisa, I need you here."

"What's up, Coach?" Lisa left the game, and wouldn't you know it? The girl who subbed in for her was passed the ball on the very next play. Whatever. Jerks.

"Mr. Braun wants to see you." Coach Spears handed her a hall pass.

"Right now?"

"Apparently."

"Should I get changed?" Lisa looked down at her gym attire.

"Nope. The note said for you to go to his office immediately. Is everything all right?"

"I don't know, Coach. I'll let you know."

Lisa shrugged at Julie's questioning expression and hurried out of the gym and down the hall to the assistant principal's office.

"Lisa Brown?" Mrs. Olsen asked. She was Mr. Braun's administrative assistant.

"Yes." Lisa's nerves were ramping up. Was her family okay? Did someone get hurt? Was there a car accident? She took a breath, trying to stay calm, but it didn't work.

"Go right in." Mrs. Olsen gestured to Mr. Braun's door.

Lisa knocked lightly on the door and then opened it. She was shocked to see Missy Matthews stand up to leave. Mr. Braun acknowledged Lisa and gestured for her to come in. Lisa looked from him to Missy and was as confused as ever. She couldn't read his expression, but Missy looked smug. This was not good, but at least it meant that her family was okay. And that, at least, was good.

"Thank you, Missy," Mr. Braun said. "You can go back to your class. Get a hall pass from Mrs. Olsen."

"Thank you, sir," Missy said demurely. Wow, she could really put it on, couldn't she?

Missy left without closing the door, probably so she could hear what Mr. Braun was going to say to Lisa. Thank God he stood up and closed it. He was a middle-aged man in his early fifties with graying hair just starting to thin out. His face seemed to have a permanent unamused scowl, but Lisa hoped that was just his game face and that there was a softer side to him in there somewhere.

"I got a visit from Ms. Lye earlier today," he said.

"Okay." Lisa's mind was racing at a million miles per hour. What was happening?

"She gave a quiz in class."

"Yes."

"I'll cut right to the chase. She found a cheat sheet under your desk."

"My desk?"

"Yes. On the footrest. Do you know anything about this?"

"Absolutely not, Mr. Braun. I don't cheat."

"Ms. Lye said she was quite surprised to find it under your desk after class."

"It wasn't mine," Lisa said. "I didn't cheat. I swear. I studied. I stayed up late to study."

Lisa couldn't read the expression on his face. Principals, especially disciplinary principals like Mr. Braun, had good poker faces, and his was the best.

"I pulled your grades, Lisa. Mostly B's. Some A's. But no A+

anywhere, except Anatomy. Can you explain that?"

"You think I cheated my way to an A+? Is that it?"

"I'm not saying that, but your grades don't support it."

Lisa could not believe what was happening. "I love the subject, Mr. Braun. I want to apply to medical school, so I spend extra time reading the textbook. It's fascinating. Just because I do well, you think I cheat." She felt her face getting warm. *Missy. It had to be.* Before Mr. Braun could say anything, Lisa added, "If the cheat sheet was on the footrest, it was under my seat. *Under* me. I don't mean any disrespect, Mr. Braun, but how could I have seen a cheat sheet if it was underneath me?"

"Lisa," he said with a sigh as if he didn't believe a word she was saying, "I'm going to have to call your parents."

"Why? I haven't done anything. All I've done is work hard. Can I at least talk to Ms. Lye?"

"She's asked me to handle this."

"How do I defend myself? I didn't do anything."

"You can go back to class now."

"Wait. What? What did Missy say? She was the one who was probably cheating. Check out the handwriting. Is it my handwriting? That should be proof enough."

Mr. Braun took a deep breath and folded his arms. "Missy said that during the middle of the quiz, you dropped your pen and took an extra-long time to pick it up. She noticed you looking at a piece of paper under your desk."

"She said what?" *That bitch!* "I'd have to be a contortionist to be able to read a piece of paper under my seat. Obviously, she's covering her own butt. She's accusing me of something she's done so that she won't get in trouble."

He stood without saying a word and opened the door to his office. "You can go back to class. Get a hall pass from Mrs. Olsen."

Lisa put her hands out in a helpless gesture. She had obviously been dismissed. She rose up to her full five-foot-eleven-inch height, held her head high, and calmly said, "I've been falsely accused, Mr. Braun. You have to believe me."

He looked her right in the eye and, without smiling, gestured for her to leave his office.

Lisa groaned in frustration, went to Mrs. Olsen's desk for the hall pass, and then stormed out of the main office door toward her PE class. The tears came before she'd made it halfway. There was no one in the hallway, thank God, but she needed to get herself together before going back to class. She stooped down to get a drink at the water fountain. The water helped cool her rage somewhat, but not enough. It was Missy. It had to be. Missy must have slipped a cheat sheet under the desk while Lisa daydreamed about softball. How low could a person go?

Lisa splashed water on her face and took a couple of deep breaths. She had never been so frustrated in her life. Oh, God. Her parents. Mr. Braun was probably calling them right now. They would be so disappointed.

Disappointed at what? A surge of anger flooded her, and she kicked the nearest locker. The sound was almost as satisfying as the jolt of pain in her toes. Too bad the locker wasn't Missy's head.

Chapter Twenty

*"Be strong and bold; have no fear or
dread of them, because it is the LORD
your God who goes with you; he will
not fail you or forsake you."* —
Deuteronomy 31:6

The day after her visit with the assistant principal, Lisa stopped at Ms. Lye's desk on the way to her seat and tried to tell her that she hadn't cheated. Ms. Lye wouldn't let her finish, saying she had handed the matter over to Mr. Braun. Frustrated, the only thing Lisa could do was sit at her desk and fume. She caught Missy's eye and shot her a silent 'what the hell?' glare. Missy just smiled with her eyes, sat down, and turned away.

Evil. Missy was pure evil.

Later that morning, Lisa's parents came in to speak with Mr. Braun. After dinner, when Lisa's siblings were otherwise occupied, her parents told her that the assistant principal was a tough cookie to crack, but he had at least agreed to let both Lisa and Missy take the quiz again. This time under direct supervision.

That Friday afternoon, Lisa sat alone in the detention room during her lunch period. She was waiting for Mrs. Olsen to arrive to administer the quiz. Since Lisa didn't want Mrs. Olsen to think she was using hidden cheat sheets, she left her backpack with Julie, who would bring it to their common U.S. History and Government class. While waiting, Lisa systematically reviewed the endocrine system in her mind.

Mrs. Olsen finally came into the room and went over the ground rules. Exactly twenty minutes and no longer. Pen down meant pen down. Lisa nodded and was handed the quiz that would vindicate her to the world. Well, at least to Ms. Lye and Mr. Braun. Hopefully. She twisted her mood ring for good luck.

The quiz was different from the first, but that didn't matter. She knew the material backward and forward. This time the essay was about the adrenal gland and its form and function. Lisa knew all about the adrenal gland since adrenaline had been racing through her body ever since she'd been called to the assistant principal's office.

Lisa put her pen down a full two minutes before Mrs. Olsen called time. Mrs. Olsen put Lisa's quiz in a folder just as the bell rang to end lunch.

"Thank you, Lisa," Mrs. Olsen said and then smiled.

"Thank you," Lisa answered, bewildered by the smile because Mrs. Olsen was known to be as hard-nosed as Mr. Braun.

At the end of the school day on Friday, there was still no official word about whether Lisa was vindicated or if the cheating accusation would stand. Lisa sat quietly in the front seat of the afternoon school bus. She was in a mood completely opposite the rest of the kids. Their happy-for-the-weekend voices did not penetrate her growing melancholy. Being accused of cheating could have serious repercussions. She could get suspended. She could be thrown off the softball team. She could have the promise of a college scholarship revoked. All because of an unproven and untrue accusation.

"Lisa?"

"Hmm?" She looked up to see kindly old Mr. Broward, the man who had driven her to and from school since she was six, gesturing toward the bus door.

"This is your stop, dear."

The rest of the kids who got off at her stop were already heading home. She stood up quickly. She was on the verge of tears and didn't want him to see. "Thanks, Mr. Broward. Have a good weekend."

"You, too, dear."

Despite the cold, Lisa shuffled her way home. She wanted to get her tears under control before seeing her mother and Bridget. She didn't want to upset them. She opened the front door to the house and hung up her coat with a sigh.

"Lisa!" Bridget said and ran toward her. Usually, Lisa would scoop her little sister up and swing her around a couple of times, but she didn't have the energy. She let Bridget slam into her legs.

"How was your day, Bridget?"

"Good. Me and Mama made sketti sauce."

"You did?" Lisa's mood perked up. Yeah, the house did smell yummy. Her mother's homemade marinara sauce with meatballs was one of Lisa's favorite meals. And she'd see Sam later, too, so the day was improving exponentially. Of course, when you're at rock bottom, the only place to go was up.

"How did it go, honey?" Her mother called from the kitchen.

"I think I aced the quiz, Mom." Lisa went into the kitchen and gave her mother a quick hug. "Meatballs, too?"

Her mother nodded. "Meatballs, too."

"What's the occasion?"

"Nothing, really. I just thought we could all use a little cheering up."

"You do believe me, Mom, don't you?"

Her mother put down the spatula she was holding and turned around to face Lisa. "If you tell me you didn't cheat, then I believe you one hundred percent."

"Thank you, Mom." Lisa hugged her mother again, this time a little longer.

When Lisa pulled back, her mother said, "Don't forget that I need you to watch the kids after school every day next week."

"Oh, yeah. Marion's going on vacation, right?"

"To sunny Florida. I'm glad she trusts me with her customers."

"Do you think you'll ever want to cut hair full time? You know, when the kids are bigger?"

"Maybe. Probably. We have a lot of college to pay for."

Lisa yawned. "Mom, I'm going to my room. I suddenly feel really tired."

"Go for it. I'll keep Bridget occupied. Is Sam coming for dinner tonight?"

"No. Maybe tomorrow. Marlee's picking me up, and we're heading to East Valley tonight. If that's okay."

"Sure, sure. I'll let you know if I hear anything from the school."

One more hug later, and Lisa was in her room, shoes off, under the covers, eyes closing. She needed a break from life; a nap was just the ticket.

"Lisa," her mother called gently.

"Hmm?" Lisa sat up and wiped the sleepy dirt from her eyes. Her room was pitch dark. "How long did I sleep?"

"Well," Lisa's mother said, "Marlee's here to pick you up."

"What?" Lisa sat up and blinked her eyes open. She was still tired. "How in the world did you keep the kids quiet?"

Her mother laughed. "We played the quiet game."

"That worked?"

Her mother nodded. "I think they know you've been going through something and wanted to help you."

"That's sweet. Did you invite Marlee in?"

"She's on the couch as we speak."

"Geez. Tell her I'll be right out."

Her mother closed the door, and Lisa flew out of bed, finding more comfortable clothes. She threw on a sweater that Sam had bought for her in New York, and after a quick trip to the bathroom, she was ready to have a carefree Friday night.

"Sorry, Marlee," Lisa said as she headed to the coat hooks. "I must have fallen asleep." Lisa looked at her still-empty dinner plate on the kitchen table. "Mom, I'm sorry. You went to all that trouble, and I slept through dinner."

"More meatballs for me," Lisa's father joked.

"Did you save me some?" Lisa's eyes were wide. This was serious business. Stealing a girl's meatballs was unforgivable.

"Yes, honey," her mother reassured her. "I made sure the vultures didn't devour everything."

"She is so mean," Lisa's father teased. "A man could starve around here."

"Oh, sure," her mother said, folding her arms across her chest.

"C'mon, Marlee. We need to get out of here before this escalates," Lisa said. She laughed to let Marlee know she was teasing.

As they headed out the door, Lisa stopped and said, "Hey Lynnie, how are your violin lessons coming?" Sam had set Lynnie up with a website that gave free beginner violin lessons. Lynnie used her new Kindle Fire to watch the lessons.

"Good, I think," Lynnie said, her face beaming. "Tell Sam I can make real musical notes with the bow."

"That's awesome. I'll tell her, okay?"

"Okay. Tell her I said, 'hi.'"

"Absolutely." Lisa turned and was just about to turn the doorknob when her brother ran over to her.

"Lisa?" he asked quietly.

"Yes, Lawrence Jr.?" She mouthed the word 'sorry' to Marlee. Marlee shook her head to say it was fine.

"If you marry Sam, will she be your husband?"

Lisa burst out laughing but quickly squelched it. It was obvious that he was trying his six-year-old best to understand. "Sorry, buddy, I didn't mean to laugh. But, no, Sam will be my wife."

"That sounds weird."

"I know, but Papa's always saying how weird we are, right?"

"You got that right," Marlee mumbled.

"Hey," Lisa laughed and playfully smacked Marlee in the stomach, "stop helping."

"So," Lawrence Jr. continued, "if I get married, then I'll have a wife?"

"If you marry a girl, then yes. If you marry a boy, then you'll have a husband."

Without saying a word, he turned on his heels and ran to the kitchen. "Mama, what's for dessert?" Lisa shrugged, and then she and Marlee headed out the door.

Thankfully the drive to Sam's house was relatively quick. Susie's car was already there, parked at the farthest end of the long circular driveway.

Sam opened the front door to the mansion for them, swooped Lisa in her arms, and kissed her right there in the foyer.

"Where are your parents?" Lisa whispered.

"Out," Sam said with a mischievous grin. "Daddy's at a political fundraiser in Watertown and won't be back until late. Mother's at an overnight spa treatment in Saratoga and won't be back until Sunday. She had so many spa treatments in Switzerland; I can't imagine why she thinks she needs more."

"So that means we're alone?" Marlee could barely conceal her excitement.

"Yep," Susie answered. "We're hanging out in Sam's suite."

"Oh, man," Marlee gushed. "No parents. This is awesome."

"C'mon, women," Sam said, "let's get this party started."

They headed upstairs to the suite where Sam had set up a cheese and cracker platter along with some fresh fruit.

"Food," Lisa said. "Fan-freakin'-tastic. I didn't eat dinner." Lisa filled a plate and had the first cheesy cracker in her mouth before they'd settled down on the couch in Sam's living room.

"Drinks are in the fridge," Sam opened her mini-fridge to show Lisa the choices.

"Wine? Sam, are you sure?" Lisa knew they shouldn't, but the one time they'd had wine before, it was okay.

"Yeah, Susie and Marlee will only have one glass since they're driving later, but we'll be fine."

Lisa relaxed and let Sam pour her a glass of the white zinfandel she'd snagged from the wine cellar. After a few sips, Lisa felt loose enough to relay the crap Missy had dragged her through that week. Sam was outraged, and Susie was ready to kick some Missy

Matthews's butt.

"Guys, guys, relax," Lisa said from her cuddly spot on the couch next to Sam. "When my teacher grades my quiz and sees how great I did, she'll know I didn't cheat."

"You guys have to understand," Marlee said. "Missy has some serious issues. She thinks she can always run to her daddy when things get hard."

"Too bad her father couldn't do her homework for her, too," Lisa said with a laugh. Sam poured her a second glass of wine.

"Oh, geez, Sam," Lisa said and pinched the end of her nose. "I don't know. My nose is already numb."

"Now I've got you where I want you." Sam laughed lecherously.

"You have me anyway, doofus," Lisa said with a laugh and smacked Sam playfully on the arm.

"Oh, yeah?" Sam retaliated with a few tickles along Lisa's sides. Lisa was especially vulnerable along her torso, especially when she and Sam had their more intimate moments.

"Get a room, you two," Susie called over to them.

Sam waggled her eyebrows. "Hey, you guys, guess what tomorrow is."

"What?" Susie answered for them all.

Sam pulled Lisa close. "Eight months for us."

Lisa inhaled sharply. She had forgotten. "Sam, I've been so busy, I wasn't even thinking about it. Eight months already?" She pulled Sam closer and rubbed her wine-numbed nose against Sam's. She tilted her head and moved in for a kiss. She sometimes felt a little awkward making out with Sam when Susie and Marlee were right there, but true to form, they started doing the same thing on the loveseat.

Sam pulled out of the kiss and looked at Lisa with so much hunger that tendrils of desire twisted their way around Lisa's body. "C'mon," Sam said and stood. She reached her hand out.

Lisa took it.

"Guys," Sam said to Marlee and Susie, who probably couldn't hear them over the steamy state they were in. "You can have the big couch. We're heading into my bedroom."

"*Excelente*," Susie said and went back to kissing Marlee.

"I'll turn your lights low," Sam said. When she didn't get a response, she and Lisa laughed. "I'm locking the suite door, too." Still no response. "And we'll knock before we come back out."

"Get gone already," Susie called to them, making everybody laugh.

Lisa followed Sam into her bedroom.

Sam pulled her into the semi-dark room, the only light coming from the outside security lights seeping around the closed blinds. Sam kissed Lisa's neck, finding all the right spots that made Lisa moan. Lisa's sweater came off, and soft lips made their way over bare skin. After Lisa's silk bra found its way to the floor, Sam's quickly followed. Their mutual desire amped up, and soon all articles of clothing lay in a heap on the floor. Lisa fell into the queen-sized bed pulling Sam on top of her. She pulled the sheet and comforter over both of them.

Sam's kisses didn't quench her thirst but fueled it. Sam's slow caresses were pure torture. Lisa cried out for release, and it wasn't long before Sam obliged. Once sated, Lisa hugged Sam tightly and cried into her shoulder.

"What's the matter, baby?" Sam stroked Lisa's hair.

Lisa couldn't answer right away. She had to catch her breath first.

"You're okay," Sam soothed. "I'm here."

"I forgot our anniversary," Lisa finally said, her voice still shaky with emotion.

"That's okay," Sam said with a laugh. "It isn't until tomorrow, anyway. You would have remembered by then."

"I hope so." Lisa took a deep breath and kissed Sam's collarbone. "Are you coming over tomorrow? Lynnie wants to show you her new violin skills."

"I wouldn't miss it. Can we do homework together? I have a big current events project in AP Enviro I have to work on."

"My parents will love that I'm doing homework on a Saturday. But why are we talking about my parents?"

"Good question." Sam snuggled closer. "Mmm, you had a good one tonight."

Lisa moaned. "No, it wasn't good. It was amazing."

"I think everyone in East Valley heard it, too," Sam said.

"Oh. My. God." Lisa smacked Sam on the shoulder. "Well, it's all your fault. You're too good. You know just how to…"

"I do, don't I?"

"Modest, too."

Lisa reached around Sam and flipped her over in the bed. After untangling the sheets wrapped around their jumbled legs, Lisa began a slow exploration of Sam's body until Sam demanded a more concentrated area of exploration. Afterward, they held each other tight, dozing off a little, until Sam said, "Baby, you have to go. I don't want you to miss your curfew."

"Mmm." Lisa didn't open her eyes. She snuggled against Sam more tightly. "I don't want to get up. I want to live with you and never have to leave."

Sam answered by kissing Lisa's eyelids, nose, forehead, cheeks, earlobes, chin, and neck until Lisa finally opened her eyes.

"One day we will," Sam said and sat up. "I promise."

Chapter Twenty-One

"For if you forgive others their trespasses, your heavenly Father will also forgive you; but if you do not forgive others, neither will your Father forgive your trespasses." — Matthew 6:14-15

Monday morning, second period, Ms. Lye silently returned the retake quiz to Lisa. She smiled and then winked before walking back to her desk to start the class. Lisa's hands shook as she slowly turned the paper over. It was all she could do not to stand up and high-five everyone in the room because written at the top in bold red ink was, "100%." Underneath that was a handwritten note from Ms. Lye which read, "You really know your stuff, Lisa. I never doubted you."

"Yes, yes, yes," Lisa mumbled to herself. She looked over at Missy, who hadn't gotten a quiz back.

Missy snarled at her. "I'm getting suspended because of you," she whispered across the aisle.

"Because of me?" Lisa said. "I didn't do anything to you, and you know it."

"Humph." Missy folded her arms and looked away.

Some people just could not be saved, Lisa thought with a slow shake of her head. She sighed and got out her notebook. Oh, well, it wasn't her concern.

Ms. Lye dimmed the lights and shined her PowerPoint notes on the pull-down screen. Oh, goody, diseases of the blood. As Lisa took notes, an unsettled feeling fell upon her. Although she had dodged the false cheating accusation, something still didn't feel right. Missy was going to continue to make her life miserable for reasons known only to her. What was it she and Sam had read in the Old Testament on Saturday? She knew that reading Sodom and Gomorrah passages on their eight-month anniversary was a weird thing to do, but Sam didn't seem to mind. Especially since they had some nice alone time in Sam's new car later that evening. She wracked her brain, trying to think of the Bible passage that was knocking on her skull.

The lights were low, and Ms. Lye was clear on the other side of the room, so Lisa chanced it. She reached down into her backpack and slowly pulled out her Bible. Keeping it in her lap, she found the yellow post-it notes she'd used to mark the Sodom passages. She opened the Bible slowly, and as luck would have it, she found the passage on the first try. Ezekiel 16:49 read, "This was the guilt of your sister Sodom: she and her daughters had pride, excess of food, and prosperous ease, but did not aid the poor and needy."

Lisa reread the last line. "Did not aid the poor and needy." She glanced over at Missy, who must have sensed it and sent Lisa a withering look. Lisa simply smiled, slid her Bible into her backpack, and refocused on the notes. Her mind made up, she would talk to Ms. Lye after class, and if she went for it, Missy was not going to know what hit her.

~~~

Tuesday evening was finally on them. Lisa tried to keep her nerves under control while Marlee drove them to the college in her van. Lisa, Marcus, Marlee, and Julie had spent every second of their common lunch periods scouring their Bibles for passages they might be able to use. If Lisa thought she'd been getting weird looks and whispers before, sitting in the cafeteria reading Bibles got her even more. Realizing that she didn't care about the whispers in regard to her and her friends reading the Bible made her wonder why it bothered her so much when people whispered about the fact that she was gay. She had always thought it was other people that suffered from homophobia, but maybe she had a form of internalized homophobia, too.

Sam and Susie were waiting for them in the parking lot in Sam's new Mercedes. Sam popped out of her car and gave Lisa a kiss that made Lisa forget all about religious debates.

When they entered the lobby of the Student Union, Lisa said, "Hey, hey, hey, I had my mind wrapped up in this debate tonight, and I completely forgot to tell you guys."

"What's up?" Sam slipped an arm around Lisa's waist.

"Ms. Lye thought it was a great idea. She ran it by Mr. Braun, and it's going to happen."

"No way," Julie said. "Seriously? You're going to tutor Missy Matthews?"

Lisa nodded. "Yup. And if Missy attends three one-hour sessions with me, she'll only have to serve a week of after-school detention instead of getting suspended."

"*Tu eres loca, chica,*" Susie said with a shake of her head.

"We all think you're bonkers, Lisa," Marlee said, "but it might

214

be the only way to reach Missy."

"That's what I'm hoping," Lisa said. "She wants to make my life a living hell? Well, I'm going to beat her to it."

"How? By forcing her to spend time with a known lesbo?" Sam's evil laugh echoed off the concrete floors of the lobby.

"More like forcing her to actually learn the science instead of cheating her way through." Lisa bumped Sam with her hip.

"Sounds like a good lesson," Julie said, "but I'm not sure she's going to be a good student. But you go ahead and keep telling yourself otherwise." Julie rolled her eyes dramatically, conveying everything Lisa was thinking.

"C'mon, we'd better get to the room," Marcus said, reaching for Julie's hand. He led the way to the room they used for the youth alliance meetings.

The room was packed with so many kids it was hard to maneuver. According to Ronnie and Jordan, the *Respect* video had been getting a lot of attention. Jordan said they were coming out of the woodwork, but Ronnie quipped, "No, Jordan, they're coming out of the closet," causing everyone within earshot to laugh.

Freddie and Rebekah were already there looking, one part curious and two parts scared to death.

"Hey, Freddie," Sam said. "Hey, Rebekah. Glad you could make it."

"We're looking forward to it," Freddie said and tugged nervously at the hem of his sweater vest. Most of the other kids were dressed down in jeans and sweatshirts, but Freddie and Rebekah had dressed up. That was nice. They were showing respect.

They chatted for a few minutes, and Lisa outlined the rules of the debate to them. Marlee added that they hoped to create something similar to the *Respect* video.

"Excuse me for disagreeing," Freddie said, "but the way you're making this sound, you're going to have something epic, something much bigger than your *Respect* video. I promise you."

"You think so?" Julie asked.

Both Freddie and Rebekah nodded.

"That would be cool," Marlee said.

Freddie tugged on his sweater again. He was clearly nervous. "I'm not sure how we can help, but we'll do what we can."

"That would be great, you guys," Lisa said. "Your support means a lot. Now, if you'll all excuse me, I have to say 'hi' to somebody."

"Okay, baby," Sam said. "Give me your coat, and I'll put it on the table."

"Thanks." Lisa gave Sam a quick kiss and headed to a group of athletic-looking girls across the room. Jessica Myers, the jerk who wouldn't pass her the ball in PE, stood among them.

"Hey, Jessica," Lisa said and watched Jessica's cheeks turn red. "It's good to see you here." Jessica brushed back a stray lock of light brown hair that had escaped her ponytail. Her black leather jacket, hip-hugger black jeans with a wide belt, and Riot Grrl t-shirt made it perfectly clear to Lisa that Jessica was family in a big way.

"Yeah, we thought we should check it out," Jessica said. The 'we' referred to her and her three friends, girls that Lisa didn't recognize.

"Cool," Lisa said. "There are drinks and snacks at the far table if you're hungry."

"Lisa," Marcus called from their podium, "we should go over our notes one last time."

"My boyfriend needs me," Lisa joked and playfully rolled her

216

eyes to the ceiling. At Jessica's confused expression, Lisa said, "I'm kidding. Sam's my girlfriend." She turned and pointed to Sam, who was talking with Alivia and Karl on the far side of the room. At least this time, Alivia wasn't rubbing up against Sam.

"No shit?" Jessica said. "Rich girl Samantha Rose Payton is your girlfriend? I was wondering what she was doing here. I thought this was one of her family's charities or something."

"No, no, no," one of Jessica's friends said, "don't you remember her picture in the paper? October, I think. She was at a Pride Fest or something and got caught. It must have been a huge scandal for her family." The gleeful tone of the girl's voice set Lisa on edge.

"You know what I heard?" another friend said. This one had blonde braids and looked like she was seventeen going on twelve. "I heard she got caught with a female Russian prostitute."

"Uh, anyway," Lisa interrupted. "I have to go. Nice to see you all here." Without waiting for a reply, Lisa turned and headed toward Marcus.

"What's wrong?" Marcus asked. "You look mad or something."

Lisa blew out a sigh, shook her head, and said, "People can be idiots."

Marcus burst out laughing. "That's why we're here, Lisa. That's why we're here." He waved his hands around to include the podiums, the cameras, and the big crowd of people.

Marcus and Lisa went over their notes and felt good about their strategy. After a kiss for luck from their respective girlfriends, they were ready to take on Alivia and Ronnie. Jordan called for order which took more than a few minutes as chairs were moved and snacks procured. It was as if people were getting ready to watch a movie. He went over the ground rules again and made it perfectly clear to the audience that they were not to react either way to the arguments presented and that he'd clear the room if they did.

"Debaters, are you ready?" Jordan asked from behind the cameras.

"Yep," Lisa said.

"As we'll ever be," Ronnie agreed.

"Ready, Anne?" Jordan asked. At her nod, he said, "The Not-a-Sin side has the first go. Two minutes to present." Jordan turned and said something to the camera operators, who all nodded. "Okay, ready?"

Lisa nodded again.

"And action."

"Our opponents," Lisa nodded toward the opposition, "will most assuredly bring out the story of Sodom and Gomorrah. Two out of many towns that fell out of favor with God and were struck down. But why did the towns fall out of favor?"

"We first find out about God's displeasure with Sodom in Genesis 13:13," Marcus said and then read from his Bible. "Now the people of Sodom were wicked, great sinners against the Lord." He nodded his head slowly. "We see it again in Genesis 18:20-21." He read, "Then the Lord said, 'How great is the outcry against Sodom and Gomorrah and how very grave their sin! I must go down and see whether they have done altogether according to the outcry that has come to me; and if not, I will know.'" Marcus closed the book. "But it still isn't exactly clear what those sins were, is it?"

Lisa picked up the point. "Ezekiel 16:49-50 reads, 'This was the guilt of your sister Sodom: she and her daughters had pride, excess of food, and prosperous ease, but did not aid the poor and needy. They were haughty, and did abominable things before me; therefore,

I removed them when I saw it.' Other than not sharing with the poor and needy, we don't know what other abominable things they did. It's not clear." She looked down at her notes for a moment and continued, "Then, of course, there was that fateful day God sent the angels to Sodom. These are the passages that seem to get everybody's panties in a wad." The kids in the room burst out laughing despite Jordan's best glares. Knowing the time clock was ticking, Lisa read from Genesis 19:4-5. "But before they lay down, the men of the city, the men of Sodom, both young and old, all the people to the last man, surrounded the house; and they called to Lot, 'Where are the men who came to you tonight? Bring them out to us so that we may know them.'" Lisa raised her eyebrows. "And we all know what the phrase 'to know them' means. If you don't know, Google it."

Even Freddie and Rebekah laughed along with everyone else. The crowd stifled itself quickly, though, because Jordan looked ready to blow a gasket.

Lisa cleared her throat. "Let me shorten this story a little. Lot pleaded with the men of the town to back off, they wouldn't, and then in verse nine, they said to Lot, 'This fellow came here as an alien, and he would play the judge! Now we will deal worse with you than with them.'"

Marcus leaned forward to make a point. "Back in history, victorious armies would often humiliate leaders of the losing army. And I don't mean to sound crass, but this often involved rape. Sure, there were beheadings and body parts mounted on sticks to scare off other enemies, but it seems to me that the issue with the men of the town of Sodom is not consensual and loving sex between men. Not even close. It was violent and intended rape." Marcus pounded his fist on the podium. "Rape!"

Lisa jumped at the violence of it. They had not rehearsed that.

"Time," Anne called.

Lisa blew out a sigh and turned to face Marcus. "That was epic."

"Sorry. My cousin was raped, and I just got really mad thinking about that."

"That sucks, Marcus." Lisa put a consoling hand on his arm. "I'm sorry that happened."

"Thanks."

Jordan turned to Alivia and Ronnie and said, "You have ten minutes to prepare your rebuttal."

"Yes, sir." Ronnie saluted his boyfriend. He hurried off with Alivia to the table where Karl and a couple of other kids sat.

Lisa and Marcus joined Sam and friends at their table.

"Great job, you guys," Sam said.

"Really good," Julie added. "I'm so proud of you." Julie tousled Marcus's hair, and his blush returned.

Lisa smiled at them. They were so cute together, and they were so amazingly awesome for helping out with the debate. Lisa was just about to suggest they figure out a Leviticus strategy when someone tapped her on the shoulder.

Jessica stood there without smiling. "Um, hey, listen, we're gonna get going, okay?"

"Come on, Jess," the girl with the blonde braids whined from the doorway. "This is so boring."

"Sorry about that," Jessica said quietly to Lisa. It was obvious that Jessica was embarrassed by her friend's outburst. "I'll see you in school tomorrow, okay?"

Lisa held her lips tight together and simply nodded. She almost felt sorry for Jessica. Almost.

Alivia and Ronnie used their full ten minutes to prepare their statements. Jordan called them back to their podiums, checked on the camera operators, and exchanged a nod with Anne.

Lisa and Marcus were ready to take notes on whatever was thrown at them. Sam and the rest of their friends gave them a thumbs-up even though there was really nothing to give them encouragement about at that moment. They had to wait and see what Ronnie and Alivia had up their sleeves.

"Everyone ready?" Jordan asked. At their collective nods, he said, "And, action."

Ronnie held up his Bible for effect. "It's quite clear what sins the Bible was referring to in the Sodom story. Jude 1:7 in the Old Testament reads thusly, 'Likewise, Sodom and Gomorrah and the surrounding cities, which, in the same manner as they, indulged in sexual immorality and pursued unnatural lust, serve as an example by undergoing a punishment of eternal fire.'" He shook the Bible and said, "They pursued unnatural lusts. Unnatural. Now," he grabbed the edges of the podium and looked straight into one of the cameras, "In the spirit of full disclosure, the words 'unnatural lust' were translated from the Greek words that mean 'went after other flesh.' And sure, sure, our opposition says that same-sex relations are completely natural. Look at the animal kingdom, they said. It's common in nature and a simple matter of biology." He grew quiet for the barest of moments. "We researched their claims. No, seriously, we did. And, you know what? It's true. I know, I know, it's hard to believe, but animals really do have gay sex. Even hedgehogs which is almost cute, but we want to remind you of something." Ronnie stepped back to make room for Alivia.

Alivia said, "The scripture I am about to read is from Genesis

1:26, the very first chapter in the very first book of the Holy Bible."
She opened her Bible and read, "Then God said, 'Let us make
humankind in our image, according to our likeness; and let them
have dominion over the fish of the sea, and over the birds of the air,
and over the cattle, and over all the wild animals of the earth, and
over every creeping thing that creeps upon the earth.'" She closed
the book softly. "It is clear here that God created humankind
separately from the animals. It's also clear that He intended for
humans to rule over them."

Ronnie continued. "This separation is made clearer in Genesis
1:28. 'God blessed them, and God said to them, "Be fruitful and
multiply, and fill the earth and subdue it; and have dominion over
the fish of the sea and the birds of the air and over every living thing
that moves upon the earth."' As you can see, God did not create
humankind to be like animals; therefore, this biology theory put
forth by our opponents is simply not valid."

Alivia stepped back up. "So, you see? Our opposition is grasping
at straws. They're bending the word of the Lord to suit their needs.
They—"

"Time!" Anne called much louder than necessary. She must
have been as annoyed with Alivia as Lisa was.

Jordan called the four debaters into a huddle. "This is amazing.
The energy in here is fantastic. We still have a little time; do you
guys want to keep going?"

Marcus looked at Lisa and shrugged. Lisa said, "It's their turn to
bring up a new argument, right?"

"Yup," Jordan said.

"I guess if they're ready to give, then we're ready to receive."
Lisa looked at Ronnie, purposely not Alivia.

"What do you think, beautiful lady?" Ronnie asked Alivia.

It took all of Lisa's strength not to roll her eyes.

"Let's go for it," Alivia said.

"Yay," Ronnie bounced up and down and clapped his hands like a three-year-old.

"It is done," Jordan said. He turned to the crowd that had miraculously remained still and announced that they would keep going with the debate. Apparently, it was a popular decision because the room filled with cheers.

"Ronnie, Alivia, do you want ten minutes to prepare?"

"Nah," Alivia said smugly. "We're ready."

"Can we have five minutes, Jordan?" Marcus asked. "We weren't expecting this and need to reprioritize our notes."

"That's all you need? Five?"

Marcus nodded, and Lisa agreed. They hurried back to their table and said, "Leviticus," in unison, causing everyone to laugh. They hastily scribbled Bible citations on their note cards and checked to make sure their pink Leviticus-defense post-it notes were in place. Pink had been Marcus's idea.

"Are we ready?" Lisa said to Marcus. The butterflies in her stomach were multiplying.

"Better than ready," he said with confidence.

As they headed back to the podium, Lisa was excited but wondered if it was boring for people in the audience. Maybe not, because everyone was still there except for Jessica and her crew. Religion and the Bible weren't for everyone, but even Marlee, the atheist, seemed interested.

"Places everyone," Jordan called. "Quiet on the set." He waited a few moments for the conversations to die out and asked, "Ready?"

Four heads nodded in unison. "And action."

Alivia practically shouted, "You shall not lie with a male as with a woman; it is an abomination. Leviticus 18:22."

Ronnie said each of his next words slowly and deliberately. "'If a man lies with a male as with a woman, both of them have committed an abomination; they shall be put to death.' Leviticus 20:13."

They stood in silence after that, looking straight ahead. The silence began to grow longer and more uncomfortable with every second.

Jordan stood up and whispered, "Is that it?"

Ronnie nodded.

Lisa and Marcus waived their right to a ten-minute planning period and let loose with everything they'd gathered to refute many of the ancient and outdated laws from Leviticus. They had their pick of the ridiculous, like the one from Leviticus 25:44, which said, "As for the male and female slaves whom you may have, it is from the nations around you that you may acquire male and female slaves," or Leviticus 10:6, "Do not dishevel your hair, and do not tear your vestments, or you will die and wrath will strike all the congregation sent." Lisa and Marcus hammered the opposition with bizarre law after law. Two minutes was not enough time for everything they had, and time was called before they were done.

Chapter Twenty-Two

"Whenever you stand praying, forgive,
if you have anything against anyone; so
that your Father in heaven may also
forgive you your trespasses." — Mark
11:25

Lisa lay her head down on her arms at their usual lunch table. The sounds of the cafeteria were getting more raucous with every passing minute.

"You look miserable, Lisa." Marlee threw her brown paper lunch bag on the table.

"I *am* miserable," Lisa mumbled into her arms. She sat up just as Julie and Marcus were joining them. "Hey, you guys."

Julie laughed and said, "You look like shit, Brown girl."

"Shut up, White girl," Lisa joked.

"We gave 'em hell last night, didn't we, Lisa?" Marcus said as he pulled a sandwich out of his lunch bag.

"Pun intended?" Lisa laughed.

"Honey," Julie said to Marcus, "that was a good one."

It was so cute how he turned red whenever she gave him attention. He was sixteen, but he was like a little boy sometimes.

"You know what, guys?" Lisa said. "Even though time got called on us last night, I don't think it mattered. I'm not sure we had enough substance to our Leviticus arguments."

"What d'ya mean?" Marlee said around a mouthful of cookies. She had gotten over her cookie trauma and was back to devouring chocolate chip cookies on a regular basis.

"Okay," Lisa said, "so we quoted all those other stupid laws from the Old Testament. Like the one in Deuteronomy that said if a man sleeps with a woman that's not his wife, they should both die."

"Harsh," Marlee said, moving on to her chocolate milk.

"And the other ones about not letting animals breed with different kinds of animals or planting your fields with different kinds of seeds."

Julie chimed in, "Or wearing clothes made from different materials. Marlee, I think your shirt is a cotton blend. You're going to hell, woman."

Marlee picked at the sleeve of her shirt. "Bummer."

"And I'm not supposed to cut my hair or shave." Marcus ran his fingers across his chin. He didn't have much, but there was some stubble there. "The Old Testament was all about ridding Israel of evil. But are these things considered evil now?"

"There were so many laws," Lisa continued. "Laws God wanted obeyed to purify the people he was bringing to the Promised Land. Laws that make no sense now."

"A lot of those laws you quoted were about sex," Marlee whispered. "Like the one that said if a man has sex with a woman during her monthlies, they were both thrown out of the town. Okay, really? Isn't that going a little overboard?"

"The laws are outdated," Julie said.

"And that's the point we made last night," Lisa said. "Tried to anyway."

"Do you think we should have done something differently?" Marcus asked.

"No, I'm not questioning our strategy." Lisa sighed and tried to figure out how to phrase her thoughts. "I guess I wanted a big slam dunk, a grand slam, a hat trick, a—"

"You've got a lot of sports' clichés in a row there, Lisa," Marlee said between bites of her sandwich.

"I know."

"Next Tuesday are the final statements," Marcus said. "And it's our turn to start."

Lisa pressed her lips together and smiled. "You know what? I think I'm just tired. And, ugh, I'm tutoring Missy this afternoon. I don't know why I thought tutoring her was such a brilliant idea."

All three of her friends wore the same disgusted expression on their faces, which made Lisa laugh, and she felt better. For a little while.

~~~

Before Lisa even made it inside the house after getting home from school, her mother was out the door. "Thank you, Lisa. I should be home by 7:30." She got into the van parked in the driveway. "The meatloaf is in the oven," she called back before slamming the driver's door.

"Okay. Bye, Mom," Lisa said to the outdoor air, knowing her mother couldn't hear her. "Have fun at work." Lisa headed into the house.

"Lisa," Bridget said and came flying at her big sister.

Lisa quickly flung her backpack to the floor, scooped her little sister up, and twirled her around three times. Bridget's giggles were good for whatever ailed you. At least, that's what her father always said. Lisa agreed.

Lisa put her sister down and hung her coat on her designated hook. They each had hooks with their respective names on them. It had been a Mother's Day gift from all the kids a couple of years ago. Lisa was about to pick up her backpack to stash in her room when she let her eye see the house the way Missy would. She was mortified. The mass of coats and boots was chaotic and messy. Bridget's toys and books covered the floor. The kitchen table still held a few dirty dishes and glasses from breakfast.

Lisa set her Anatomy book and notebook on the kitchen table and then flung her backpack into her bedroom. She went into overdrive, cleaning and straightening the living room and bathroom. She straightened anything that Missy might see. Bridget, bless her, helped in her own way.

"Hey, Sweetpea, can you wipe the kitchen table with a rag the way Mama showed you?"

"Kay." Bridget ran to the kitchen to get the rag.

Way too soon, the doorbell rang.

"Shit," Lisa said and immediately regretted it.

"Shit, shit, shit," Bridget sang. "Shit, shit, shit."

Oh. My. God.

"Bridget, let me get the door, okay?"

Bridget's pout and quivering bottom lip almost broke Lisa's heart. Oh, God, don't let her start crying.

"Okay, okay. Come on, Sweetpea, let's see who's at the door. Put the rag on the table first."

Bridget did as she was told and ran to the front door, curls flopping behind her.

Lisa undid the deadbolt and then helped Bridget open the front door. Missy stood on the front stoop, looking less than pleased to be there.

Lisa reached over Bridget and opened the outside storm door. "C'mon in, Missy." Lisa nudged Bridget away from the door. Her little sister seemed mesmerized by the stranger at their doorstep.

"Bridget, this is my friend Missy." Lisa almost choked on the word, 'friend.'

Bridget backed up as Missy came in.

"You can hang your coat on any of these hooks." Lisa pointed to the empty hooks. All the coats, extra scarves, gloves, and snow suits were piled on her bed. She'd put them all back when Missy left.

"Bridget, where are your manners? Say hello to Missy," Lisa said to her almost four-year-old sister, wondering where sixteen-year-old Missy's manners were. She hadn't said a word to either of them.

"Hi," Bridget said shyly. "You have nice clothes." She ran back to the kitchen table to wipe it like Lisa had asked her to.

"Thanks," Missy mumbled. She tried to hang on to her backpack while she took off her coat.

"Here," Lisa said, "let me take this for you."

"I've got it," Missy growled.

Lisa held both hands up and backed away. "We'll study at the kitchen table."

"Is anyone else here?"

"My other sister and my brother should be home from school in about an hour."

"No adults?"

"Missy, I'm not going to attack you. Geez. I told you my mother had to go to work and that I was babysitting this afternoon. You knew that."

Lisa grabbed a dishtowel to dry the kitchen table and then sat down and opened her Anatomy textbook. She grabbed a pencil and started to make notes in the margins of her notebook, wondering if Missy would make it any further into the house. Out of the corner of her eye, she watched Missy standing by the front door, one arm folded across her chest, the other clinging to her backpack.

"Is this some kind of 'turn the other cheek' thing?" Missy asked, not moving any closer.

Lisa looked up. "What do you mean?"

"I see all you guys at lunch with your Bibles."

"Oh, that. We're doing a project for our youth group, that's all."

"I thought you'd be all 'an eye for an eye and a tooth for a tooth' or something. See? I know the Bible, too."

Lisa just shook her head. She never thought getting even with somebody was the right thing to do. As the silent seconds ticked on, Lisa realized something. Missy was nervous. Well, that was interesting.

Missy took a tentative step toward the kitchen table but veered off when she noticed the framed photographs on the bookshelf. Still clutching her backpack, Missy looked over the photos as if trying to get a sense of what she was up against.

Bridget, unsure of this unfriendly stranger in her house, crawled into Lisa's lap. Lisa barely noticed since it was a common occurrence.

"What d'ya think, Sweetpea?" Lisa said quietly to Bridget, letting Missy explore at her leisure. "Do you want to learn about blood with us?"

Bridget giggled. "No. You're silly, Lisa."

"I know. I am silly. So, what did you and Mama do today?" So, this is what it came down to, small talk with Bridget.

Before Bridget could answer, Missy screeched. Lisa looked up to see Missy holding a picture of Lisa and Sam at the infamous Snowball Dance, the dance that had been the catalyst for Lisa's public outing.

"Are you okay?" Lisa figured Missy was repulsed by the obvious fact that Lisa and Sam were a couple in that picture.

"Are you wearing an Yves Fornier Roux gown? No, don't even answer. I know you are. Oh, my God."

Lisa was shocked. It was the longest string of words the girl had put together since her arrival.

"God," Missy said again, "this is so disgusting."

"Listen, Missy," Lisa's temper flared, "I know you think I'm repulsive and all of that, but we have to do one hour of tutoring today, or your deal with Mr. Braun is off, so why don't you…" Lisa trailed off, not sure what to say next. Geez, what had she gotten herself into?

Missy turned and shot Lisa a mischievous smile. "Your little sister's right. You are silly. I mean, it's disgusting how in love you two are. In a good way, I mean. I wish Brad looked at me the way your girlfriend is looking at you in this picture." With a sigh, Missy put the photo back on the shelf and plopped down in the seat next to Lisa.

Missy pulled the books she needed out of her backpack and tossed the pack on the floor. "Marnie and Collette said I was crazy for coming over here."

Lisa agreed with the crazy part.

231

"But I told them you were a Bible thumper and wouldn't break your little commandments or whatever."

Lisa's lips were pressed so tightly together that they were probably turning white.

"What's a manment?" Bridget asked.

"Like the ten commandments in the Bible, Sweetpea. You'll learn about those in Sunday school."

Bridget squirmed out of Lisa's lap. "Can I go read now?"

Lisa laughed. Bridget didn't know how to read yet. She was stealing a page from their sister Lynnie's book whenever Lynnie wanted to ditch an uncomfortable situation. "Okay, how about you read on the couch while Missy and I do our homework?"

"Are you gonna kiss her like you kiss Samtha when Mama's not ?"

"Bridget Mae Brown, go get your book and start reading!" Lisa couldn't hold back a laugh. She covered her face in her hands. "I'm so sorry about that. Sam and I did homework together on Saturday, and it was our eight-month anniversary, and—"

"No, no, no, I get it. The same thing happens when Brad and I try to do homework together."

Lisa's stomach was jittery. Missy had changed her entire school schedule, trying to escape her, but she was now sitting at Lisa's kitchen table. Lisa hoped her scheme would work. Letting Missy's fear and ignorance of gay people remain unchecked would only mean bigger trouble down the line. And Lisa had another year and a half of high school left. That was far too long to suffer at the hands of Missy Matthews's prejudice. And, besides, if she could win Missy over, then Missy's entourage would undoubtedly follow, and that might convince a lot of the other kids that being gay was not that big a deal.

Lisa mentally crossed her fingers, hoping Missy would see that she wasn't a threat. She cleared her throat and said, "Well, should we get started?"

"Sure," Missy said, and much to Lisa's amazement, reached down into her backpack and took out a pair of glasses. "I know. They're the ugliest things on the planet."

"I didn't know you wore glasses."

"You cannot tell a soul."

"Your secret's safe with me." Lisa put one hand in the air in promise. "Do you wear contacts at school?"

Missy sighed. "I'm supposed to, but they bother my eyes. It always feels like there's a boulder underneath one or the other."

"So you walk around blind all day?"

"No."

Lisa waited. She had three siblings and knew a lie when she heard it.

"Okay, fine." Missy sighed. She took her glasses off. "Like, without them, I can tell that the front door is brown, and I can see that there's writing over the hooks, but I can't read it unless I put these on." She put her glasses back on. "Oh, how cute. You all have your names up there. That's so sweet."

"So, I have a question for you."

"Hmm?"

"How do you read the notes on the board or Ms. Lye's PowerPoints?"

Missy twisted her mouth back and forth. "I don't."

"You don't." It was a statement, not a question.

"Nope, but I listen, take notes from what I hear, and then read the textbook later. Well, sometimes." Missy took her hair and twisted it up into a bun behind her head. She stuck a pencil in it to keep it together.

"Well, I think we've figured out half your problem." Lisa tapped the table with her fingers. "You know, those glasses aren't ugly. And please don't freak out at my next statement, but you kind of have a sexy librarian thing going on with your glasses and your hair like that."

"I do?"

"If you wear your glasses, maybe Brad will look at you the way you want him to, eh?"

"Hmm. That's something to think about. And you know what?"

"What?"

"I've always loved your hair. The way you wear it in a braid all the way down your back."

"Thanks," Lisa said. "Okay, we should get to work. The kids'll be home soon, and I'll have to get them snacks and get them settled somewhere. So, let's get busy."

"Thanks."

"For what? We haven't done anything."

Missy sighed and looked down at her notebook. "I panicked. I wasn't ready for the quiz, and I couldn't figure out a way to get my cheat sheet back out from under your desk, and then Mr. Braun called me in, and, like I said, I panicked."

"How were you able to see the cheat sheet?"

Missy blushed and said, "I wrote really big with black marker. It didn't really help me, anyway."

"Missy, what you did wasn't cool, but let's make a deal that you don't ever do that to me again. I almost had a heart attack when I got called in."

"I know. I'm a bitch."

Lisa did not deny it, and they settled down to study the veins and arteries of the circulatory system.

After an extremely productive study date, they set up another session for the following Wednesday, same time, same place. Lynnie and Lawrence Jr. burst into the house just as Missy was leaving. Perfect timing. Lisa didn't want to subject Missy to more of her family than she could handle in one day.

After hanging the family snow gear back on the hooks by the front door and setting the table for dinner, she plopped down on her bed to unwind and write in her journal.

> So, it's been a while since I've last written, and a lot has happened. Missy Matthews just left. Yep. THAT Missy Matthews. Long story. She was all nervous when she walked in. She said something weird about an 'eye for an eye,' like I was going to beat her up for trying to frame me for cheating or something. She also asked if I was 'turning the other cheek.' That's from the New Testament.

Lisa put her journal down and dug her Bible out of her backpack. "Where is it?" she mumbled as she thumbed through the book of Matthew. "Ah, here you are." She wrote the passage in her journal.

> That's in Matthew 5:38-40, and I quote: "You have heard that it was said, 'An eye for an eye and a

tooth for a tooth.' But I say to you, Do not resist an evildoer. But if anyone strikes you on the right cheek, turn the other also; and if anyone wants to sue you and take your coat, give your cloak as well."

Okay, giving somebody my coat might be going too far, but I guess the idea is good. Can you imagine if everyone did that? Turned the other cheek? And how about the Golden Rule? That's a good one. Now I quote Luke 6:31: "Do to others as you would have them do to you."
Wouldn't that be freakin' amazing? If people treated each other the way they wanted to be treated? Nope, that's never going to happen.

With a sigh, Lisa finished her journal entry and was just about to put it away when it came to her.

"That's it," she said and punched her comforter. "Oh, my God. It was there all along. I knew there had to be something else. I have to call Marcus. We need one more round." She leaped off the bed and ran for her cell phone.

Chapter Twenty-Three

*"Take heart, daughter; your faith
has made you well."* — Matthew
9:22

For an entire week, Lisa and her friends planned and plotted
their strategy for the next and last debate session. Her team
had kind of taken a defensive stance, refuting the claims from the
other side, but it was time to take the offensive. Lisa hoped it would
be the grand slam she was hoping for. In the group chat, Marcus,
Julie, Susie, and Sam seemed really excited about it. Even Marlee was
swept along by their enthusiasm.

The van ride to the college that Tuesday evening was fun.
Everyone was full of energy and excitement. They had finally found
a way to smash Alivia and Ronnie to bits.

"Hey, Lisa," Julie said from the back seat of the van. "I saw two
of the weirdest things today."

"Oh, yeah, what did you see?" Lisa turned from the passenger
seat. Julie and Marcus were sitting as close together as their seatbelts
would allow. It was cute.

"First of all, I saw Missy Matthews say hello to you in the
hallway. And she wasn't being mean or sarcastic or anything."

Lisa burst out laughing. "It just shows you that a little honey does better than vinegar."

"Whatever you say." Julie shook her head and laughed. "And the second miracle? Jessica Myers actually passed you the basketball in PE."

"I know. Wasn't that awesome? I even scored a few times."

"It's been, like, opposite week or something. The mean girls are being nice."

Lisa laughed, but it was kind of true.

They pulled up to the college, and before getting out of the van, Marcus said, "No matter what happens tonight, we know we're giving it our best shot."

"And hopefully," Marlee said, "this video will help people who are struggling with this."

"Here, here," Julie raised an imaginary glass. "Here's to helping people. Not only the oppressed but the ignorant assholes, too."

They raised their invisible glasses and toasted.

Within moments of entering the meeting room, Jordan had them behind their podiums and ready to go. He said something about this being the final performance, and he wanted to make sure there was time for both sides to make their points.

That didn't sit well with Lisa. Maybe Ronnie and Alivia had come up with something else to sling at them. She took a deep breath and flashed a smile at Freddie's nod of encouragement. Amazingly, Jessica from PE class was there, too, this time without her so-called friends.

"Ready, leading lady?" Marcus said, sounding like Ronnie.

"Ready, leading man," Lisa answered.

"Both sides ready to go?" Jordan asked. They all nodded. He smiled warmly at them before saying, "And, action."

Marcus spoke first. "Having outlined many of the outlandish laws set down in the Old Testament, we realized something. Christians no longer live under the law." He paused for the briefest of moments. Here it was, their big grand slam swing. "We live under grace."

Ronnie's eyebrows shot up so high that Lisa almost lost it. She kept herself together and quoted John 1:17, "The law indeed was given through Moses; grace and truth came through Jesus Christ." Lisa flipped to Romans 12:6-7 in her Bible. "We have gifts that differ according to the grace given to us: prophecy, in proportion to faith; ministry, in ministering; the teacher, in teaching."

Marcus opened his own Bible and read, "This is from Galatians 5:4-6. 'You who want to be justified by the law have cut yourselves off from Christ; you have fallen away from grace. For through the Spirit, by faith, we eagerly wait for the hope of righteousness. The only thing that counts is faith working through love.'"

"'Love,'" Lisa echoed. She was pleased to see that Alivia and Ronnie were frantically writing down notes, and it even looked like they were arguing back and forth on paper. Good! Let them squirm for once.

"Galatians 5:22-23," Marcus continued. "By contrast, the fruit of the Spirit is love, joy, peace, patience, kindness, generosity, faithfulness, gentleness, and self-control. There is no law against such things."

"In Matthew 22:34-40," Lisa went on, "one of the Pharisees asked Jesus which commandment in the law was the greatest, and Jesus said, 'You shall love the Lord your God with all your heart, and with all your soul, and with all your mind.'" Lisa smiled in an attempt to convey that she personally followed this commandment without question. She continued the verse, "This is the greatest and first commandment. And a second is like it: 'You shall love your neighbor as yourself.' On these two commandments hang all the law and the prophets."

Marcus looked straight at the camera and repeated, "Love your neighbor as yourself." He looked back at his notes and said, "This idea is also found in the Old Testament. Leviticus 19:18 says, 'You shall not take vengeance or bear a grudge against any of your people, but you shall love your neighbor as yourself: I am the Lord.'" Marcus looked at Lisa, and his body language softened. This was her cue to say their final line. They may have overstated their point, but Lisa didn't care. They were going to use their full two-minute allotment.

"In Romans 13:8-10, the apostle Paul reminds us, 'Owe no one anything, except to love one another; for the one who loves another has fulfilled the law. The commandments, 'You shall not commit adultery; You shall not murder; You shall not steal; You shall not covet;' and any other commandment, are summed up in this, 'Love your neighbor as yourself.' Love does no wrong to a neighbor; therefore, love is the fulfilling of the law."

Lisa folded her hands on the podium. With a second to spare, Anne called time.

Lisa and Marcus fell on each other exhausted. "Phew," Lisa said with a sigh. "That was a lot. Too much, maybe."

"Nah," Marcus said. "It was just enough."

After Jordan reminded Alivia and Ronnie they had ten minutes to prepare rebuttal arguments, Lisa and Marcus returned to the table with their friends.

"Amazing, baby," Sam said and wrapped Lisa with a hug.

Lisa slipped an arm around Sam's waist. "Thanks. But it ain't over yet. Jordan wants us to make closing statements tonight, too."

"And he has a script for us to use at the very, very end," Marcus said.

Freddie smiled at Lisa and said, "Thank you."

"For what?" Lisa asked.

"For reminding us what's important. We got so caught up in religious dogma that we forgot what matters. You guys are right. Loving each other. That's what matters."

"What he said," Rebekah echoed and reached for Freddie's hand.

"Thanks, you guys," Lisa said. She turned to Marcus and said, "We should go over our closing statements."

"Agreed," Marcus said.

The entire table put their collective heads together, Freddie and Rebekah included, and went over their closing.

All too soon, Anne called time, and they had to head back to their podium. Lisa's smile faded when she saw the confident smirk on Alivia's face. Ronnie's face was unreadable, but he was a great actor, and you never knew what he was thinking.

Jordan called, "Action," and Alivia moved closer to the podium as if she were in no particular hurry. Lisa frowned at her cocky demeanor.

Alivia said, "Our opposition spent a lot of time talking about not living under the law anymore, so let's examine this further. Romans 3:31 in the New Testament says, 'Do we then overthrow the law by this faith? By no means! On the contrary, we uphold the law.' Using the version of the Bible that they asked us to use in this debate, let me read from 1 Timothy 1:8-11." Her eyes narrowed as she read. "Now we know that the law is good, if one uses it legitimately. This means understanding that the law is laid down not for the innocent but for the lawless and disobedient, for the godless and sinful, for the unholy and profane, for those who kill their father or mother, for murderers," Alivia paused and looked right at Lisa, her eyes boring into Lisa's soul as she slowly and deliberately quoted the next two words, "fornicators, sodomites," she looked back up to the cameras and finished, "slave traders, liars, perjurers, and whatever else is contrary to the sound teaching that conforms to the glorious gospel of the blessed God, which he entrusted to me." Alivia sounded like she was speaking to dimwits when she said, "Fornicators and sodomites. It's pretty clear, isn't it?"

Lisa's stomach clenched. She wanted to shout out that they had already gone over the sins of Sodom. Rape, selfishness, and all-around bad manners. And the word fornicator? They had come across the word early in their research. Marlee told them the word fornicator was from Latin and meant people that go to prostitutes.

Lisa's blood boiled. Why did everyone think that gay people were out-of-control regarding sex? That was the problem with the world. People wanted to assume the worst of others. A wave of anger flooded over her. Whose side was Alivia on anyway? Maybe she really believed the things she was saying.

Oddly, Ronnie sounded gleeful when he quoted Romans 1:26-27. "God gave them up to degrading passions. Their women exchanged natural intercourse for unnatural, and in the same way also the men, giving up natural intercourse with women, were consumed with passion for one another."

"Hallelujah," Alivia said with a righteous grin.

"Time," Anne called.

It must have been Alivia's smug look or the way she high-fived

Ronnie that sent Lisa over the edge. Didn't they know how serious this was? Didn't they know this was about her life? And other people's lives? Lisa tried to hold back her tears as she bolted past Alivia and Ronnie. She ran out the door and down the hallway, her face in her hands, the tears coming fast and furious. All the frustrations and setbacks during the debate came rushing to the forefront. Maybe Alivia was right. Maybe Reverend Rinaldi, Freddie, and Rebekah were right. She was a sinner. Footsteps approached her, so she turned away and faced the wall trying to stop crying but unable to.

"Lisa?" It was Alivia. The last person in the entire universe she wanted to see at that moment. "I—"

Lisa whirled around and snarled, "Why is my life and what I do so important to you? Seriously, do you have nothing better to do?"

Alivia backed away slowly, stunned.

Lisa groaned. She hadn't meant to unleash her frustration that way and struggled to keep her tears under control as Sam approached.

But before Sam reached her, Freddie put a hand out. "Can I try?"

Sam looked at Lisa, silently asking if it was okay for Freddie to approach. Lisa nodded once, and Sam stepped back.

"Walk with me," Freddie said to Lisa, keeping a respectable distance between them. They walked to the farthest end of the hall and then turned the corner, far enough so no one from the youth group could see or hear them. "Mark 9:40 says, 'Whoever is not against us is for us.'"

"Are you including yourself in the 'us?'"

He nodded. "You're doing good works, Lisa. Even I can see it.

243

And Alivia, too. She is a good person."

"Sure she is." Lisa rolled her eyes.

They leaned back against the cinderblock wall and stood in silence for a while until Lisa said, "What's your take on all of this? Is my side losing?"

He laughed. "I don't think it's about winning or losing. It's about reaching people. Some people, like the old me, are simply not reachable. Then there are others who might not have thought about the things you're bringing up, and I include myself in that group now. Hopefully, people will choose to think for themselves, make their own judgments."

"'Do not judge, so that you may not be judged,' Freddie," Lisa quipped. "Matthew, something or other."

"Matthew 7:1. I've been doing a lot of research on the subject lately. But listen. All is not lost. They gave you an opening."

"They did?"

Freddie nodded. "Their last Bible quote, the one from Romans about the men who have sex with, you know, each other?"

Lisa pressed her lips tight so she wouldn't smile at Freddie's deepening blush.

"Yeah, what about it?"

"They took that passage completely out of context."

Lisa narrowed her eyes as she thought back on why the passage was talking about carnal lust in the first place. She inhaled sharply when she realized. "Freddie, you're a genius. Come on." She tapped him on the chest with the back of her hand. "We have to get back." She took off running down the hall, leaving Freddie laughing as he tried to keep up.

Chapter Twenty-Four

*"Bear with one another and, if anyone
has a complaint against another,
forgive each other; just as the Lord has
forgiven you, so you also must forgive."*
— Colossians 3:13

"Places, please," Jordan called. "The Not-a-Sin side gets a two-minute rebuttal, and then we're segueing right into closing statements."

"Are you sure you're okay?" Marcus said as he adjusted their notecards on the podium.

"Yes, I lost my mind for a moment, but I'm good." And she was. How ironic that it took Freddie to talk her off the proverbial ledge. The same Freddie who had been against her and all gay people. Standing out in the hallway, she realized that if she could convince him, then there must be others that would listen, too. She gave her mood ring a quick twist and was ready.

"We need quiet on the set." Lisa almost laughed out loud. Jordan was really taking his director's role seriously. "And, action!"

Lisa opened. "Our opposition brought up a point in Romans 1:26-27, about God giving up on people who gave in to their carnal passions. Out of context, it's a pretty damning passage, but the opposition didn't give us the whole story. Yes, Romans 1:26-27 talks about how God gave up on the men who were 'consumed with passion for one another' and the women who did the same. But in the preceding verses, Romans 1:23-25, we realize that the apostle Paul is talking about idol worship and altar desecration." She pointedly tapped the podium with each of her next words. "Idol worship. Altar desecration."

She shook her head in disgust, "I quote, 'And they exchanged the glory of the immortal God for images resembling a mortal human being or birds or four-footed animals or reptiles.' Sounds like idol worship to me. It goes on to say, 'They exchanged the truth about God for a lie and worshiped and served the creature rather than the Creator, who is blessed forever! Amen.' It was this idol-worshipping sexual fervor, these pagan orgies, that God was displeased with. Paul was not referring to loving, caring same-sex relationships."

Marcus took over. "And, come on, let's talk about this whole sex thing. We've heard the words fornicator and sexually immoral used to describe gay people. Talking about sex is often uncomfortable. Thus, many ears don't hear. But let me ask you this. Why do some of you automatically assume gay people are fornicators and sexually immoral? Most gay people, just like most straight people, live in or want to be in loving, caring relationships. They don't go out seeking prostitutes. That's what the word fornicator means. Did you know that? And sexually immoral? Loving someone and showing it in a personal private way is immoral? Really? Come on, people, open your hearts so your ears can finally hear and understand."

She and Marcus stepped back to indicate that they were finished with their rebuttal statements. Lisa's heart was beating a thousand miles an hour. She glanced up at Sam, who was standing behind the cameras next to Jordan. She shook two fists in triumph. With the barest of nods to Sam, Lisa bit down a smile.

"Cut," Jordan called. "Ready for closing statements?" At the four nods, he said, "Cameras ready?" The three camera operators, all classmates of Jordan's from Southbridge High School, nodded. "Remember there are no time limits on closing statements. Quiet on the set, please." He paused to let the conversations die out, then said, "And, action."

Lisa spoke first. "It seems to me that sometimes we don't listen to each other. When I read Acts 28:27, it strikes a chord. 'For this people's heart has grown dull, and their ears are hard of hearing.' This is how it feels to me as a gay person. So many people want to judge me without first listening and finding out who I am." In the back of her mind, she realized that she had just come out to the entire world, but so be it. She was being open and honest about who she was. God had made her, after all, so the world had better get used to it.

Marcus quoted Luke 6:42, "And how can you say to your neighbor, 'Friend, let me take out the speck in your eye,' when you yourself do not see the log in your own eye? You hypocrite, first take the log out of your own eye, and then you will see clearly to take the speck out of your neighbor's eye." Marcus then looked directly into the camera. "In John 8:7, Jesus said, 'Let anyone among you who is without sin be the first to throw a stone at her.'" He shifted his gaze toward Lisa.

Lisa said, "'Do not judge, and you will not be judged; do not condemn, and you will not be condemned. Forgive, and you will be forgiven.' Luke 6:37."

Marcus continued. "'Why do you pass judgment on your

brother or sister? For we will all stand before the judgment seat of God. Each of us will be accountable to God. Let us therefore no longer pass judgment on one another but resolve instead never to put a stumbling block or hindrance in the way of another.' Romans 14:10-13."

Lisa paused for a moment. She was glad they didn't have the two-minute time constraint. "Remember what is written in 1 Samuel 16:7. 'The Lord sees not as man sees; man looks on the outward appearance, but the Lord looks on the heart.'"

Marcus moved Jordan's script on top of their notecards. Following Jordan's instructions, Lisa and Marcus looked over at Alivia and Ronnie, who, in turn, looked at them.

Ronnie said, "'In everything do to others as you would have them do to you.' Matthew 7:12."

Lisa nodded at Ronnie in reconciled agreement. She said, "Luke 6:31. 'Do to others as you would have them do to you.'"

"These both, of course, refer to the Golden Rule," Alivia added.

"Let's try to live this way," Marcus said.

Ronnie looked toward the camera, which was their cue to move together between the podiums and link arms. Ronnie quoted 1 John 2:9, "Whoever says, 'I am in the light,' while hating a brother or sister, is still in the darkness."

Lisa pointedly looked at each one in turn and said the final statement directly into the camera, "'Let everyone be quick to listen, slow to speak, slow to anger.' James 1:19."

They held their gaze at the camera, waiting for Jordan to call, "cut," but he didn't. Instead, he simply stood there, arms crossed, grinning.

"Okay, then," Ronnie said, breaking character. He turned to

Lisa and said, "So, who's 'Grace,' and why do we live under her?"

The entire room burst out laughing.

"Cut!" Jordan yelled. The entire room burst into applause. "That was amazing, you guys!" Jordan yelled over the din. He hugged the four debaters, thanked the camera people, and gave special thanks to Anne, their youth group leader, for letting them tackle such a huge project.

Sam ran over to Lisa and grabbed her by both forearms. "Baby, that was so good. Now can we go back to being heathens?"

"Sam!" Lisa pulled her arms free and smacked her lightly on the shoulder.

"Actually, baby …"

"What?" It wasn't like Sam to be so reticent.

"I want to start going to church with you and your family."

Without a word, Lisa hugged Sam, twirled her around again, and then kissed her all over her face until Sam giggled and begged for mercy.

"Hey, Lisa," Alivia said. She and Karl had been standing off to one side.

Lisa stopped kissing Sam and frowned. Geez, Alivia was such a buzz kill.

Before Alivia could say anything, Freddie and Rebekah walked up to congratulate them on a well-done endeavor.

Freddie said, "I'm glad I was able to break my bindings and open my ears."

"Me, too," Rebekah said. "I was doing some research and found this info for you online. I don't know if it's something you're interested in, but here." She handed a one-page printout to Lisa.

"Metropolitan Community Churches," Lisa read out loud. Sam

moved in closer so she could also read it.

"It's, like, a gay church or something." Rebekah pointed to the paper. "Here, look at their mission. It says they want to change people's hearts and that God's love includes everybody. See?" She stepped back and reached for Freddie's hands. "They're doing the same thing you guys did with your video."

By this time, a crowd was gathering around them. Marlee and Susie, Julie and Marcus, Ronnie and Jordan, and even Jessica from PE stood close.

Jessica said, "There's an MCC church in Rochester."

"There is?" Lisa asked. No wonder Jessica had come back to their debates without her friends. She must have been struggling to find a church that accepted her, too. "Too bad it's so far away."

"Road trip," Susie announced, causing a spontaneous chant of "road trip, road trip, road trip."

Lisa smiled when she noticed that Jessica, Freddie, and Rebekah joined the chant.

Before the chant was finished, Alivia let go of Karl's hand and threw herself on Lisa, wrapping her arms around her in a tight hug. Alivia sobbed in Lisa's ear. "I'm sorry. I'm so sorry."

Lisa looked wide-eyed at Karl, whose own wide eyes told her nothing. She patted Alivia on the back, stiffly at first, then more genuinely. "What are you sorry for, Alivia?"

Alivia sniffled her sobs back and let Lisa go. She stepped back and reached for Karl's hand, pulling him to her. "I was so mean to you. I wasn't sure about you. I couldn't let her get hurt."

"You couldn't let who get hurt?"

Alivia looked over at Sam, whose eyes were now as wide as Karl's. "Me? You don't have to protect me, Alivia. And not from

Lisa."

"I know that now, but those kids at school were so mean to you when that stupid newspaper reporter outed you." She turned to face Lisa. "You should have heard the mean things they said to her and Susie."

Marlee raised a questioning eyebrow at Susie. Apparently, Susie had been shielding Marlee from the truth about the name-calling and homophobic slurs she and Sam had been getting at school.

Alivia turned to Sam. "I didn't want to see anyone else stomp all over you."

"Why did you think Lisa was going to hurt me?" Sam's tone was soft.

Alivia's face turned bright red. She let go of Karl's hand and reached over to rub Lisa's upper arm, making Lisa a little uncomfortable. "I'm sorry. I thought maybe she was only after your, uh …"

"Fame and fortune?" Lisa suggested.

Alivia nodded.

"Alivia, you're a good friend to worry about Sam that way." Lisa put her hand over the hand that was rubbing her arm raw. "Thank you for looking out for her, but I am in no way after her riches. In fact, I didn't know who she was when she first asked me out. Did you know that she was the one that kissed me first? It was on that very same day."

Ronnie led the whooping and hollering. "And they say gay guys are promiscuous."

"Shut up, Ronnie," Sam said and smacked him in the stomach.

"Oof." Ronnie recoiled, pretending to be hurt.

"I'm sorry for judging you too soon." Alivia stepped back and reached for Karl's hand again. He took it, kissed it, and then put a comforting arm around her.

"How about this," Lisa suggested. "I won't judge you, and you don't judge me."

"Fair enough." Alivia nodded. "Fair enough."

Chapter Twenty-Five
"It is finished." — John 19:30

Sunday morning, Lisa held tightly onto Sam's hand as they bravely walked from the family van toward the steps leading up to the Presbyterian Church of Clarksonville. She wanted the members of her church to see her walking proudly with the love of her life. If she'd learned anything from the youth group debate, it was that love was never wrong.

Lawrence Jr. ran to catch up to them and reached for Sam's free hand. "Happy Birthday, Sam. We're having cake for you when we get home from church." Before Sam could respond, he blurted, "Are you guys getting married today?"

Both Lisa and Sam burst out laughing. Sam answered first, "Uh, no, buddy. I'm just joining your family this morning."

"You know what I know?" Lawrence Jr. asked, an excited grin on his face.

"What's that?" Sam exchanged a worried glance with Lisa. You never knew what was going to come out of a six-year-old's mouth.

"When you do get married, you will be Lisa's wife. And you know what else?"

"What?" Sam's grin was widening.

"Lisa will be your wife, too."

"I know," Sam said, looking relieved. "And that is very, very exciting to me."

Lisa's mother cleared her throat loudly behind them. Lisa laughed at the severity of Sam's blush.

Lawrence Jr. let go of Sam's hand, raced up the steps as fast as he could, and disappeared into the lobby of the church. Bridget ran up and grabbed Sam's newly freed hand.

Several people had to walk around Lisa's large family as they slowly made their way toward the church, mainly because the family walked at Bridget's pace.

Mr. and Mrs. Maynard said, "Good morning," as they walked past them, but then Mrs. Maynard turned back around and did a double take as she took in Sam and Lisa holding hands. Her surprised expression almost made Lisa laugh. Mrs. Maynard turned back around and whispered something in her husband's ear. He waved her away as if he didn't want to hear any gossip and increased his pace. She had no choice but to follow.

Other people weren't as kind. Some outwardly frowned at them, while a handful clucked their tongues in disapproval and shot angry glances their way.

"What's up with them?" Sam whispered to Lisa while helping Bridget navigate the stone steps. "Who do they think they are judging us? They don't get to judge us."

Lisa nodded. "You're right. They don't. Especially not on someone's eighteenth birthday."

Sam waggled her eyebrows.

"I can't believe you wanted to go to church with us on your birthday," Lisa said.

"With you is the only place I want to be."

Lisa's heart pumped a little harder at that moment.

They found their usual pew and squeezed together so Sam would fit in with them. The kids were unusually squirrely that Sunday morning, and it took all Lisa, and her parents could do to calm them down. They were either suffering from the North Country's never-ending winter syndrome or from the fact that Sam was with them. Probably a little bit of both because Lisa also felt a little squirrely with Sam there. But it was a good squirrely.

Once the kids were relatively settled and the service was moments away from starting, Lisa looked up toward the pulpit and groaned. "Oh, no."

"What's wrong, baby?" Sam followed her gaze.

Lisa nodded with her chin. "It's another visiting reverend."

"At least it's a woman this time," Sam offered, nodding her head toward the middle-aged woman in pastor robes.

Lisa reached across Bridget and squeezed Sam's hand. "You're right. Maybe she won't be a Reverend Rinaldi."

Lisa's mother said, "Reverend Owens announced his retirement."

"He did?" Even though Lisa wasn't sure Reverend Owens approved of her, she still had a big place in her heart for him. He had been the only reverend she had ever known. Not that she remembered, but he had baptized her almost seventeen years before. And he had baptized her sisters and brothers. Her heart hurt a little.

Her mother nodded. "Our guest is Reverend," she looked down at her program, "Cross. Now that's an interesting name for a reverend."

Lisa and Sam laughed. It was a great name.

"She pastored a church downstate in a town called Norwich. I think that's near Binghamton. Anyway, she's on the search committee's short list for Reverend Owen's replacement."

Lisa whispered to her mother. "Fingers crossed that she's not a bigot like Reverend Rinaldi."

Lisa's mother nodded her agreement.

"Hello, Leslie," Mrs. Maynard said to Lisa's mother. She stood at the end of their pew. "Hello, girls," she said to Lisa and Sam, completely ignoring Lisa's father and siblings.

"Hello, Mrs. Maynard," Lisa said. "This is my girlfriend, Sam." She was proud of herself for being honest and open. That's how she hoped life would be from now on.

"You girls must be really excited."

Lisa exchanged a glance with her mother.

"About what, Miriam?" Lisa's mother asked.

"The Presbyterian Church just voted to allow gay marriage. Didn't you know?" Lisa's shock must have shown on her face. "Oh, it's true, dear. The General Assembly voted, and pastors can now perform gay marriages in New York. Of course, you're both too young to be thinking about marriage, but this would be a first for our little church, wouldn't it?" Without letting anyone reply, she added, "They're even changing the marriage language in the Book of Order to read 'two persons' instead of 'a man and a woman.' Isn't that something? My, the world is changing." She turned abruptly to face the front. "I'd better get back to Joe. He hates when I'm not seated at the start. Bye, girls, and good luck."

Lisa's head was spinning. The one thing she desperately wanted was to be able to get married in her own church. She looked at Sam and saw just what she knew she would see. Love. Hope. The promise of a real life together.

This time it was Sam who reached across Bridget to squeeze Lisa's hand. She held on for a very long time.

Lisa's mother cleared her throat to let them know that the service was starting. Sam let go of Lisa's hand but turned her head toward Lisa's mother. Lisa's mother tried to remain stoic but burst into a rapturous grin after catching Sam's eye. She reached over both Lisa and Bridget to squeeze Sam's hand.

Tears formed in Lisa's eyes, and a quick glance around showed her that she wasn't the only one. Her father, mother, and Sam were each blinking back tears. Lisa's mother sighed, let go of Sam's hand, and dug into her purse for tissues.

"Hey, Papa," Lawrence Jr. whispered, "is Lisa getting married today?"

Lisa squeezed her lips together. It simply wouldn't do to burst out laughing.

"One day, son, but I don't think it's today."

Sam, obviously hearing the exchange, whispered to Lisa, "One day."

Lisa nodded and quoted John 8:32, "And the truth will make you free."

~~~ THE END ~~~

Bible Quotes Source

The New Revised Standard Version (NRSV) of the Holy Bible used in this work was used with permission from the following online source:

"BibleGateway. New Revised Standard Version (NRSV)."
National Council of the Churches of Christ, 1989. Accessed 31 Oct. 2014.

https://www.biblegateway.com/versions/New-Revised-Standard-Version-NRSV-Bible/

Newsletter Signup

Sign up for Barbara L. Clanton's newsletter to stay on top of new (and revised) releases. She also likes to provide writing tips for newbie (or oldbie) writers in addition to recommendations for books to read (other than her own, of course).

Sign Up on the official website:
www.blclanton.com

About the Author
Barbara L. Clanton

Barbara L. Clanton is a native New Yorker who left those "New York minutes" for a slower-paced life in central Florida. While in middle and high schools, she played any sport she could find—softball, volleyball, basketball, and field hockey. She could even be found in the upstairs gym playing handball with her friends during high school. She played softball at Princeton University and was the team captain during their Ivy-league champion senior year.

Her career has been spent teaching mathematics at college preparatory schools in both New York and Florida. She also coached softball and basketball in both states as well. She was inducted into the ASANA's (Amateur Sports Alliance of North America) Hall of Fame as an amateur softball player.

Somewhere in adulthood, she picked up a new hobby. "Dr. Barb" plays the bass guitar and has been in several pop-rock bands, playing such notable events as Gay Days Orlando.

When asked why she started writing, she said she was writing the books she wished she had in high school to help her make sense of her "differentness." Although the world is evolving, it's still not easy to come out to yourself or the world. She hopes her books will help.

Barbara L. Clanton's Website:
http://www.blclanton.com

Barbara L. Clanton's Instagram:
https://www.instagram.com/barbara.clanton14

Barbara L. Clanton's Facebook:
https://www.facebook.com/BassGuitarGirl

Barbara L. Clanton's Goodreads Page:
https://www.goodreads.com/author/show/3072442.Barbara_L_Clan
ton

Barbara L. Clanton's Author Page on Amazon:
https://www.amazon.com/Barbara-L-Clanton

Books by Barbara L. Clanton

THE CLARKSONVILLE SERIES (Young Adult)

The Clarksonville Series follows four high school girls in upstate New York as they maneuver the difficult process of coming out to themselves, each other, and their families. And it doesn't always go well. The four friends have a mutual love of softball which helps them bond and find love. Each book is from a different character's point of view, but all four main characters are present in each book. There are currently eight books in the series.

Out of Left Field: Marlee's Story (Book One in the Clarksonville Series)

High school junior Marlee McAllister lives and breathes softball. She's the pitcher for the Clarksonville Cougars in the North Country of upstate New York. With the season opener approaching, Marlee and her best friend, Jeri D'Amico, go to scout their rivals, the East Valley Panthers. The Panthers' star pitcher, Christy Loveland, took the All-county pitching title the preceding year. It is a title Marlee covets. Marlee and Jeri settle in for the game, but as the Panthers take the field, Marlee finds herself staring at Susie Torres, the Panther left fielder.

For reasons Marlee doesn't understand, she's drawn to Susie. Over the next few weeks, Marlee and Susie will slowly act on their mutual attraction. But suddenly, Susie pulls away without explanation, and Marlee realizes it has to do with Christy. Susie won't explain the bond she and Christy share, but whatever it is, it threatens Marlee's burgeoning relationship with Susie.

Struggling to maintain her grades, dealing with the ever-increasing estrangement from her best friend Jeri, and handling the pressures of the All-county pitching competition, Marlee also has to confront the bittersweet realities of what it might mean to be gay.

ISBN: 978-1-953734-04-4 (eBook)
ISBN: 978-1-953734-16-7 (Paperback)

Tools of Ignorance: Lisa's Story (Book Two in the Clarksonville Series)

Lisa Brown is the starting catcher for the Clarksonville Cougars High School softball team, and she has a major crush on her pitcher Marlee. Lisa continues to carry her torch for Marlee, even when Sam, a rival softball player, flirts sweetly. However, Lisa becomes more confused than ever when Tara, the first girl she ever kissed and the first girl who ever broke her heart, resurfaces. Since Marlee doesn't know Lisa's alive, should Lisa give up on her once and for all?

Sam seems to have secrets of her own, but Lisa wonders if she should overlook them and allow her fledging attraction to grow for the pretty blonde, or should she fan the tiny flame still burning in her heart for Tara? Lisa faces these problems and deals with society's tools of ignorance in her quest for love and acceptance.

ISBN: 978-1-953734-06-8 (eBook)
ISBN: 978-1-953734-17-4 (Paperback)

Going, Going, Gone: Susie's Story (Book Three in the Clarksonville Series)

Susie Torres planned to spend most of the summer before her senior year of high school with her girlfriend, Marlee McAllister, but that's proving to be quite challenging. Marlee works at D'Amico's restaurant, and Susie babysits for Mrs. Johnson, her mother's boss. Susie hates the job because she not only works like a slave but almost gets paid like one. Susie is desperate to take her physical relationship with Marlee further, but she knows she has to go at Marlee's slower pace. Complicating things is the attention that a pretty blonde softball player from another team shows Marlee, and Susie falls into a funk when Marlee seems to enjoy it.

On top of that, nothing she does seems to be good enough for her summer softball coach. Frustrated with life, Susie accidentally, on purpose, comes out to her mother. It would be an understatement to say that her mother didn't take it well. Can Susie deal with a girlfriend whose head has possibly been turned by another, an employer who treats her like dirt, a coach who doesn't respect her, and a mother who tells her she is unnatural? Can she get her life back on track before senior year starts?

ISBN: 978-1-953734-05-1 (eBook)
ISBN: 978-1-953734-18-1 (Paperback)

Stealing Second: Sam's Story (Book Four in the Clarksonville Series)

Samantha Rose Payton likes girls, but her parents don't know that. And Sam would like to keep it that way because her parents are ultra-conservative Republicans. They live in a mansion and have servants and chauffeurs. However, instead of playing the dutiful debutante who plays the violin and still has a nanny at age seventeen, Sam would rather watch ice hockey on TV and play second base on her summer softball team. Having to hide her relationship with her girlfriend, Lisa, from her parents is becoming an agonizing struggle. Not only are her friends pressuring her to come out to her parents, but they are also trying to convince her to attend a very public gay pride festival at the local college.

At least she has her nanny Helene to confide in, but for how much longer? Sam is acutely aware that the time for Helene to move on may be fast approaching. And if that isn't enough, Sam's summer softball coach gives her no end of grief after an error-filled game and isn't afraid of making an example out of her. Will Sam remain the perfect princess her parents expect? Will her beloved nanny leave her forever? Will her girlfriend get fed up about being kept hidden? Will her friends continue to pressure her about coming out? Will Coach Greer make her life miserable? All of these questions are answered in Stealing Second: Sam's Story.

ISBN: 978-1-953734-07-5 (eBook)
ISBN: 978-1-953734-19-8 (Paperback)

<u>Out at Home (Book Five in the Clarksonville Series)</u>

Marlee McAllister just wants to fit in. She didn't know she didn't fit in until Kate and Rita - the prettiest girls in the senior class - pointed it out. Even Marlee's grandmother declared that Marlee's too old for "this tomboy nonsense." All the other girls at school have long hair except Marlee. All the other girls wear something other than jeans, a t-shirt, and sneakers to school every day. Except for Marlee. All the other girls fit in except Marlee.

Marlee decides to grow out her short hair, buy femmy girly clothes, and pretend she has a boyfriend named Ronnie. Really, though? She has the most amazing girlfriend in Susie Torres. Susie is everything Marlee hoped for - sweet, sexy, kind, athletic, pretty. And best of all? She loves Marlee as much as Marlee loves her. Although their parents know about their relationship, not many other people do.

Marlee is out at home, but not to anyone else. And if anyone else finds out she's into girls, Kate and Rita especially, the entire school and her grandparents will know within a day. Life as she knows it will be over.

Out at Home is the story of Marlee McAllister's life-altering struggle to fit in.

ISBN: 978-1-953734-20-4 (eBook)
ISBN: 978-1-953734-24-2 (Paperback)

Tools of the Devil (Book Six in the Clarksonville Series)

Seventeen-year-old Lisa Brown loved going to church. Oh sure, sometimes she'd rather sleep in, but she liked the calming and empowering strength of her faith. Sundays revitalized her spirit when she thanked God for the wonderful things in her life, like her loving family and amazing girlfriend, Samantha Rose. One day she hoped to marry Sam, have a house and yard, and have babies together. One day.

But then it happened. That fateful Sunday, the guest preacher stepped behind the pulpit and spoke four words that would change Lisa's world forever. "Homosexuality is a sin," he said. Had she heard him right? When her mother put a hand on her forearm, she knew she had. Every muscle in her body tensed, and she forgot to breathe. What was happening?

The church she'd been baptized in, grown up in, and wanted to get married in had, in one instant, turned against her. Still not quite believing what she'd heard, she mumbled, "Ignorance is a sin, Reverend." Never one to back down from a challenge, she scanned the congregation but didn't find a single soul who looked upset by his statement. On the contrary, many nodded in agreement. Under her breath, she muttered, "Game on, people. Game on."

ISBN: 978-1-953734-21-1 (eBook)
ISBN: 978-1-953734-25-9 (Paperback)

Going Under (Book Seven in the Clarksonville Series)

Susie Torres is a second-semester senior with devoted friends and an amazing girlfriend in Marlee McAllister. Susie's father has the kind of job that takes him away from home on frequent business trips, but lately, his trips seem to be longer and more frequent. Tensions rise at home when Susie's mother challenges him about that. At first, Susie and her younger brother Miguel hide in her room when their parents' frequent squabbles elevate to out-and-out yelling matches. But as her parents' war escalates further, Susie finds other ways to escape the tension.

A fake ID becomes a clear and easy way to anesthetize herself with alcohol. Her crumbling home life becomes momentarily forgotten whenever she swims in a sea of peaceful drunken bliss. Unfortunately, Susie doesn't realize that she is alienating everyone around her with her attempts to cope with her parents' possible divorce. Including Marlee. Her best friend Sam tries to warn her that her excessive drinking is driving away all of her friends, but Sam's well-meaning advice isn't heard. Will Susie finally realize that it is her own actions that are making her life fall apart around her? That her new love of drinking is getting in the way of everything good in her life? That her amazingly patient girlfriend isn't going to put up with much more?

ISBN: 978-1-953734-22-8 (eBook)
ISBN: 978-1-953734-26-6 (Paperback)

<u>Stealing Hope (Book Eight in the Clarksonville Series)</u>

Sam Payton is a high school senior with a bit of an identity crisis. Raised in a well-to-do family, she dutifully plays the role of Samantha Rose Payton, the wealthy debutante. Now, almost one full year into her life-changing relationship with Lisa Brown, Sam is hit with many life-challenging events. Her best friend, Susie Torres, struggles with alcohol addiction and a wrecked home life as her parents go through a bitter divorce, and Sam tries to help her friend keep her head above water. In another struggle, two friends cross the line between friendship and intimacy—a line that should not have been approached. Sam finds herself trying to make them see how incredibly egregious the transgressions are for all involved. And to top it all off, Sam's mother is diagnosed with a serious illness.

Through the love of her parents and her girlfriend, Sam navigates these challenges the best way she can, all while trying to fulfill everyone's varying expectations of her. Sam struggles to break free of the preconceived roles she seems to be bound by to figure out who she really is. It ultimately comes down to whether Sam can make everyone see that she is both a softball-playing ice-hockey-loving lesbian named Sam as well as a classically-music-trained debutante named Samantha Rose.

ISBN: 978-1-953734-23-5 (eBook)
ISBN: 978-1-953734-27-3 (Paperback)

THE WHICKETT SERIES (Young Adult)

Art for Art's Sake: Meredith's Story (Book One in the Whickett Series)

High school senior Meredith Bedford is a social outcast. Her family recently moved from the Catskill Mountains to the sprawling suburbs of Albany, the capital of New York State. Shy and self-conscious about her acne scars, she stays to herself and tries to remain invisible. Her twelve-year-old brother, Mikey, has Down Syndrome, and she tries hard not to blame her troubles on him. Despite verbal and sometimes physical harassment, she survives because she has her art. She was selected to be part of the elite Advanced Placement art class and is quite good at capturing the emotions of her subjects in her portraits. Besides her family, art is the one thing that helps her cope with her outcast status.

One day, at a senior class meeting, she sees Dani Lassiter, president of the senior class and captain of the lacrosse team, and knows that she must paint this enigmatic young woman. One class period later, Dani manipulates things to have Meredith as her partner for a history project. Meredith is suspicious of Dani's motives but takes a chance. And it pays off. Meredith slowly sheds her invisibility cloak and allows Dani in - a little at a time. They explore an old Victorian house for their history project and become close with Esther and Millie, the two older women who own the house and who've lived together for about forty years. But, when Dani reveals to Meredith that she is gay, Meredith simply can't deal with the news. How had she not known? What is it that won't allow her to come to terms with this unexpected news? Will Meredith control her own homophobia, or will she reject the one person who had taken a chance on her and made her feel human?

<u>Dani's Story (Book Two in the Whickett Series)</u>

<u>< Coming Soon ></u>

THE GRASSE RIVER SERIES (Young Adult)

Quite an Undertaking: Devon's Story (Book One in the Grasse River Series)

Devon Raines, a sixteen-year-old journalism nerd, was happily minding her own business when wham her life was turned upside down. She struggled with grief when her grandmother died from a sudden heart attack. But it was at her grandmother's wake that she locked eyes with the most beautiful black girl she'd ever seen. No, Rebecca Washington was the most beautiful girl she'd ever seen, period. Would this beautiful dancer freak out if she knew Devon was gay and attracted?

Enter Jessie Crowler, Rebecca's basketball-playing best friend. Or were they only friends? Devon tried to hide her attraction for the ebony dancer, but would fate allow Rebecca to look her way? Would Jessie get in the way? Would the difference in skin color keep them apart? All this adds up to quite an undertaking in Devon's formerly quiet existence.

Rebecca's Story (Book Two in the Grasse River Series)

< Coming Soon >

THE GIRLS' SPORTS SERIES (Children's Books Ages 9-12)

Bases Loaded

Sixth-grader Mackenzie Kelly's first love was soccer until her best friend talked her into playing summer softball. Now Mack is eager to be on her school's softball team and dreams of playing in the Olympics with her idol, Cat Osterman. But first, she needs to bring up her failing English grade to stay on the team. When she learns softball has been cut from the Olympics, she's determined somehow to get it back into the Olympic Games so she can fulfill her dream.

"I just wanted to let you know I received the book and I think it is FANTASTIC!"
– Jessica Mendoza, *US Olympic Softball Team*

ASIN: B0094IT3RK (eBook)
ISBN 978-1-934452-79-0 (Paperback)

Side Out

Seventh-grader Dina Jacobs feels like she's landed on another planet when her family moves from Long Island, New York to Indiana. She tries out for the seventh-grade volleyball team, and her new friend, Christine, introduces her to Olympic volleyball. Now Dina dreams of playing in the Olympics like her newfound idol, Logan Tom. Indiana doesn't seem so bad until Dina's Jewish faith crashes against her coach's win-at-all-costs attitude. Miserable, Dina is torn between staying true to her religious customs or putting them aside to play the game she loves.

ASIN: B005HM9CUU (eBook)
ISBN 978-1-934452-65-3 (Paperback)

Live, Love, Lacrosse

Addie Coleburn, fresh out of the sixth grade, is spending the summer at her grandmother's house in Syracuse with her mother and brother. Kimi Takahashi, a girl who lives up the street, invites Addie to go to the park and play lacrosse. Addie hasn't the first clue what lacrosse is and would rather sit on Grandma's front porch eating potato chips, drinking sodas, and reading books. But then again, spending the summer dealing with her younger brother isn't that appealing, either, so she goes to the park with Kimi. Within a week, she's hooked on lacrosse. She's overweight and can't keep up with the faster, stronger girls. She has to find a way to lose her excess weight quickly or risk getting cut from the team.

ASIN: B09GPYMHDK (eBook)
ISBN 978-1-943837-50-2 (Paperback)

www.ingramcontent.com/pod-product-compliance
Lightning Source LLC
Chambersburg PA
CBHW061549170626
46811CB00001B/144